FOURTH DOWN
IN TEXAS

by

MATT WIXON

Designed by Vince Pannullo
Printed in the United States of America by RJ Communications.

ISBN: 978-0-578-20258-7

Many of the high schools mentioned in *Fourth Down in Texas* are real schools, but although I worked for more than two decades as a sports writer, this is not a work of journalism. It is a novel, which is a work of fiction, and it is set in the future.

All names, characters, events, and incidents are either the product of my imagination or used in a fictitious manner. Any resemblance to actual persons, living or dead, or actual events is purely coincidental.

For those who win and lose with grace, judge success in moments and years, and stand for what they believe in while respecting others who do the same.

CHAPTER 1

AT least thirty thousand fans are here already. That's my guess, anyway, as I look up at the crowd at AT&T Stadium, home of the Dallas Cowboys and whatever mass-audience event rolls through North Texas. This place is huge. Science-fiction huge.

I'm not sure what that means, but it's just what comes to mind as I peek out of the tunnel that leads to the field. Maybe it's the video board, the thing so enormous that it's both impressive and ridiculous, that hangs from the roof. I think back to growing up, when the family TV had like five channels, and there was no remote, and you had to twist around the antenna to make Bugs Bunny and Elmer Fudd come into focus. Now I'm standing under a screen so monstrous it's like I've been pulled into a cartoon.

All of this is a little hard to believe, even for a high school football coach like me. I've been coachin' up kids long enough to see just about everything, but the magnitude of everything now is astounding. This is a pro football stadium, after all, and it's filling up for a high school game. I bet there will be close to forty thousand here by kickoff, or soon after, because of the traffic jam near the parking lots. Yeah, traffic is brutal out there. You might find that surprising for a high school game, but this is Texas. We're the fifty-yard line of football in America.

I could say, "This is Texas, *y'all*," but why fuel the stereotype? Some joke that y'all is the most common word used in Texas, but I've been in the state for more than half my life, and I don't use it much. Maybe it's because my wife is an English teacher who cringes when she hears something like "might could."

This stadium will be rocking soon, and the players standing next to me are the reason why. They're shoulder to shoulder, internally pacing, waiting to take the field. They're both thrilled and terrified, the unforgettable combination of being simultaneously fired up and scared shitless that

I remember from the last time I put on shoulder pads in high school. Even then, as a teenager who rarely thought farther ahead than my next Whataburger order, I thought about becoming a coach. But that was going to be after my NFL career, you know, because as a high school senior I was still a couple years from the dose of reality that eventually hits 99.99 percent of football players.

The players standing across from me aren't worried about that right now. They're thinking about the game plan, and their assignments, and whatever other thoughts flash through a teenager's mind minutes before he takes the field. I can't remember what used to go through my mind, and I won't pretend to know what the teenagers of today might be thinking. I probably know less about that with each passing year, as I get older and they look younger.

God, they look so young. So young that it scares me.

"Thirty thousand?" I ask them.

"I bet that's forty," says Mickey, a starting receiver who's also a kick returner, punter, backup quarterback, and occasional safety. He can do a bit of everything, which is not surprising because he's the son of a coach. Mickey is my oldest, the boy who roughed me up as a new father and then jumped from six years old to six feet tall in a blink. Well, nearly six feet tall. In cleats, I guess, and on the football roster, where the kids always beg to be listed a little taller and a little heavier.

Mickey peeks out from under the tunnel, trying to get a better look.

"Definitely forty," he says, his voice muffled by his helmet. Mickey really has no idea, but he doesn't lack for confidence in anything. Even when he's proven wrong, he just kind of shrugs his shoulders like he's unconvinced.

Standing next to Mickey is one of the nation's top recruits, a speedy, yet huge, receiver who has twenty-two touchdown receptions this season. His parents, who are of Nigerian descent, gave him a perfect big-play name: Kingsley.

Kingsley Savage.

"Hey Beast," Mickey says, using Kingsley's nickname. "Whatcha think?"

"I'd say forty. Place holds eighty, right?"

"No, a hundred," says another player.

Kingsley shakes his head and shoves the player in the shoulder.

"Nah, Sticks, that's with all the standing-room-only fans. I'm just talkin' seats."

"Oh."

"I tell you this," Kingsley says, "the crowd is on point."

That's the final word, because Kingsley is the ringleader.

I smile as I watch them absorb a memory they'll never forget. Then I walk out of the tunnel onto the artificial turf, and the crowd erupts. Half of it, anyway. The crowd is catching a glimpse of the enthusiastic blur of blue and silver, the Putnam High School Panthers, preparing to take the field.

I think football in Texas is the best in the country, but even if it isn't, it's certainly different than anywhere else. We had nearly sixty thousand fans for a championship game. We had forty-six thousand for a second-round game. We have stadiums that look like college facilities and indoor practice facilities that NFL teams use.

Texas high school football games draw bigger crowds than a lot of college bowl games, and the games are often better. Each week is big and intense. That's not always a good thing for the players, or the fans, or coaches like me who can stew over losses more than we celebrate wins. But Texas high school football is incredible. It's as rich a part of the culture here as barbecue and Big Tex at the State Fair. The cheerleaders, drill teams, color guards, marching bands—and oh, man, the stadiums on Friday nights. It's just . . .

Sorry, lost my train of thought for a second. The other team just rushed onto the field, and that crowd boom always gets me. When you're on the field and that roar comes down from your side, that's something you never forget. You don't forget the way your heart races, your skin tingles, and how the energy can buckle your knees.

That's what the Putnam High School Panthers, minutes away from playing in a state quarterfinal game, are about to experience.

I look up and see a boy, maybe eight or nine years old, who reminds me of Mickey. He's waving a blue towel as the Panthers emerge from the field entrance and gather behind a large inflatable football helmet. Yeah, we've now got inflatable entry tunnels. Gone are the days when we just ripped through butcher-paper banners to get on the field. Gone are the days of playing on real grass, too. It's artificial turf now, surrounded by gorgeous stadiums with state-of-the-art scoreboards and multiple camera decks so the game can be captured from every angle. In high-def, of course, for broadcast on national networks like ESPN.

The helmet tunnel seems too small for the players' swelling spirit, and it jolts and bounces as they funnel into it. A fog machine adds to the scene, and the tunnel looks like it will explode.

I step to the side as the players walk toward the stadium field. The crowd continues to build as the Putnam players pass by in sharp navy jerseys and scuffed silver helmets. Their cleats clack on the concrete walkway and then squish into the artificial turf. I look up again at the boy above me with paw prints painted on his cheeks. He's looking down at the Panthers.

In awe, I suspect, because these are his guys. To him, these guys are huge.

They're pretty huge to me, too. The helmets and shoulder pads make them look bigger, which is true with all football players, down to the pipsqueak grade schoolers who are like animated bobbleheads. But the high school football players these days are just big, period.

When I played high school football, I was six-foot-two and about 230 pounds. Three decades have passed since then, and I've gone from a solid physique to a solid devotion to barbecue. I'm not obese, but I'm pushing fifty, and my priorities have changed.

My name is Tuffy Nehls. I'll now pause to let you laugh, or cringe, or whatever you do when you hear of a man named Tuffy. But there are other men out there who go by names like Tuffy, and they probably have stories like mine.

My parents named me Gordon Samuel Nehls, a perfectly fine name. But when I was a sophomore in high school, a coach pointed out how I was doing well against guys who were bigger than me. I was small, he said, but tough. My last name is pronounced "nails," so one of the coaches, such a clever guy, started saying I was tough as nails. Eventually, I became Tuffy.

I was an offensive lineman in high school and then played college football at Stephen F. Austin. I was a starter, not a star, but it was a good run. I got my education paid for, and I met my wife, who might've passed on our first date had she known she'd be called "Mrs. Tuffy."

The thought of being a coach's wife could've scared Christine off. The long hours, the emotional ups and downs, the moving from job to job, the games when she was surrounded by complaining fans. I'm sure Christine has felt like a single mom sometimes during the season, but she knows how much our kids mean to me, and she knows how much coaching means to me.

Christine stayed home with the boys until they got into grade school, and Mickey is now eighteen and Andrew fourteen. She went back to work for three years before our daughter Emma came along. Emma, now nine, is sometimes assumed to be a "whoopsie baby," but she was planned. Everybody who knows Christine knows that, because everything Christine does is well-planned. Outside of coaching, I'm pretty much the opposite. The yin-and-yang thing applies.

We thought we were done after the boys, but as we both approached forty—with me in front, as Christine would surely point out—we had a change of heart. Christine did, mostly, but I was fine with adding to the family. After all the sacrifices she had made for me, only an asshole would put up a fight.

Let the wifey call an audible on ya, huh?

I heard that a lot. I would smile and tell them that it was Christine's fault. She just found me too irresistible.

Nobody has ever really found me irresistible, but back in high school, I was a big man on campus. After my growth spurt, six-two and 230 was considered pretty darn big back then.

Not anymore. But as big as the players get, they're still kids to me. They might look different than they did twenty or thirty years ago, but they haven't changed. They might feel invincible, and they might act like they know it all, but they're still figuring things out. That confidence, that swagger, that attitude—that's what we see with teenage boys. But I can look past the wispy mustaches and scraggly beards and see the anxiety on those baby faces.

For most of the Putnam Panthers, there are no more than three football games in their future. They'll be football players for three more hours, or maybe another couple weeks, and then life will go on. They'll mourn the end of something that for years has been part of their lives, part of their direction, part of their self-worth.

But right now, as the crowd keeps filing in, the Putnam Panthers are about to experience a forever moment. They're tightly bunched as they prepare to head through the inflatable tunnel and onto the field, bouncing in place as three captains in the middle deliver a message I can't hear. I step back from the pack and stand with a couple of the booster club parents who will deflate and roll up the tunnel after the players run through.

A second later, the Panthers emerge from the tunnel, flanked by back-flipping cheerleaders and guys with large blue flags spelling out P-U-T-N-A-M. The crowd erupts, horns blare, drums pound, and confetti flies in the stands as the players spill onto the sidelines and look up to see themselves on the cartoonishly huge video board.

This is one of those knee-buckling moments. It still feels that way to me, too, even after coaching more than two hundred games. Today, however, I'm not a coach. The Putnam Panthers aren't my team, and I'm not sure I even have a team anymore.

Why?

To me, it's simple. Some people want to kill football.

CHAPTER 2

L ET me take you back to a year ago. We'll go back a little more than a year, actually, to when my career felt more solid. A lot of things felt more solid then.

My ninth season as head coach of the Creekside High Knights had gone about as I expected, with a young team taking its lumps early and then going a couple of rounds in the playoffs. We finished with seven wins and five losses, and it was both disappointing and encouraging. We could put up some points, but injuries sapped our thin defense, and a rugged Longview team bullied us in the second round.

Injuries are part of football, and sometimes your team must limp through the final weeks of the season. It's easier to have roster depth at the largest high schools, which can have four, five, or even six thousand students, but we've got a little less than two thousand at Creekside. We play in the second-largest classification for Texas public schools, a notch below the monstrous schools in the Dallas suburbs around us.

So back to last year. It was the Monday before Thanksgiving, just three days after our final game, when my friend Dave Holgate called me. Dave's on the Creekside School District's board of trustees—I think he's been on there for about six years—and is a big football fan. He also cooks some amazing barbecue, and as I'm far better at eating than cooking, I appreciate the invitations to his backyard feasts.

Looking back, I should've seen it coming, or at least something coming, but a football season is like a black hole. It devours your time, energy, focus—everything. That's why I started telling my assistant coaches to stay away from the office, as well as planning, email, phones—all that— on Sundays. For one day, just get away. You've got to have some balance in your life, or at least try for it.

But obviously I have trouble following my own advice, because I barely felt a breeze from the gathering storm. That all changed at lunch one day when Dave, an accountant and no-nonsense kind of guy, told me that football was on the table.

"Football's on the table?"

"As in, it's being considered," Dave said. "They're building the budget for the next school year, and it's getting looked at."

"Cuts again?"

There had been cuts to the athletic program in recent years, including the elimination of one of our freshman football teams. Until two years ago, we had Freshman Blue and Freshman Red, with the more advanced kids playing on the blue team. We always have enough freshmen to field two teams, and I don't like to turn away a kid when he's that young. You never know how he'll develop.

I hated the cuts, but it's not like the athletic department was being targeted. The state was sharply reducing its education funding, and districts had to tighten things. The slash in funding was like nothing I had seen before, and hundreds of districts sued the state, alleging that the finance system wasn't adequately providing for public education.

"Is the state cutting more?"

Dave shook his head as he looked down and stabbed at a couple of pieces of salad. I was having a chicken sandwich and losing my appetite.

"It's not about that," Dave said. "Maybe worse."

"Worse?"

"Here's the thing. There are lots of reasons why, and I think they're huge overreactions, and I certainly don't support them . . ."

Mr. No Nonsense was stalling.

"Huge overreactions?"

"Tuff, they're talking about dropping middle school football."

I leaned back in my chair and stared at him for a few seconds.

"Who's 'they'?"

"Bashum," Dave said, referring to Creekside superintendent Charles Bashum. "He wants it in the budget discussion for the next school year. He's got some support from the school board."

I was still leaning back in my chair. It felt like there was an actual, physical weight on my shoulders, like I was hauling buckets of water.

Dave was looking at me, waiting for a response or to call the paramedics. But I broke into a half smile and picked up my sandwich, although I didn't want another bite.

"They're not going to cut football," I said.

Dave took a deep breath and shook his head.

"It seems ridiculous to me, too. The budget's always tight, and football is a real expense. But it's football."

"So what's changed?"

"I don't know," Dave said. "Maybe nothing. Bashum just might be looking at another way to trim the budget. But there's also all the new talk about head injuries. And, you know, Chris Dozier."

"The kid with the concussion."

"Yeah."

"I thought that was over. Sovereign immunity."

I can't really explain sovereign immunity, but it prevents lawsuits. Dave has told me about all these different interpretations from the courts, and listening to the explanations gives me the kind of tired head I get when trying to figure out playoff tiebreakers.

"The parents, and their lawyer, are trying to push forward with a lawsuit."

"It doesn't have anything to do with me."

"But it has everything to do with football," Dave said.

I sighed and shook my head. I don't even know what really happened with Chris Dozier. I never even met him.

Chris was a freshman at Lakeview Christian High School and never attended Creekside. But in eighth grade, he played football for Bevell Middle School, which is in the Creekside school district. Chris suffered a concussion when he was playing offensive guard in a game. That's one of the few things that Chris' parents, his doctor, and the coach of the eighth grade team agree on.

The coach said Chris was injured while blocking on a play, that he might have lost consciousness briefly, and that he was woozy as he was helped off the field. Two weeks after the concussion, Chris was having headaches and hadn't attended school since the injury. He was still feeling dizzy and nauseous at times and couldn't focus or sleep through the night.

The parents claimed Chris suffered two concussions in the game and that the symptoms from the first were ignored. A second concussion, they said, is what caused more serious damage. Their son was once an honor student and now struggled to keep up in school.

"I doubt the case will hold up," Dave said. "But it's another lawsuit, another black eye for football. There's already the NFL's billion dollar settlement with its players. And now high school cases keep popping up, like the kid in Pennsylvania whose family was awarded nearly three million last year."

I remembered that one. It was horrible, and as much as I'll defend my fellow coaches and give them the benefit of the doubt, those coaches were an embarrassment. We're working with kids, you know? We need to look out for them because God knows they won't look out for themselves. I came home one day a couple of years ago and found Mickey and a couple of friends doing flips off a ladder into the pool.

"So that's why they're talking about dropping the middle schools?"

"Bashum hasn't said that," Dave said. "But the lawsuits are making people sweat. Insurance premiums are shooting up, and some insurance companies refuse to cover football at all."

"So this is about lawsuits?"

"It's about the lawsuits and the NFL and the concussions and a lot of things. . . . I think it's just accelerating the idea with Bashum. Gives him another argument. Another arrow to shoot at the target."

"And the target is football?"

"Seems so."

Yeah, the target was football. That was clear to me. It wasn't about cutting costs. It was about cutting football.

As I tell you this now, you might be thinking, "But it's only middle school football." Just seventh and eighth graders, right? Is that really a big deal?

Yes, it's a big deal. It's the whole deal.

It's pretty much a death blow to any high school program. Middle school feeder programs provide the football players for the high school teams, and middle schools are where kids learn the fundamentals, or at least the proper ones after years of playing in some youth league where the coach is some fanboy with a whistle.

You don't just cut middle school football and stop there. You cut middle school football because no superintendent or school board, at least in places where people care about football, can cut it from high school and avoid burning up in the firestorm. The only way to do it is piece by piece, year by year, slowly heating the water to a boil with the unwitting frog in the pot.

Take away middle school football first. Then, as potential players move out of the district, let the high school program flounder and slide toward irrelevance. Then make the final cut when parents, fans, and the community are numb with apathy.

I can tell you that, as I talked with Dave, my thoughts were not that crystallized. My head was spinning, and I'm sure I looked more pathetic than stoic, even with my attempt at the shrug-it-off smile. Mickey was much better at it than me.

"Cut middle school football and you'll kill the high school program," I said. "You can't compete."

"I guess that means you'd leave?"

I threw my hands in the air.

"Of course I'd leave. How could I stay? I mean, what kind of district cuts football? We're not some little private school."

"Yeah, I know," Dave said, backing away from the table a bit and raising his hands in front of him as if he might need to push me away.

"I know, Tuff. I do." Dave paused, took a deep breath, and then let it out with a combination of exhaustion and frustration that would become familiar over the next few months. "But . . ."

"But what?"

"Fontana is a 5A school, and it dropped football completely," Dave said. "And with expenses, more and more districts are talking about . . ."

"Yeah, but Fontana is a perennial loser, and it didn't have great participation numbers. And that's down in the Valley, where football means soccer. We've got kids at Creekside who want to play football."

"Of course we do."

"And all the talk about expenses is just the same ol' talk," I said. "Just posturing and threatening, especially when admins are always prepping for another bond vote."

I leaned forward and stared at Dave.

"Can you imagine Creekside without football?"

"No," he said with a sigh.

"This is Texas, so tell me what the hell is going on. Does Bashum suddenly hate football or something? It hasn't seemed that way before."

Dave leaned back and rubbed his forehead.

"Maybe this isn't all new. Could just be that Bashum thinks the time is right."

"The time is right?"

It pissed me off to hear something like that.

"I'm just saying you can't put this all on him. Look where things are now. Ten years ago, who talked about concussions? Who talked about limiting hits in practice? Who would've thought some college football teams would stop all tackling in practice?"

"But they're not cutting football."

"No, but football has problems, right? And if Bashum is on some safety crusade, he has support. Remember that doctor in New Hampshire who proposed banning football a couple of years ago?"

I almost laughed as I remembered him, and my tone turned more to disgust.

"That guy? Come on. Nobody took him seriously."

"Bashum did," Dave said.

"Great. I'll suggest we put all the kids in bubble wrap."

I looked down at a fist squeezed so tightly that my fingernails were digging into my palm. I tossed a mashed napkin on the table, took a breath, and tried to relax. Overreacting was a hallmark of my younger days, but one upside of getting older is that it's easier to keep emotions from revving to the red line.

"I guess Bashum doesn't know the kind of backlash there will be," I said.

"No doubt about it. It will be a shitstorm."

"A huge fucking shitstorm," I said.

Even under the circumstances, I was surprised to hear myself. Since the kids were born, or at least since Mickey was old enough to mimic me, I had tried to clean things up. Nobody wants to hear a kindergartner dropping f-bombs.

Profanity is the sign of a limited vocabulary, my wife tells me. But as Dave sat across from me, profanity was just the sign of someone feeling angry and confused. Even betrayed, I think. Not that anything was owed to me, but it felt like betrayal.

"I hope there's some way that it doesn't move forward," Dave said. "But I think Bashum feels empowered, and I wanted you to know before he talks to you."

"When's he going to talk to me?"

"Not sure. Before he puts it up for public discussion."

I sat back and smiled.

"That public discussion will certainly be interesting," I said. "Hey, we're going to drop football, everyone. Come tell us what you think!"

I leaned forward, rested my elbows on the table, and sighed. Did my focus on the football season blind me to some big culture shift? It felt like it came out of nowhere.

"Maybe I shouldn't have waited until now to say something, but I know what it's like for you during the season. And who knows what's going to happen? It might be nothing changes."

"Or it might be that I'll be looking for a job."

Dave looked down at his phone, I assume to check the time. I started gathering up my trash.

"I just can't believe it's even possible."

"Anything's possible," Dave said. "The state funding, the safety questions about football, the parents filing lawsuits. Three mill for the kid in Pennsylvania, and before that, that eight-million deal for the kid in New York. And the NFL is even having some hard times. As much as I hate it, Bashum has stuff to talk about. He has ammo."

I didn't like how Dave was building a defense for the indefensible. A school in Texas cutting football? Come on.

"It's bad, Tuff. That's all I can say. And you know, construction begins next year on the new middle school, and construction on the second high school is just a few years away. If Bashum is going to do something about football, now's the time."

"You think he's been planning this for a while?"

"I don't know what to think. It's just like a perfect storm."

I shook my head and sighed—again.

"A perfect storm," I said. "Remember that movie? Everyone dies at the end."

CHAPTER 3

BASHUM waited until after Thanksgiving to turn my stomach. He didn't want to cut anything, he said, but football shouldn't be some kind of untouchable sacred cow. Apparently several superintendents shared that thought at a national conference where they could talk confidently about things they know little about.

"Others are considering cutting football?" I asked Bashum. "In Texas?"

"They're considering everything," he said as we talked in his office. "With every department and student affected, it's not fair to take anything off the table."

And so, for the December school board meeting, middle school football was on the table. Bashum said it would be listed on the agenda as a discussion of aspects of extracurricular programs, including athletics.

"Word will get around you're talking about dropping football."

"That word won't come from me," he said.

"If you cut middle school football, it will be tough to compete in high school."

"Middle school students can play through the CSA," he said, talking about the Creekside Sports Association. "The CSA said it can expand beyond sixth grade and add leagues for seventh and eighth. They'd still get to play."

Yeah, they'd still get to play. But what would they learn? Who would they be learning from? They would be split into multiple teams, not learning the offense and defense we run, and be coached by a few dads who think they know what they're doing. No real coaches. No real learning.

"And no trainers," I told Bashum. "It's not safe."

Bashum said his responsibility was to serve all students, and that students might be served better with the football dollars used elsewhere. And he said he didn't think there's "any real way to make football safe."

"Is there any real way to make anything safe?" I said.

I'm always frustrated when I hear that football needs to be made safe. Safer, yeah okay . . . we should always work toward that. But yes, there will be injuries in football—and in life. Football isn't going to be checkers, and neither is life. If everything needed to be safe, we couldn't have cars. Or bikes. Or lives. How do you make the world safe?

I wasn't going to ask Bashum about the Dozier lawsuit, but sometimes my mouth gets ahead of my brain.

"Is this a reaction to the Dozier kid?"

I immediately regretted jumping to that. The tone wasn't right, and it was too aggressive. Nothing had been decided yet, and no matter what happened going forward, a bad relationship with the superintendent would do me no good.

Bashum didn't flinch. He talked to me calmly and clinically, like he was giving an insurance seminar or explaining employee benefits. That's kind of his style. He's sorta military, but not in a macho way, in an "I'll eat dinner at six o'clock sharp every night" sort of way. He's not a big dude, maybe five-foot-eight or so and in pretty good shape for a guy in his late fifties. He's a real neatnik, too, and always looks ultra-organized. I don't think I've ever seen him with a whisker.

"This is not about the Dozier lawsuit," Bashum said. "But of course it's a concern. So are the lawsuits in other places, and the rising price of catastrophic insurance, and all the new information about concussions."

"But we've got concussion precautions," I said. "Ours are as protective as anyone's. We're all about protecting the kids."

"I know you do your best to protect the kids."

"So then what's going on?"

"Coach, we're not targeting football. We're exploring possibilities. Nothing's been decided."

As Bashum spoke, I noticed the photo on the shelf behind his desk. A black-and-white photo of a football player in one of those old school poses. He had the ball cradled in his arm while kicking his leg into the air, hurdling some imaginary defender in an empty field.

Is that Bashum? I wondered if the photo was brought in for our meeting, or at least brought out from some dark corner of a bookshelf so it would be in my line of sight. Bashum reaching for some football cred or something.

I thought it was funny, and I wanted to tell the assistant coaches about the photo. But I didn't want it to get back to Bashum, so I only told Jim Hartline, my longtime offensive coordinator. We had a good laugh.

I told the other coaches that my meeting with Bashum was fine and that we wouldn't really know anything until the next school board meeting. I told Jim that Bashum seemed dead set on taking down football, even if it meant the superintendent might get taken down with it.

✳ ✳ ✳

Word leaked quickly in the coaching community about "a discussion of aspects of extracurricular programs, including athletics." It lit up coaching message boards and was discussed on Twitter, and not long after that a newspaper reporter called me. I told him I couldn't talk about it.

"What about off the record?" the reporter asked.

"Sorry, no."

"So they're considering cutting middle school football?"

"I don't know what they're considering. I'm waiting like everybody else."

"I can't see it happening," he said. "Not around here. Not at a place with a coach who has won a state championship."

Leaning on me with flattery, I guess.

"Sorry, Lee. I know you're just doing your job, but, you know . . ."

"Yeah, okay."

I knew Lee Fountain would hit me up about it some other time. Lee has been covering high schools for the newspaper since before I moved from Waco to take the job at Creekside. He's fun to shoot the breeze with, and his name sounds like a character from an action film. A James Bond associate or something. *Lee . . . Lee Fountain.*

I joked with Lee about that, and he told me that Tuffy sounds like the name of a talking hamster in a Disney movie. Fair enough.

Lee called Bashum's office looking for information, so the superintendent might've thought the football coaches were whipping people into a frenzy. But nobody was. It's just that if you mess with football, people are going to notice, and Bashum should know that.

I got a lot of calls and text messages from coaches, and the support was nice. Coaches are intense competitors by nature, and sometimes things can get nasty. But for the most part, we support our own. We all go through a lot of the same things, have the same challenges, the same frustrations.

"Same deal here," the coach at Parker Hills, a high school near San Antonio, sent me in an email. "Not sure what's coming."

Several districts were talking about cutting middle school football, apparently.

"First step toward cutting everything," the Parker Hills coach said.

I wasn't ready to panic, but the outpouring of support actually made me feel worse about the situation. It made it seem more imminent. And, you know, responding to texts and emails is exhausting.

* * *

I was sending one of those emails on a Thursday morning, just three days after my meeting with Bashum, when I heard Mosey's voice in the hallway. He was loud, as always.

"Oh hey, Mrs. Adamson, how are you? . . . yeah, doing great . . . nah, we stayed in town, had family in . . . ha, ha! . . . oh, yeah, of course!"

And then Eric Posey, known as "Mosey" since his days as a cornerback for one of my first Creekside teams, brightened the office.

"Morning, Coach!" he said.

I turned and smiled. It was hard not to smile when Mosey came into a room. Everyone at Creekside loved his laid back personality and that wide smile that was both endearing and a warning of trouble. Mosey, back when he was a player who could launch a thousand coaching headaches, reminded me of Eddie Murphy in his *Saturday Night Live* days. I guess he still does.

Mosey stopped and his smile became a pained expression.

"Wait. Coach, come on . . . Springsteen again?"

"No, no," I said. "Bob Seger."

"Huh. Sounds like Springsteen. I can't really tell the difference between your old man rock."

"*Classic* rock," I said.

"Classic old man rock."

"Well then, Mister Deejay," I said, still smiling. "What do you suggest?"

"Glad you asked, because it reminds me . . . You do know I'm going to be on Saturday night, right? You gonna tune in?"

"Of course. Nine o'clock on 93.1."

"Coach," he said with a sigh, "it's 93.7 . . . The Groove."

It's fun to play around with Mosey.

"I'll be listening, Mose," I said.

I generally went back and forth on calling him Mosey and Mose. He responded to both, of course, as well as several other nicknames. Guys with that much personality usually have a ton of nicknames.

"And I'll tell all my old man classic rock fans to give the hip-hop station a listen Saturday night, at least for the deejay."

"It's not a hip-hop station, all right? They play more than that," Mosey said. He looked down at his phone and brushed at the screen with his finger. "And hey, seriously . . ."

He looked up.

"Make sure you're listening because I'm going to throw some tunes your way. Some old school stuff that you'll like."

"Old school hip-hop? What would that be?"

"Old school R&B for you. They told me I could play anything for my hour."

"Anything? Woooow . . . celebrity swagger."

"Well, almost anything," Mosey said with a slightly embarrassed grin. "It's my show."

"So you can play Bob Seger?"

"Only if I want people to turn off the radio."

I looked back at my computer. Man, I hate email.

"So, Coach, what do you got for me today?"

"Well . . ." I said, leaning back in my chair and folding my arms. I was taking my time, enjoying the distraction of my favorite former player and realizing I didn't have a lot for him to do that week.

"Can you chop up some video?"

"Sure, no problem."

All our game footage is now uploaded onto computers, and the kids have access to it. Some are so tech savvy that they can have highlight reels put together in minutes and then blasted out on Twitter and other places. Mosey is great at everything tech, and he can do just about anything, it seems, on his iPhone or iPad. He's like my personal I.T. guy.

"Great. Pull some highlights for Ferguson and Beaz. It would be great to start building some tape of those guys as sophomores."

"Good and bad stuff?" Mosey asked. "Or just good?"

"Just good for now. We can put together something for instruction later."

"Okay. But wait, Coach, before I get to it, you gonna tell me what's going on?"

"With what?"

"Come on, Coach."

Oh yeah, of course. Mosey's so plugged in, he obviously knew. He probably knew more than me.

"I don't really know, Mose."

"No way they cut football," he said. "Just blowin' smoke, makin' threats, acting important."

"Hope you're right."

"They don't how important football is. There's some kids who wouldn't go to school if they didn't have football."

"I hope they'd still go to school," I said.

"You know what I mean. There'd be a huge hole. It's like their life. It was like my life, you know."

"I do," I said, "and that's why I'm grooming you to be the next football coach here. You can take over for me when I get old."

"You're already old."

"When I get *older.*"

"Hey, hey," Mosey said. "I like it, I like it."

He flashed the big smile that draws everyone in. When Mosey was just a sophomore, the newspaper picked him as athlete of the week after he had a big interception and returned a kickoff for a touchdown. The first line of the story was about how, even after his monster game, Mosey was still best known for his smile.

"So you're not worried about the board meeting and all that?"

I shrugged.

"I've got plenty of things to worry about. I've got a football season to prepare for and a team to bring together. I'm not worrying about anything else until I know more about what's going on. I only worry about the things I can control."

"Okay then . . . as long as this doesn't affect my pay," Mosey said.

"You're safe," I said. "That's the great thing about an unpaid internship."

We don't actually have internships, but Mosey is kind of like an intern when he comes into the coaches' offices for a few hours each Thursday, and he's certainly important. Mosey is a technical wizard and a morale booster. He's one of those guys everyone wants to be around.

"I can probably finish that video today," Mosey said. "If I finish early, maybe we can work on expanding your music repertoire."

"Ah," I said with a chuckle.

I got up from my desk chair, feeling the strain in my lower back from jogging a day earlier. It was the first time I had run in a month, and my body wasn't reacting too well. I needed to get back into some kind of routine, but my days had been anything but routine lately.

"Well, Mose, I've got to talk with the coaches. Anything you need from me?"

"Nah, I'm good," he said as I gathered some papers and grabbed my phone.

Across the room, the soft hum of an electric motor began as Mosey scooted his wheelchair in front of the desk. I turned toward the door to the larger adjoining room shared by the other coaches and then turned back to watch Mosey as he reached behind his wheelchair and hooked his fingers around the drawstring of the pack hanging from the corner of the backrest. The neon green pack was one of the flashes of color that Mosey always brought into the room. He had a huge collection of baseball hats, which always looked fresh and crisp, and who knows how many pairs of sneakers.

"Nikes only," he once told me. "Air Force Ones."

Pretty slick. Mosey was always pretty slick, even when he was cutting in front of receivers, picking off passes, and talking trash.

"I don't talk trash," he told me. "I talk truth."

Good ol' Mose. He scared the crap out of a few receivers. But he also cracked them up as he was shutting them down. Mose was like a Deion Sanders starter kit, attitude included, when he was sixteen. Creekside had never seen anyone like him.

At twenty-four years old, Mosey can still talk truth. His truth now is God, he says, although he's not one to throw out a lot of Bible verses. He talks a lot about having faith that everything happens for a reason, even when we don't understand God's plan. I'm sure that belief helps him make sense of his world now.

Mosey can talk about anything, which is why I told him he needs his own talk show. Sports, music, religion, politics, anything. Put him on *The View*, and he would win over the other hosts, I promise you. He'd just give that smile.

But as Mosey grabbed his pack, he wasn't smiling. His face showed the concentration and effort it took to turn his torso, lift his arm, and place the pack on the desk. He tapped the control stick on his wheelchair a couple of times to scoot tightly under the desk that years earlier had been set up for him. He slowly pulled his iPad out of the pack and then, with his right arm, slid the headphones that were around his neck over his right ear. He lifted his left arm, which trembled slightly as it raised, and slid the headphone over his left ear.

"What are you listening to today?" I asked.

His smile was back as he looked over his shoulder.

"Not sure yet. Starting with Soulja Boy."

"Is that your favorite right now?"

"Nah, Soulja Boy's all right. Just wanna hear Crank That. Reminds me of football."

"Pregame warm-ups?"

"Yup."

"I remember some of your dancing out there."

Mosey scooted back in his wheelchair and turned toward me.

"Oh yeah, I loved me some Soulja Boy back then. But we had to make sure we got the clean version."

He broke into a smile.

"I know how you feel about that cussin'."

He obviously hadn't heard me lately.

CHAPTER 4

A S people filed into the meeting chamber of the Creekside government center, I decided on a spot near the front, but off to the side. Jim Hartline and three other varsity coaches sat with me, and I saw a few coaches for the younger kids, down to the middle schools. I looked at the agenda for the school board meeting and there it was: "discussion of aspects of extracurricular programs, including athletics."

The agenda said citizens would have the opportunity to address the board regarding new policy, revised policy, or proposed policy. Each speaker would be limited to three minutes, apparently. Good luck with that.

The meeting chamber was pretty crowded, and I was a little nervous. I also remember thinking, as the agenda papers ruffled and the hum of conversation grew in the room, how old I felt. A day earlier my wife and I had taken Emma to see Santa Claus, and I wondered if that would be the last time. She had never really said much about Santa, and her brothers were good about keeping quiet, but I figured she was just playing along. Time moves on; things change.

At the same time, I was thinking about the other high school football coaches who were still preparing for games. The state semifinals were that weekend, and I remember the rush of pride, excitement, and anxiety—not unlike what I felt as a player—when my teams made deep playoff runs. My teams had done it twice, including once at Franklin, the small school I coached for five years. My Franklin team lost in the semis.

But in my third season at Creekside, we won it all.

I can't deny that being one of the largest schools in Class 3A helped that year. It was our last season before our growing enrollment pushed us into 4A. The team was flourishing with Coach Hartline's spread offense, and we could score quickly or outmuscle just about anyone. We had some players that doubled up on offense and defense, but not as many as most schools in 3A. That kept our team fresh.

We also had a few game-changers, including Mosey, a talented, boisterous, hilarious, frustrating sophomore. He started the season as someone we expected to be pretty good at cornerback, and by the end of the season, he was our most indispensable player. He shut down receivers, returned kicks, and added offensive punch with his big-play ability. In the championship game, we put him at quarterback in the Wildcat formation, and he ran for nearly a hundred yards on only seven carries. Everything just came together that season.

And now the football program was being picked apart.

School board president Fisher Henderson called the meeting to order, and for thirty minutes, the board rolled through items such as a proposed increase of student lunch prices, the recognition of Teachers of the Month, and a vote for authorization of a job order for fencing and concrete work at one of the middle schools. It was like sitting through rinky-dink bands before a concert's headliner.

More people filed in as the meeting progressed, and with most of the seats filled, they began lining up along the back wall. Two security guards stood up front, flanking the seven school board members and superintendent Bashum, who were on the raised stage, seated behind a large C-shaped desk adorned with microphones and shiny nameplates. They looked very important.

"Next on the agenda is a public hearing regarding the budget for the next school year," the board president said. "Dr. Bashum, can you provide some information about the consulting firm and the printouts and where we are in the process?"

Heads turned toward Bashum, who adjusted the microphone in front of him and looked out at the crowd.

"As in past years, we've been evaluating programs and services as we track this year's budget and prepare the next one. This has been especially needed since 2011, a couple of years before I was here, when state funding was reduced."

I caught the eye of Dave Holgate, but he didn't react. He looked down at some papers as Bashum continued.

"Data from the cost-containment analysis—some of it—is what you see on the handouts. It includes a breakdown of extracurriculars, net costs and revenues, and what the cost-containment analysis defines as recoverable dollars."

Coach Hartline looked at me, shook his head, and pretended to fall asleep.

"Thanks, supe," he whispered to me, "for making this so easy to understand."

There was enough data to make your head spin, and it was jammed onto the front and back of one page. The type size wasn't much bigger than fine print on a car advertisement, and Bashum sounded like a car commercial as he spoke. You know the ending of the ads when they talk real fast with all the disclaimers, like certain-restrictions-apply-you-may-not-qualify-your-results-may-vary? Something like that.

The handout seemed like an all-out blitz on football. Other sports were on there, and so were extracurriculars such as theater arts, band, and choir, along with expenses and revenues. Our varsity football team doesn't draw the huge crowds of some other schools, but we come close to breaking even. If there's a "financial albatross," as Dave Holgate mentioned, it's the lower levels of football. But without freshman and junior-varsity teams, there won't be a varsity team. Varsity football players don't parachute into the program.

On Bashum's printout, the costs of the lower-level teams stood out like Tom Brady in a Pop Warner game. But that's because football is the king of high school extracurriculars. At the high school, we've got more than nine hundred boys enrolled, and more than a hundred and fifty are on football teams. Our speech and debate team has twelve members. Doesn't that need to be mentioned when comparing costs?

Behind the big C-shaped desk, with the audience in the darkened rows of seats looking up at him, Bashum continued. I would be sweating if those bright lights were bearing down on me, but he was almost robotic. Well-rehearsed, I imagine.

"And so, with some difficult, painful, decisions ahead of us," Bashum said, "with the help of our chief financial officer, I have prepared several options for the trustees. Those will be presented formally in the coming months, and all will include at least a slight pull from the district's reserves. But the rainy-day fund has been hit hard since 2011, so we're reaching a point with the budget where we need to aim for better long-range fiscal sustainability."

There were a couple seconds of silence, probably because much of the audience didn't know what the hell he was talking about. Then Bashum looked over at Henderson, which I guess signaled that he was done. The board prez looked a little surprised. I bet he thought Bashum would specifically address football.

"Thank you, Dr. Bashum," Henderson said. Stares swung back toward him, but I kept looking at Bashum, who wouldn't look my way.

"One of the options you mentioned involves football," Henderson said. "Before we open for public comments, can you talk about the budget proposals relating to that?"

Bashum nodded and looked deliberately serious, like a newscaster about to deliver the story of a bus crash.

"The proposal relating to football is for the seventh and eighth grade teams," he said. "If those teams were removed from the budget, there would be a substantial savings in equipment, insurance, travel, and also staffing."

"So," Henderson said, "you propose eliminating football at the two middle schools?"

"That's correct."

There was lots of reaction in the room, but I was too proud to show any. I knew people would be looking at me. I sat stone-faced, masking my emotions the way I do, or at least try to do, on the sidelines.

"It's a difficult decision," Bashum continued, raising his voice over the discontent. "It's one other school districts are making, and some school districts have never had football teams at the middle school level."

"What districts?" shouted a member of the audience.

"Districts throughout the country," Bashum said. "Others are eliminating it because of the need to cut budgets and because participation numbers are decreasing."

"Thank you, Dr. Bashum," Henderson interrupted. He looked down at some notes, tapped his hands on the table, and took a breath.

"I think now, um . . ." he said, pausing to look out at the standing-room only crowd. "I believe this would be a good time to open up for public discussion."

A line formed down the middle aisle, and people stepped up to the microphone. It was emotional and repetitive, as people said that cutting football would be ridiculous. It teaches kids more than about sports, they said. It teaches discipline and teamwork and personal responsibility.

I would've said a lot of the same things, so I was glad I declined to speak. It sounded better coming from the audience.

"Aren't we always hearing about our youth being overweight?" one woman said. "Take away sports and the kids will have another reason to play video games and stare at their phones."

"I want to be clear," Bashum said, "that we are not trying to take away sports. We have cut back on music and arts programs in recent years."

"But why football?" another person asked. "Why not basketball or volleyball or track or tennis or another sport?"

"Cutting those sports would not save a considerable amount of money," Bashum said. "Football incurs far higher costs for equipment, staff, insurance, and other aspects."

The public discussion went on for more than an hour. One man said he was tired of watching arts programs get slashed while sports were untouched, which made me want to send him the phone numbers of the two football coaches whose positions were eliminated two years ago. Another man said the district needs to make other programs more of a priority instead of worrying so much about football.

But the vast majority of the public discussion was in support of football. One man talked about how the sport was the last bastion of discipline for teenage boys. "Keep them in diapers too long and they won't know how to take a crap in the real world," he said.

Not the most graceful way of getting an idea across, but at least he showed up to support football. He didn't show up to support me, though.

"What we really need is a new head coach," he said. "Mr. Superintendent, you said middle school participation numbers are down? That's because the varsity team isn't good. Tuffy Nehls has let the program slip into mediocrity. Kids want to play for a winner, and whatever Coach Nehls is doing ain't working."

If you allow public comments on a football program, there's sure to be one person saying the coach doesn't know what he's doing. More than one person, actually, and they'll be saying far worse than "he doesn't know what he's doing." That's just the way it is. Everyone is an expert.

But when I took over, Creekside's program had been to the playoffs only twice in eight years, and since then we've had only two losing seasons. I'd rather be great than good, but let's be real. It's football in Texas, and it's going to be as competitive as anywhere.

Maybe that state championship set the bar too high, too quickly. Funny thing is, we almost lost in the second round that year. We actually got a little lucky, and if you ask a coach who's won a championship, he'll probably admit there was a lucky break or two along the way.

"Thank you for your comments, but I believe Coach Nehls does a great job," the board president said.

The commenter who caught me off guard was a doctor who got rolling about how football should be eliminated completely. For all grades. Not because of the cost, but because it's too dangerous. Football is just organized violence, he said.

"Why don't we leave it up to the parents to look out for their kids," was the response from the next person in line to speak. "You don't want to play? Don't play."

When the time for public comment was over, Bashum thanked

everyone for sharing their thoughts and then returned to his insurance-seminar delivery.

"It's never easy to cut anything," he said. "But we are facing difficult decisions."

Bashum could've stopped there. But then the superintendent, on a chilly night two weeks before Christmas, decided to drop a lump of coal in the stocking of every high school football coach in Texas—and beyond. Intentional or unintentional, he allowed our school district to be the spark of a national debate about high school football.

"It might be that, one day, the Creekside Sports Association will be better positioned to serve students with football than the high school," Bashum said. "It might be that way in other communities, too. Students might play for football select teams or clubs like the baseball and soccer and hockey teams that many of our students play for."

Bashum hesitated for a second, and someone in the crowd started to say something but then pulled back. Most of the crowd was silent, either in shock or numbed by boredom. Maybe they were exhausted from the parade of comments or simply didn't recognize the magnitude of what Bashum was saying.

I certainly did.

"The cost for high school football is rising," Bashum said, "and the number of participants in youth football is decreasing. It might be that the high school athletics program is not the right environment for a football team."

CHAPTER 5

AFTER a week of questions, emails, long talks with coaches, longer talks with my wife, and generally pondering the future, I had a permanent headache. Watching the state championship games at AT&T Stadium would be a nice break, and I arrived midway through a matchup of schools with enrollments of less than one thousand each. The championship weekend starts with tiny schools, with enrollments of less than two hundred, and finishes with schools that sometimes resemble small colleges.

Many of the games are televised live, but they still draw huge crowds. The games also draw a lot of coaches and athletic directors, who often congregate in the press box. I usually go up there and shoot the breeze for a while, but I thought about skipping it. I was tired of talking about Bashum and cuts and what might happen. I appreciated the support of the other coaches, but talking about it was a repeated kick to the gut.

Bashum's proposal to cut middle school football had hit the news, and it was treated as a big deal. Lee Fountain used the comments from Bashum about high school not being the right environment for football, and when he linked his story on Twitter, it went viral like a one-handed touchdown catch.

School district in Texas considering cutting football. Could football's days be numbered?

The hashtag #footballdying was soon trending on Twitter. People from all over the country were weighing in, piling on, positioning themselves as authorities—and as is usually the case on the internet, being jackasses. People were just trying to get attention. That's kind of what America has become, you know. We're the nation of reality stars, pseudocelebrities, and people who are famous for being famous.

"First domino might be falling for football" was one headline. "Is football past its prime?" was another. When school districts were asked if they have considered cuts to football, most said no. But when a few said yes, especially in Texas, it was treated as a monumental thing.

It was a bonanza for the news outlets because, in Texas, anything related to football is pretty much golden. Some newspapers from other states picked up the scent, and then one of the national newscasts pushed it hard.

"Some have said tackle football shouldn't be played by anyone under the age of fourteen," said one doctor. "But it's not unreasonable to consider banning football for anyone under eighteen."

Things had blown up in just four days, sparked by Bashum's proposed cuts to middle school football. And he hadn't even mentioned anything about concussions or injuries.

In the two previous years, three small Texas school districts had dropped middle school football, and one had dropped football completely. It barely made a ripple in the news. But now the football environment was changing. The way football was perceived was different. There were the stories of former NFL players whose dementia was linked to head injuries. There were autopsies of former players whose brain showed chronic traumatic encephalopathy, a degenerative disease they say is the result of repetitive blows to the head.

Football was under a microscope. More than that, football was on trial. It was challenged to defend its existence. That made it easy for Bashum— Mr. "I played football myself"—to turn a campfire into a bonfire.

I was talking about that with Coach Solomon "Solo" Barnes as we sat in the back row of the AT&T Stadium press box. In the rows in front of us, coaches, media, scouts, and others who managed to get a pass were watching Felton High put the finishing touches on a state title.

Yeah, I had decided to go to the press box. It would mean some questions I didn't want to answer, but it was the best place to see the games, and I wanted some time to talk with Solo, who saved me a spot next to him. I filled up a soda, bought a bag of peanuts, and sat down for a few hours of football.

"What's going on? Solo said as I sat down. "This one's almost over."

"I know, I know," I said with a sigh. "Family stuff."

"Yeah, I get it. And there was probably a line of coaches with something to say."

"They all mean well."

"They're probably worried, too."

"It is what it is," I said with a shrug.

Solo was wearing a coach's short-sleeve polo despite the freezing weather outside. He always wears tight shirts that prove he's a workout fanatic. He was a defensive back at Texas A&M-Commerce and is probably in better shape now than he was in college. (That makes one of us).

Solo is a few years younger than me and has two daughters in middle school. We've known each other since we were assistants on the same staff years ago, and he's now the head coach at another school in suburban Dallas.

"I bet my superintendent wishes he could pull back some of this now," I said.

Solo nodded as we watched Felton's stud defensive tackle make another sack. This kid named Tyus Graham, he's like six-two and 270 pounds, and he had sacked the QB three times in one quarter. Almost impossible to block.

"He's a monster," I said. "I haven't seen anyone that dominant this year, even at the bigger schools. Committed to the Sooners?"

"He *was* committed to Oklahoma, but he's looking again. You know how those commitments go. They change in a blink."

"Or a Twitter post."

"Right," Solo said. "A Twitter post with an action photo and a bunch of logos and some stare that makes him look like a badass."

It's true. That's what recruiting has become.

"Every recruit's a rock star now," Solo said. "They're hashtag-blessed to get their fortieth scholarship offer and need a press conference to announce fifteen finalists."

I grabbed a handful of popcorn.

"Hey, aren't we all hashtag-blessed?" I said with a smile.

Solo rolled his eyes.

"Remember the kid I had a couple years ago? Dabney? He changed his commitment at least three times. Who knows how many recruiters he was blowing smoke at. One recruiter was mad at me because I couldn't convince him to stick to his commitment."

I laughed.

"If I could control what any teenager does, I would have a lot less to worry about. I can't even control what my own teenagers do."

"No doubt," I said.

"So how are the kids? How's Mickey?"

"Oh, he's fine. He's down there somewhere," I said, pointing to the stands. "I'm not sure who he's with today. Hopefully he'll stay out of trouble."

"He will. You lucked out with him. Now if you had a teenage daughter . . ."

"Oh man, I don't want to think about that. I'm already worried about Emma."

"It scares me so much sometimes, Tuff. I see these teenage boys every day."

"Does the dating policy still stand?"

"Absolutely. Alicia knows she better not be telling me about any boyfriend before high school. I don't even want her going on, like, one-on-one dates next year when she starts high school. Maybe when she's a sophomore."

"Good luck with that."

We watched as the media guys stood up and headed out of the press box to take an elevator to the field. Less than a minute was left and the Felton crowd was chanting "Fel-ton Fal-cons."

Solo and I rolled our chairs forward to let a pair of reporters walk behind us.

"If you talk to Graham," one said, "ask if he's committed."

"He's not," the other said, adding sarcastically, "but I'll ask if he's going to announce with a fireworks display or by jumping out of a plane."

As the Felton players stormed onto the field to celebrate a title, I thought of the championship season at Creekside. It'll probably never happen again, but so many coaches never get a ride like that. I'm hashtag-blessed like those rock-star recruits.

"I don't think I have any recruits this year that will be shooting off fireworks," Solo said. "One going to UTEP, a few others getting calls from small schools, but it's pretty quiet. Recruiters still calling about Cason?"

"Not really. Boston College is a done deal. He's enrolling early."

Alex Cason, my starting QB for three seasons, decided on Boston College over several other schools. He was probably going to be the only kid from Texas on the BC roster, but the school was somehow special to him. He spent his early years in New Jersey and wanted another taste of the Northeast.

Alex is six-foot-four, has a strong arm, and is really smart and mature beyond his years. He's never been overwhelmed by any moment or challenge, even way back when he was a fifteen-year-old sophomore making his first start.

Without Alex last season, we wouldn't have made the playoffs. It's hard for me to admit that, considering his backup was Mickey, but I need to look through some serious Dad-tinted glasses to make Mickey look like a star QB. He's not even a star wide receiver, but that's where he's much more comfortable and productive. I planned to move him to quarterback as a senior, but only because our quarterback pool was so shallow.

We looked good at receiver, had a hard-nosed running back and decent size on the lines, and even had two kickers who could nail field goals. Some years we struggled to find a guy who could simply make short point-after kicks, and suddenly we had two guys who could nail a field goal from close to fifty yards. But what I needed was a QB.

"I wouldn't be surprised if Cason plays as a freshman," I said. "Always a step ahead of everyone. He's probably watching Boston College games right now, breaking everything down."

"Hey, you're not so bad off," Solo said. "I'd take Mickey in a heartbeat."

"As a quarterback?" I said with a smile. "Uh . . . I don't know. Mickey's good at a lot of things, but throwing the ball isn't one of them. Not accurately. I'd love to keep him at receiver, but what good is a receiver if there's nobody to throw it to him?"

"Yeah . . . well, maybe you'll get the coach's dream. Say your prayers, Tuff."

"Star QBs aren't moving into my district," I said, chuckling. "The families of the star QBs always seem to find houses, or apartments, or some kind of address for the powerhouse schools."

"Coach Nehls," Solo said as he leaned back and gave a look of surprise. "Are you saying that kids are transferring for athletic purposes?"

"Coach Barnes, I am as stunned as you are."

We looked down at the field as the teams for the next championship game began warming up. Highlights from the previous game were flashing on the giant video board, a band was playing a cover of Ozzy Osbourne's "Crazy Train," and the booster-club dads were unrolling deflated tunnels as preparation began for another dramatic entry.

Some fans from the earlier game were leaving, but many were going to hang around. On a cold Friday evening in North Texas, AT&T Stadium was a good place to be. Even for a coach who realized he would probably never get back to a championship game and was leading a program getting hacked by its own leadership.

"Maybe I shouldn't even worry about a quarterback," I said. "Bashum might decide we don't have enough money for that position and force us to go ten-on-eleven."

CHAPTER 6

I'M not a Scrooge, but December 26th is one of my favorite days of the year. Once we get through Christmas, and everything gets cleaned up and put away and kind of back to normal, I get a week or so of relaxation before school begins again. A little bubble of calm.

But not last December. Before the year was over, I knew that one of my assistants would be leaving and that another was looking to leave. I'm sure all my assistant coaches were wondering about the future as our school district took aim at the football program.

Less than three weeks had passed since the school board meeting, and it was hard to be optimistic. I'd even heard that some families with kids in middle school and elementary school were looking at homes in other school districts.

Sounds drastic, right? Probably helps cement the stereotype of the over-the-top sports parent. But I get it.

Parents do whatever they can to help their kid succeed. Parents want their kids to get a good education, of course. But what if a boy or girl shows enough potential in a sport that a college scholarship is a possibility? Go to a school with a strong athletic program, with administration and community support, financial resources, and good coaching, and a kid has an advantage.

If you have a kid who's interested and talented in music, wouldn't you seek out the best school? Nobody would question parents' priorities if they move their kids to a school with better arts or music programs. What if a school was making big cuts to the funding of a marching band? If your kid has been spending time practicing and dedicating time to learning and improving, you'd want to move to another school if you could. It just makes sense.

It made me worry more about what was happening, and would

eventually happen, to my football program. I spent nights lying in bed, staring into nothing, considering things I thought I would never consider. I wished school would start again so I wouldn't have so much time to think.

One thing the winter break did allow time for was a going-away lunch with Alex Cason, who graduated early so he could enroll at Boston College in the spring semester. Some top high school recruits do that so they can go through spring practice with the college team.

We planned to meet on the last Friday of winter break so that Mosey could come along. Alex and Mosey are pretty close, but you wouldn't know it if you listened to them talk. Or maybe the way they annoy each other is a sign of that closeness.

I got to the restaurant first—a chicken-tenders place, as selected by Alex—and waited out front. My phone buzzed as a text came in from Mosey telling me that his "staff" was running a little behind. Mosey's parents and his aunt, who is one of the nicest people you'll ever meet, take care of what he calls his "personal needs." On this day, Auntie Rae was driving the wheelchair-accessible van, and she pulled up a minute or two after Alex arrived.

Alex and I waved to Auntie Rae as she got back in the van, and Mosey came toward us. He was in the manual wheelchair, which he now used most of the time instead of the electric one. His arms were getting stronger every day, he said. He was having more feeling in his chest, too. Someday he was going to walk again.

"It's God's plan," he often said. "I'm just getting ready for it."

The wheelchair had a red sports bag, one of the dozen or so brightly colored sports bags in Mosey's rotation, hooked over the backrest. The cherry red matched the swoosh on his white sneakers, which looked like they could be on display at the store. He wore dark jeans, a silver Cowboys windbreaker, and a black hat with a gray-and-red checkered pattern along the brim. His iPhone was on his lap, and a Bluetooth was clipped to his ear.

Looking sharp, as always.

"There he is," Alex said, reaching out to Mosey for a fist bump.

Mosey smiled and raised a loosely clenched fist. "What's up, Mr. Boston?"

"Not much."

"Wait. Where's your car?" Mosey said. "Did ya pahk the cahr in Hahvud Yahd?"

"Oh, here we go," Alex said, turning toward me. "How long has he been waiting to say that?"

I smiled and shrugged. I figured Mosey had said that before.

"Wait a second," Mose said, "are you saying that my Boston accent is not wicked awesome?"

"I am indeed saying that," Alex said, "and you're a wicked chump."

Alex turned toward the restaurant and started walking. I gave a fist bump to Mosey as he passed and then walked behind the two. Alex held the door open, and Mosey rolled past.

"Thanks, chowdahead."

Alex shook his head and looked over at me.

"He's just making sure you're ready for Boston," I said, tapping him on the chest as I walked by.

We got our food and headed for a table that had been wiped "clean" but still had a slightly greasy feel. Alex carried Mosey's basket of chicken fingers to the table and took the lid off three dipping sauces: honey mustard, barbecue, and creamy gravy. Healthy stuff.

Mosey took over from there. He nudged the basket into position in front of him, picked up one, dipped it in the honey mustard, and started eating. Sometimes it's hard to watch as Mosey completes tasks we take for granted. He bites down hard and squints as he concentrates intensely, and when he tries to lift something that's heavy for him, and I can see his arm tremble, it's hard to resist stepping in.

But once everything is in reach, Mosey doesn't need any help wiping out a basket of chicken fingers. He started in on his favorite food, washing it down with sweet tea, as the exit interview began with Alex.

"Exit interview?" Alex said.

"That's right. Just like when you leave a job and the boss asks what you really think of the place, what things can be done differently, all that."

"You do this with all the players?"

"Some. . . . But usually not while they're eating chicken fingers."

Alex pulled off his maroon Boston College hat and now looked like a surfer dude, with his straight sandy blond hair that almost reached his shoulders. He finished off a piece of chicken while dipping another in sauce, eating like chicken fingers were available for one day only. He's six-four and solidly built, and he looked even bigger as he sat next to Mosey.

"Uh, okay . . . what would I do differently. Hmm . . . ," Alex said, wiping his thumb on one of the napkins piled between him and Mosey. "Well, I wish I could play another year."

"We could certainly use you," I said.

"Mickey will be fine," Alex said. "But I would really like to play some more. High school went by too fast."

"Yeah, well, you're only really halfway through senior year," Mosey said.

"Right now, I kinda wish I hadn't graduated early."

"You'll have a blast in college," I said. "Boston will be great."

"Wicked awesome," Mosey said.

"You already used that one," Alex said to Mosey.

"Sorry, chowdahead."

Mosey went back to his chicken fingers. Alex shook his cup around, rattling the ice before he took a long sip.

"If I was still at Creekside this spring, I could play basketball, hang out with friends, and kind of coast to graduation."

"But you'll have a head start at BC," I said. "That's a good thing."

"I know. But I guess these last few months of high school seem more important now than when I was committing. It still seemed like I had so much time. I was always so worried about the future."

"That you didn't enjoy the present," Mosey said.

"Yeah. See, Coach, I told you Mose is more than a smartass. He's kind of smart, too."

"Obviously," Mosey said.

"Well, I'm glad you want to stay around here," I said. "But I think the time's right. And I hope I didn't put too much pressure on you. I know Coach Hartline and I expected a lot."

"No, no. I appreciate all that stuff. And you know, playing high school football and hanging out with the guys, and even the practices . . ."

Alex smiled.

"At least some of the practices. I mean, those were just the greatest times. Most fun I've had in my life."

"Well, I wish we had won more games to keep things going longer, but I know you'll do great at BC. You probably caught on to things faster than any player I've coached."

Mosey cleared his throat.

"Okay, you and Mosey caught on to things faster than anyone."

"So what's next?" I asked. "You've got like what, three or four days?"

"Leaving Tuesday. Hanging out with the guys Saturday night, and Sunday night we're having a big family dinner. I've still got to pack, too. And, you'll be happy, Coach . . . I'm going to get a haircut."

"No man, you can't!" Mosey said. "Think of the girls. You're gonna go and break their hearts like that?"

"It's college, so I'm kinda changing things up."

Mosey shook his head and smiled.

"Coach, looks like our Alex is growing up. So . . . you said you're hanging out with friends Saturday night?"

Alex nodded as he took a bite of another chicken finger.

"Okay, man, then you've got to tell them to listen to my show."

"Nine P.M.," Alex said. "93.7."

"Look at this guy," Mosey said, turning to me. "He knows what's good."

"Tell the people at the station that their internet stream is spotty," Alex said. "I might want to stream it in Boston. Maybe I can get you some new listeners."

"Wicked awesome," Mosey said.

"God," Alex said with a sigh, "I don't know why I do you any favors. . . . But Coach, it's a good show."

"Yeah, yeah, Coach," Mosey said. "Alex might look like a Ken doll, but he knows his music."

Mosey and Alex bumped fists.

"So," Alex said, turning back toward me, "are they really going to cut into football?"

"They're going to cut something from football," I said. "Just waiting to see what it's going to be."

"So it's for sure?"

"Nothing's for sure."

"Who makes the final decision?"

"The school board."

"So are they gonna vote? And when?"

"I don't know, and I'm trying not to worry about it."

"You don't have any say?"

I chuckled.

"I can say a lot of things, and I have, to the superintendent and the school board members. But they don't have to listen."

I cut myself off and leaned back in my chair. I didn't want to be ranting to a high school student.

"I read about it," Mosey said, "but it should be a bigger deal. They're trying to kill football. Why aren't more people going crazy?"

"People might not believe it," I said.

"So why are you so calm?" Alex asked.

"Do I seem calm?" I laughed. "It's just that I can't do anything about it. I can't talk with the media. Coaches aren't allowed to do it."

"That's crazy," Alex said. "This guy says he's going to whack football and you're not allowed to talk about it? That takes some serious hubris."

"Hubris?" Mosey said as he started to laugh. "Dang, dude. Hubris? I guess you're like Mr. College Man, right?"

"Wicked awesome," Alex said.

Mosey winked and nodded, and Alex started to crack up.

"But . . ."

Alex wanted to keep talking, but Mosey was staring hard at him and nodding. Then Mosey began shaking his head.

"What now?" Alex said.

"Just trying to picture you in Boston."

"What do you mean?"

"I don't know, man," Mosey said. "You're going to the northeast, so I think you need like, um . . . a harder edge or something."

"What?"

"What do you think, Coach? What can we do to toughen up the golden boy? A few tats? Some scars?"

Alex dropped his head into his right hand and rubbed his eyes. I had a flashback to years earlier when Mosey was playing for me. I had the same reaction when Lil' Eric Posey did all his big talking. When he was a freshman, before he became our beloved Mosey, a couple of linemen jammed him into a locker.

"Anyway, Coach," Alex said as he gently punched Mosey's shoulder, "what I was saying was . . . I just don't get the superintendent. Won't he get run out of town if he tries to cut football?"

"I don't think he knows what cutting middle school football would do. Most people in the city probably don't know what it would do."

"If you don't have guys playing football before high school, isn't that pretty much a killer?"

"It would certainly make things difficult."

"So what do you think is going to happen?" Alex said.

I took the napkin out of my lap and crumpled it in the plastic basket in front of me. Alex had been looking down at his hat, curving the brim, but then he looked right at me, waiting for an answer. On my right, Mosey was doing the same. I guess these guys really thought I knew what was going to happen.

I leaned back, took a deep breath, and lied.

"I really don't know."

CHAPTER 7

YEAH, I pretty much knew.

I had known from the moment I told Bashum that it would be dangerous for middle schoolers to be funneled into the Creekside football league. The coaches in that league are, at best, well-meaning but largely unqualified. At worst, the coaches are know-it-alls who actually know nothing and can be dangerous to a kid's physical and emotional health. They think that screaming can mask a coach's incompetence. It doesn't. Neither do color-coordinated hats and Under Armour coaches' shirts.

I told Bashum that, but he still went forward with the plan to cut middle school football. His words: "The school district cannot provide everything for everyone."

Cutting middle school football was going to be a huge blow to the high school program. Instead of freshmen arriving with some fundamentals, as well as the experience of playing in the offensive and defensive schemes we use in high school, most would be starting at zero.

And what about the kids whose parents couldn't pay the fees to play in the Creekside football league? There was discussion a few years ago about having participation fees for high school athletics, which some other districts have, but the board decided not to do that because it might create a hardship for families. Wasn't this creating a hardship?

It was creating a disaster, I'd say.

But Bashum knew he had the votes. He only needed four, and after another contentious and pointless round of public input, the Creekside school board made it official. Whether the cut would be permanent would be determined later, but it was out of the budget for the school year. Dave Holgate told me he was embarrassed to be on a board that could be so shortsighted.

The next day, Lee Fountain came by the athletic offices. I warned him that I couldn't offer much information, but he came anyway. He's been to the school enough times that they pretty much wave him through the front desk and send him my way.

"So, slow day, huh?" I said as he closed my office door.

"Yeah," he said, taking a seat on the other side of my desk. "Just a school district in the epicenter of the high school football world cutting the legs off its football program. So nothing much, really."

"Well, at least I don't have to play it up to you," I said. "Some people are like, big deal . . . it's just middle school teams."

"But where do the high school players come from?" Lee said.

"Exactly."

"So it really is like cutting the legs out from under the program. Or at least a kick to the nuts."

"Eloquent, Lee."

Lee pulled a pen and notepad out of the backpack he always carried around. He shook his head and sighed, mirroring my emotions.

"Sorry, Tuff. Shitty situation."

"No argument."

"So, are you allowed to talk now? Has Bashum lifted the media ban, or whatever it is?"

"It's not really a ban. He just said any questions needed to go through the communications department, and I didn't want to talk about it anyway."

Lee nodded like he understood. But he had come to the school that day, so maybe he didn't, because I really didn't want to talk about it. I knew he was just doing his job, though, and we've known each other a long time.

"So what brings you here today?"

"I'm writing a follow-up story on the budget decision, and I wanted to get some kind of comment. I talked with Bashum after the meeting last night, and he gave me the same line about how he wishes nothing had to be cut."

I nodded, but I still didn't want to talk about it.

"Oh, I don't know . . ."

"You don't have to comment on the decision, but what about the challenges this creates? You're going to have to do some things differently, right?"

"When we start getting freshmen who never played middle school football, definitely."

"So, just for this story, is there something I can use from you? Or I can say you declined comment or that you referred questions to someone else."

Lee knew that would get me to say something. I always thought that when a story said someone declined comment, it made the guy look like he was angry and bitter, and even if that's how I felt, I didn't want to come across that way.

"Okay . . . here you go," I said. "We've got great kids in this community and great families and support for the football program. Our goal will still be to teach kids not only how to play football, but how to be successful off the field, to work hard and work together, and to be leaders and not make excuses."

Lee jotted on the notepad.

"How do you even read what you're scribbling?"

"I'm recording," he said, raising his phone off his lap. "Anything else?"

"Not really."

"What about transfers? Are you worried that kids and their families will move out of the district?"

"Of course, but that's off the record."

"Okay then," Lee said, flipping the notebook cover back to the front and sticking his pen across the top of it. That could mean he was about to leave, but not on this day.

"You know, if you just added in that this was a real kick to the nads by the administration . . ."

"You'd have a better story?"

"A much better story. A much truer story."

Lee leaned back in his chair.

"So, off the record, how are things?"

I shrugged. Lee was one of the few reporters I would talk to at length, even off the record, about what was really going on, or how I felt, or whatever.

"I've still got a job a lot of people would love," I said. "Hard to complain."

"But if the cuts make it impossible to do that job, then what?"

"They don't make it impossible to coach. They just might make it tough to win. I've already lost two coaches, and others are looking around. Some kids are leaving, too."

"Middle schoolers?"

"I'm sure there are families of middle schoolers looking to move, but I don't know much about them. But three high school players are leaving . . . so far."

"In the middle of the year?"

"One of them—a sophomore named Shawn Simon. Big, strong kid who was going to be on the offensive line, and maybe defensive line, next year. He played varsity in the last half of the season. He's heading to Rockwall. The others, another sophomore and a freshman, are moving after the semester."

"Are they moving just because of the football cuts?"

"They won't say because they need me to sign the transfer papers. But Chandler Carter—he's the freshman—is a linebacker who had a chance to make varsity next season. His dad told me straight out that he knew what cutting middle school football would do. He's not shopping his kid around, but he's checking out schools. Chandler won't be back."

"So he's moving for football?"

"Oh yeah. But I'll sign his form and let him transfer clean. I don't want any kid who doesn't want to be here, and especially if his parents don't want him here. And what district is going to contest the eligibility of a kid coming from a program that just got whacked? Well, unless it was Alex Cason, because he was so damn good. Perfect time for him to leave for college."

"What about you? Sounds like a good time for you to go."

"Go where?" I laughed.

"Not many coaches around here have won a state championship."

It was nice of Lee to bring up, but I had given very little thought to moving. If I were ten years younger, or maybe if Emma hadn't come along—and to be clear, I wouldn't change that for a dozen state titles—then maybe I wouldn't need to think hard before applying for jobs. After my third year at Creekside, when our three-season run had included thirty-two wins and a state title, I could've jumped to a bigger program and tried to create a powerhouse. I was in my early forties, and I had some skins on the wall. The time was right.

But I don't know. Could be I didn't have the ambition or ego or confidence to try to drive a powerhouse. I also felt some loyalty to the players and the superintendent who had hired me—the guy before Bashum. Had I left after just three years, even if people understood why, it would've felt like a betrayal.

I was fortunate to win a state title early in my career. I would love to win another, but that carrot on the stick, the one so many coaches chase unsuccessfully for decades, didn't drive me the same way. Creekside felt comfortable. Maybe I had become complacent and wasn't pushing forward with the same energy, but we were still coaching up the kids, leading them, molding them, developing them. We just didn't have a lot of the raw material of guys like Alex Cason, or Daeshon Watts, the bull of a running back I had years ago, or even good ol' Mosey.

I never got to see Mose's full football potential, but as a sophomore, especially in our smaller classification at the time, he was amazing out there. The speed, the grace, the intuition—and good Lord—the swagger. Mose would've driven me crazy if he wasn't so damn lovable.

My goal has always been to build a competitive team. Then, in the years when we're blessed with a sprinkling of truly dynamic players, I hope for deep playoff runs. But you know, the best teams don't always win, and neither do the best coaches. Busby Merchant, who is the best high school coach I've known, didn't win a state title. People brought that up when Merchant, whose staff I worked on for three years, retired a few years ago. He had three hundred wins, but hey, he never won the big one!

Coach Merchant won the big one. He coached thirty-five years and won the admiration, and then adoration, of his players. They played out of their minds for him, and he was a father figure to all of them, even the kids who had great dads themselves.

A couple years before he retired, he took his team to the state finals for the second time in his career, and it looked like he would get his fitting ride into the sunset. Then his star quarterback held the ball too long, got blindsided in the pocket, and was flattened in the first quarter. Broken collarbone.

His team still almost won. It was heartbreaking. But after it was over, what did he do? Pulled his crying players together, told them how much they meant to him, told him he would never forget how they had worked and their time together as a family. That's a coach.

I'm not trying to build a juggernaut at Creekside. I had forty-seven kids on my varsity roster last season, and other than Alex, I might have one that'll play college football. Maybe two or three, including Mickey, if you count small colleges. But what I had last year was forty-seven kids who got to experience something really special, something that people who haven't played football will never understand. What makes football what it is, or makes it so worth it, are the relationships. Teammates, coaches, friends forever linked. That's what stays with you. That's what you want to stay with you.

Across from the desk, Lee unzipped his backpack and pulled out a manila folder.

"Here," he said. "I meant to give this to you last time I was by."

"What is it?"

"Open it up."

I unfastened the clasp and slid out a group of photos that made me smile and cringe at the same time. Man, I looked so young. It wasn't that long ago, but I looked so young. And, geez, how much weight have I gained?

I was on the sidelines with a headset slightly crooked on my head, pointing at something. In the next photo, I had my arms raised in a touchdown signal, waiting for the official's call after our running back fought into the end zone in the championship game. And then there was a photo of Mose, at the height of his glory, effortlessly sidestepping a tackle at the start of a punt return for a touchdown. And finally Mose coming off the field with his arms spread apart like he was flying, his helmet pushed back, his mouth wide open, his eyes so bright that they seemed to be reflecting the stadium's lights. I was to the side, waving him off the field, already worrying about the next play. I wish now that I had taken more time to appreciate the moments of that day.

"These are awesome. Where'd you get these?"

"They're from a photographer who used to do freelance work for the paper. I've known him for a long time, and he said he heard Mosey on the radio a few weeks ago, and he remembered he still had his files from the championship game. He thought Mosey would like to see some of them. They only used one photo in the paper, and they didn't post all the photos on the website the way they do now."

"Oh yeah, Mose will love these. Does the photographer want them back?"

"Nope, those are yours."

"Great," I said with a smile. "Tell him I said thanks."

"I'll tell him. He knows Mosey's story well, and he was happy to hear him on the radio. So he's a deejay now?"

"Yeah, but he's kind of breaking into it. Mose is really good, but I don't tell him that because, you know, he already thinks a lot of himself. He has a show on Saturday nights."

"On The Groove."

"You're hipper than me," I said.

"Doubtful," Lee said.

"I wish Mose was here right now. He'd certainly entertain you. He'd also give you some of his business cards. Guy knows how to network."

"Yeah, I'm sure," Lee said. "Maybe he's the next big thing."

"Who knows? He's taken a bunch of broadcasting classes. He has a podcast too where he interviews people."

"The kid's sharp. . . . Well, not a kid anymore, I guess."

Lee picked up his backpack, put it on his lap, and started packing away his stuff.

"Sorry again that this is all goin' on," he said. "You know, maybe I'm just too close to high school football, but I really thought this would be a bigger deal. People are upset, but it's not how I thought it would be. I figured if you did something like this to football in Texas, people would be coming with torches and tar and feathers."

"People don't understand," I said. "They know the high school team will still be playing."

I shrugged. I did a lot of that in those early days of the football take-down when so much was out of my control.

"Wish I could say more, Lee, but it's a tough deal. If I push how terrible this is for the program, I'll just scare off more kids and families. And you know, I've never been through anything like this. I have no idea what the effect will be."

"Guess we'll know in a few years," Lee said. "And not just with you guys. Massington dropped middle school football last year, and although I didn't think much of that because Massington is never that great, that'll be interesting. A couple more districts in South Texas are considering it, too, and I guess it doesn't raise eyebrows anymore in other areas."

"It's a different culture in other places. My wife has family in Colorado, and it's just not the same. They think it's nuts down here."

"In some ways, it is," Lee said. "Think of how high school football has changed. All the recruiting stuff and the kids holding press conferences and the nationally televised games. But in other states . . ."

"It's different, no doubt," I said.

"And the concussions, the threat of lawsuits, the worries about inju-ries, it's got to be some trickle down from NFL and college. Is it trickling into Texas?"

"Probably inevitable," I said. "All the safety training we do now, all the safety protocols we have, all the hoops we jump through."

"A lot has changed since I played," Lee said.

"A lot has changed in just the last few years," I said, "and, yeah, it really is a good thing. I mean all the medical stuff we know. But with all that has come some fear of football, and some of it is irrational."

"Like what's going on with the NFL and concussions?"

"No, no. That stuff—we're still off the record here—I get it. Years and years of playing in the NFL . . . those guys take some licks. It doesn't surprise me. Saddens me, doesn't surprise me. But the NFL is so different than high school football. It's just . . ."

I stopped for a moment and shook my head, knowing I was headed for a rant that I wanted to avoid. But it ended up making me feel better. At least a little.

"Look what's always on TV now," I said. "This mixed martial arts and ultimate fighting crap, where guys are just bludgeoning each other in a ring. But it's football that's on the firing line?"

"I know what you mean," Lee said. "But kids aren't in the ring."

"Yeah," I said. "It's about the kids, I guess. Your son is now, what, nine?"

"Just turned ten."

"He plays football."

"Yeah . . . flag," Lee said. "Some of his former teammates played tackle this year, but Josh stayed with flag. I'm not sure football is his favorite sport, though. He likes baseball."

"So what does his dad think?" I said with a smile.

"You know, Tuff, I loved everything about my, ahem, modest football days, and I'd like Josh to experience something like that. But all this new information . . . I don't know . . . I'm just not hurrying him into tackle. I think Josh is going to want to play football, but if he doesn't . . ."

Lee leaned forward on the backpack in his lap.

"Don't you worry when your sons are on the field?" he said.

I smiled and sighed.

"Lee, I worry every time my sons leave the house."

CHAPTER 8

I didn't tell Lee about everything. Even if it was off the record, I didn't feel like sharing all that was going on. That included how it looked like I would need to find a new quarterback. Not to replace Alex Cason, who was now a few weeks into his college experience and busy tweeting out photos of snowy scenes around his dorm. I knew Alex was gone, but now I needed a replacement for the guy who I thought would be Alex's replacement.

A replacement for Mickey.

It's kind of a long story. Kind of embarrassing, too, although I've told myself I shouldn't feel that way because I didn't start all this crap. But so here's the thing. I decided to let Mickey leave for another high school. Yeah, yeah, I know . . . after all the times I've talked with Solo and others about transfers that are officially "not for athletic purposes," I let Mickey leave for Putnam High.

Call me a hypocrite. Fine. But this was not like parents selling a million-dollar house and moving to a new city so their son could be a starting quarterback. I'll admit, though, that I was a lot like those parents in one respect. I was trying to do the best thing for my son.

Still, I guess you can call criticize me. But you weren't the coach getting the calls from parents saying they were moving their kids out of the district because of the cuts to football. You weren't the coach who watched players he expected to be starters take off for other places. You weren't the dad seeing the potential that his son's senior year of football could be a disaster.

Mickey was not transferring for athletic purposes. Of course not. He transferred to be part of an academic program unavailable at Creekside, and because Christine teaches at Putnam, he was eligible to enroll from outside the attendance boundary. We live a mile from the Putnam attendance boundary, anyway. Mickey's girlfriend, whose family we know pretty well through church, also attends Putnam.

That last part won't be listed on the Prior Athletic Participation Form, and neither will the fact that, after the elimination of our middle school football program, Creekside was bleeding out. Nine high school players had left for other schools. Five freshmen left and so did three sophomores, including one who I expected to be our top running back in the fall. A junior linebacker who was one of our team's leading tacklers transferred to a school in Mesquite.

Transfer number ten was Mickey, and I hated it. I really did. But for years he had talked about his senior season like a trip to the moon. I watched him work toward it, too, as he tried to maximize every bit of football ability in a body limited by his parents' genes.

I said Mickey was nearly six feet tall. He's really between five-ten and five-eleven. He runs terrific routes as a receiver, has great hands, and knows how to find soft spots in coverages. But breakaway speed? Forget it. Mickey is the king of the eight-yard reception.

That might sound like a putdown, but you run into third-and-eight a lot. Throw it to Mickey and he won't drop it. The problem I had at Creekside was that I didn't have a quarterback to throw it to him, so the plan was to put Mickey at quarterback and try to develop some receivers.

And then Michael Greer, the head coach at Putnam, called me. Coach Greer and I have known each other since he took over at Putnam six years ago. Our schools are only about eight miles apart, but we never play each other because Putnam is in 6A, the biggest classification, and Creekside is in 5A. Putnam has six thousand kids. It's one of the biggest schools in Texas and the only high school in a city of about 70,000.

When Christine went back to work full time a couple years ago, she took a job teaching English at Putnam. Coach Greer and I became more friendly after that. He's got a strong football program—a lot of kids to work with, obviously—but there's also some pressure. He hasn't won a state title, and the Putnam fans seem to think it's just a matter of snapping your fingers and raising the trophy.

We've got lots of talent, we've got the money behind our program, and look at our stadium and our state-of-the-art workout facility! Why haven't we won a state title?

Because nice facilities can't throw a touchdown pass or make a big defensive stop, that's why.

Anyway, Coach Greer gave me a call. We talked for a few minutes before he got to why he was calling. His defensive coordinator was leaving for a head coaching spot, and he wanted to know if I was interested.

I never would've got the call a year earlier. Head coaches don't usually step back to assistant positions unless they're unhappy with the school they're at, or they know the administration is unhappy with them. I didn't like what was going on at Creekside, but I wasn't ready to move.

Apparently a lot of other head coaches thought I might be ready, because they kept calling. For the first time since Creekside was basking in the glow of the state championship, I was a hot commodity. Or at least a warmish commodity.

But not as a head coach. I was in demand as a defensive coordinator, and all the attention was frightening. It hammered home the point that others thought Creekside was a toxic situation. I had to want out, right?

I didn't want out. I just wanted a different superintendent, and I wasn't ready to give up a head coaching position at a school I really liked. Pride was clouding my thinking, too. I worked for a long time and paid my dues, and I didn't want to take a step backward, even if my school district was backpedaling.

I had no trouble declining all the offers. Except for one, because going to Putnam made sense. There would be a pay cut, but it wouldn't be dramatic. I wouldn't have the athletic director duties I had at Creekside, and I wouldn't be sweating through budget discussions every year or be worrying about kids leaving. I'm sure Putnam has been affected by the state's pinching of education funds, but it's not reflected in the school's sports. Putnam's new stadium is like a high school football Taj Mahal, and that enormous high-definition video board, framed by glowing signs for well-heeled sponsors, looks like it was plucked from a college stadium.

But if I became the defensive coordinator at Putnam, that might be the end of the line for me as a head coach. Coach Greer isn't much older than me, and he isn't going anywhere. He doesn't want to coach at the college level, and he's got one of the plum jobs around. Everyone wants a head coaching job at a district with one high school because there's no division of financial resources and no division of the athletic talent. You have control over all the district's middle school teams, giving the kids two years of instruction tailored to your high school program. That was one of the things that originally attracted me to the Creekside job.

Eventually the Creekside school district plans to open another high school and an athletic director will oversee both schools. My master plan, pie-in-the sky thought, or whatever from years ago was that I would slide into that AD spot. I'd get into my fifties and start looking to cut back on the crazy hours of coaching, because although I do love it, there comes a time when it wears on you. I know some great coaches, some legendary guys, who have coached into their sixties and even a few into their seventies, but I know that won't be me. I don't know if I'd use that cliché of it being a "young man's game," but your body handles it differently as you get older. And your priorities change, of course.

By my mid-fifties, both my boys will be through high school and Emma, Disney princess Emma, sweet little "I want a puppies calendar" Emma, will be a teenager. God knows that will create enough drama. Solo tells me to start game-planning for that right now.

But at the same time, I knew the athletic director position wasn't a sure thing. And did I want to be athletic director of a district where football was either in a no-win situation or didn't exist at all?

There was a lot to think about, and Christine knew it was weighing on me.

"Bottom-line it," she said, stealing a line I use when I want someone to get to the point. (That someone is never her, of course, because even when Christine gets rolling on some topic, I know better than to ask her to boil anything down. I think I'd rather wear a Cowboys jersey in a circle of Eagles fans.)

"You're a bottom-line guy," Christine said. "Use it on yourself."

I tossed the TV remote on the coffee table in front of us. We were sitting in the living room, looking at the television but not really watching it. Emma was already in bed, and the boys were in their rooms, so Christine and I had a chance to talk normally instead of in parental code.

"Bottom line is that I don't want to go to another school. I still want to be a head coach, and when the district adds another high school, I'll be in line for the athletic director position. That's not happening anywhere else."

"Probably not," Christine said.

"And I like the people, and I don't want to walk out on the kids. I don't want to walk out on coaches who've been with me for years. I know some of them don't want to move. I don't want to move, either. I don't want anything to change."

"So stay at Creekside."

"But things are changing. The athletic department might get slashed more. That athletic director job might not happen."

"You can't stop change," Christine said. "That's true wherever you go. Just do what feels right for right now. It's not like this Putnam job is a once-in-a-lifetime thing. Couldn't you still be an assistant somewhere in a couple of years? Wouldn't those opportunities still be out there?"

"Not as good as Putnam."

"But maybe even better, right?"

"Always the optimist."

Christine is always the optimist, and that's usually a good thing. She's like a rock in all these situations. I think she's naturally that way, and years as a coach's wife probably added to that even keel. But sometimes her "it will all work out" perspective feels like a "you worry too much" judgment of me.

I do know that I worry too much, though. I think that just gets built into you when you see all the things that can go wrong in a season, even when things are going right overall. You plan for the worst, so it's naturally always playing out in your head.

"I just don't want you to give up something you love out of worry," she said. "Don't just give up because one superintendent is creating a problem. Superintendents don't always stay, you know."

"Yes, I know that very well."

The best one I had ever worked for, the guy who hired me at Creekside, had retired four years earlier.

"So you still want to be a head coach and still want to be at Creekside. I'd say that, bottom line, you don't have much to think about."

"Maybe not," I said, sinking back into the couch. Chester, our beagle-basset hound mix that is unofficially the world's laziest dog, looked up from his spot on the couch, annoyed by the disturbance.

"But it could be a tough year. I've lost three coaches, and bringing in new ones and fitting the staff together will be messy. And kids are transferring out. I'm sure I'll coach some kids through spring practice that will be somewhere else in the fall."

Christine shrugged and nodded at the same time.

"So that's why you're still thinking about it? Worried about a losing season?"

"No. It would hurt my pride, sure, but I think about Mickey. He's worked his butt off for years and dreamed of his senior year. I already feel bad about moving him from receiver to QB because we're so desperate. This is it for him. Remember after we won the state title, how the boys used to pretend they were playing for the championship?"

Christine smiled.

"They'd put on those old Creekside jerseys that hung to their knees," she said.

"They looked so small in those," I said. "And then they threw each other bad passes so they could dive for them. They did crazy celebrations, those flying chest bumps, and pretended to kiss trophies."

"They made banners to run through," Christine said. "They were always asking me to bring butcher paper home from school."

I smiled, thinking of Mickey at age ten, still so innocent and hopeful. But that memory also made me feel worse about what was going on at Creekside.

"Now look what Mickey's big moment has become. He's worked so hard for this, dreamed about this, and he's never played for a losing team."

"Losing is as valuable an experience as winning," Christine said.

"Yeah, yeah. But for Mickey, it could be memorably miserable. If he plays receiver, there's no QB to throw to him. And I'm not even sure what receivers he'll be throwing to. Who knows what will be left next season."

"Nothing you can do about that."

"Not if I stay at Creekside."

We sat in silence for a few seconds. I think Christine was waiting to see if I had anything else to say, but I was done. I was already way over my average. I'm usually the nodder in our conversations. In football terms, Christine dominates time of possession.

"I really don't want to leave," I said. "But if I go to Putnam, Mickey could play for a team that will definitely make the playoffs. Mickey would actually play for something. He could play in that stadium, get something a lot closer to the dream he's always had."

"So go to Putnam, then."

"Thanks, hon. Very helpful."

She smiled and rubbed my right shoulder, which on other days might've been an invitation to something but in this case was just the supportive-wife thing.

"Mickey knows about the Putnam offer," Christine said, "and I haven't heard him talk about it. Has he said anything to you?"

"I told him I wasn't going to take it. . . . Pretty much."

"Do you even know if he would want to move to another school? Going to a new place for your senior year?"

"But he has friends over there. He knows the football players from camps. And you know, the girlfriend."

"You can say her name, you know. It's not like that makes them married. Kirsten is a nice girl, but it won't last. It's high school."

I knew it wouldn't, but I still wasn't crazy about it. Hormones and teenage brains are a frightening mash-up.

"So you don't think he would mind moving to Putnam?" Christine said, snapping me back on track.

"Not if I went over there."

"What about if you didn't go over there?"

"Without me?"

I acted like I hadn't thought about it, but I had thought about it. I couldn't stop thinking about it, in fact.

I was 99 percent sure that nobody would block Mickey's transfer. The coaches and athletic directors on the executive committee for Putnam's district, who vote on the eligibility of transfers, were all guys who knew what my program was going through. And, as I mentioned, it wasn't an all-state player moving to a new school.

Still, I didn't like that I'd basically be lying when I said the transfer wasn't for athletic reasons. Also, if the coach's own son transfers out, isn't that a sign of trouble? It might be like flashing "program collapsing" on the Jumbotron. It could be the start of a full-scale exodus.

Most importantly, I wanted to keep coaching Mickey. I wanted to be part of his season, be there for his games, do everything I could to make his final year of football a fitting finish line. And so, after talking more about it with Mickey, I decided that I needed to take the Putnam job. I needed to do it for him. I didn't want to leave Creekside, but the time was right, and as bad as I felt about telling my longtime assistant Jim Hartline about my decision, I knew he would understand.

I thought it over for nearly a week, and because I didn't want anyone to know that I was considering leaving, Christine was my only sounding board. I don't know if I was looking for a response, but talking with her helped me get a handle on things, and when I told her about my decision, she seemed relieved. She didn't stop what she was doing—reading through a stack of essays from her students—and responded with a simple "okay."

"Okay and . . ."

There had to be more. I don't care how much I had worn out Christine with the discussion of whether to stay at Creekside, she is not the kind of person who just says "okay." I waited a few seconds, and sure enough, there was more.

"I'm glad you figured it out," she said.

"So am I."

"And you're sure about this?"

Oh man. She wouldn't let me off easy.

"I won't ever be sure," I said. "But how much more can I think about it?"

"You don't need to think more about it. If you've made a decision, go with it and don't second-guess it, because I'm not going to. I just want you to be happy."

I sat down by her at the kitchen table where she was grading papers.

"Do you think I won't be happy if I'm not a head coach?"

"No, I think you would be very happy over at Putnam," she said, turning toward me. "And now that we'll be at the same school, we can eat lunch together every day."

I smiled because I knew she was joking. We love each other, but we don't need to see each other that much. There's no way she wants to see me that much.

"Okay, then good," I said. "It's done . . . and I'm done thinking about it."

"Okay."

"Okay and . . ."

"Just okay," she said. "We're done talking about it, right?"

"Yes we are."

I looked down at my feet for a few seconds, feeling relieved that the decision was really made, but also somewhat in disbelief that I was going to leave Creekside.

"Yes we are," I said again, trying to convince myself. "So . . . anything else you want to talk about before I head to the store?"

"How about this," she said, handing me a student's essay. "Read the start of the second paragraph and tell me if anything jumps out."

I began reading, stopped a few words in, and laughed.

"Prolly?" Christine said. "Really? Prolly?"

"Wow," I said. "But that's the language of today."

"The language of texting and tweeting. But this is an essay about what patriotism means to the student, it's an essay that's being graded. Does he actually think that prolly is a word?"

"Defs," I said. "He defs thinks it's a word he can use in the essay." Christine sighed.

"Sometimes these kids make me feel so old," she said.

"But my dear," I said, getting up to leave, "you don't look a day over twenty-one."

"And you, my dear, should prolly get your eyes checked."

✳ ✳ ✳

So it was all settled. Boom. Done.

And then, like so many times in life when you think you've got something figured out, everything changed. It all blew up when Putnam's defensive coordinator had a last-second change of heart and decided not to leave for a head coaching position. Apparently he wasn't happy that he would have to keep most of the assistants of the coach who resigned. There were some other complications, too, none of which mattered to me. It only mattered that I wasn't going to Putnam.

Everything happens for a reason. I don't know if I've ever really believed that, but I actually felt some relief when Coach Greer told me the position was no longer open. He was apologetic, even though I had never accepted anything.

The only disappointment I felt was for Mickey, who had warmed to the idea of playing for Putnam. When I told him I was staying at Creekside, he was let down. He tried to hide it, but it was obvious.

I can only guess how he'd built up Putnam in his mind. I think all his dreams of Friday night glory, back to those days when he and Andrew were pipsqueaks putting on pads just to play catch in the park, were rekindled by the chance to play for Putnam.

"So we don't need to move?"

That's about all Mickey said, which wasn't surprising. He doesn't say a lot. That made it even more impactful, a day later, when Mickey came to me and started talking about Putnam. I was putting together our tax return, the annual joy of March, when he walked through the kitchen and into the study.

"Do you think I could've been a starter for Putnam?"

"I think you could play for any team," I said without looking up from my pile of forms.

Mickey stood in the doorway, not saying anything more. He had his classic Sunday afternoon garb on. Gray hoodie, blue sweatpants that he preferred a size too big, and black Under Armour sandals. It was like fifty degrees, and he was wearing sandals. It all seemed to fit with that patchy beard he was trying to grow into a mountain-man look.

"Seriously, Dad," Mickey said. "I mean, Kingsley Savage is a stud, but Putnam's other receivers are graduating. I wonder what they've got coming up."

"I don't know."

The microwave beeped, and Mickey walked back to the kitchen. He got whatever he was cooking out and grabbed a bottle of water out of the fridge.

"Mickey, come in here."

"What?" he said, twisting around the corner with eyebrows raised and a fork in his hand.

"Come in here."

"But I just heated up . . ."

"You can bring it in."

Mickey came in with a dish of leftover lasagna.

"Dinner's in like an hour," I said.

"I'll be hungry again."

"Yeah, I'm sure."

Mickey sat down in the other chair by the large U-shaped desk Christine and I share. Behind him was a collection of family photos, including multiple shots of him and me on a football field. At that moment, as I prepared to give up a final year of coaching him, I wasn't sure if that back-drop was fitting or completely out of place.

"You know, Mickey, you can still go to Putnam."

"Yeah, I know."

"So you've thought about it?"

"Sort of."

"Do you not want to leave friends?"

He shrugged.

"Do you feel bad about leaving teammates?"

"All that, I guess."

Mickey took a deep breath, then sighed, and then looked over at the wall of photos. Just staring into space as he took a couple more bites of lasagna.

"I just want you to know you can go," I said.

"But what about Creekside? Who's gonna play quarterback?"

"Mickey, if that's what's holding you back . . ."

I smiled and waited a second for Mickey to look up.

"Mickey, listen. I know how long you've waited for this. Don't worry about me."

"It just doesn't seem fair to you, the way it's all working out."

"Don't worry about me. And don't talk about fairness. It's probably unfair how much I've been given in my life. If everything is supposed to come out even at the end, I've got some tough times coming."

Mickey smiled. Relieved, I think, although he's hard to read.

"Give it some thought," I said. "Coach Greer would love to have you."

"It sounds like you want me to go."

"It's not what I want," I said. "But if you want to go, it's what I want for you."

CHAPTER 9

MY longtime offensive coordinator, Jim Hartline, was standing behind our three "as of now" quarterbacks as they took turns throwing to receivers. The QBs are expected to be rough around the edges in the spring, but this was ragged. You could see how it was going by watching Jim, who had his arms folded tightly across his chest, probably so he couldn't slap his forehead.

The QBs were throwing hitch, slant, and hook routes. Short stuff, basically. Easy stuff. But nothing was going to be easy or basic for us that year. After a particularly bad throw, so wobbly that it suggested there was something wrong with the football, Jim turned his head my way, tipped down his sunglasses, and stared.

It was only the second day of our four-week run of spring practices, but we needed to find a quarterback. At some positions, you can kind of wait it out and expect leaders to emerge, but having a muddled quarterback situation keeps an entire team in neutral. I was hoping one of the QBs who had split time on the junior-varsity team would rise to the occasion.

"Give me something positive," I said to Jim after practice. He had walked into my office with a defeated look, and when he plopped into the chair across from me, he let out a deep, gravelly sigh. It seemed like an especially dramatic sigh—an intentionally exaggerated, feel-sorry-for-me sigh.

"Positive, huh?"

Yes, positive. I needed something we could build on. Something that would ease the frustration of working with a slew of new coaches and a roster hit hard by graduation and player transfers.

"Well," Jim said, "I like this Springsteen song."

"No . . . come on. Nothing's ever as good or bad as it seems. Give me something positive."

Jim looked out the window of my office into the hallway at the players walking by. They were shuffling slowly, staring down at their phones, talking, laughing, somehow still energetic after a long practice. Many wore the big, bulky headphones that are now crazy popular and might be the greatest scam since that Miss Cleo psychic and five-dollar bottles of water.

In the middle of the group, and yet alone, with his head bobbing inside a bubble of blasting headphones, was Tyreke Abrams.

"Check him out," Jim said.

"Tyreke?"

"Yeah. Wow. Is he not the cockiest S.O.B. you've ever seen?"

I laughed.

"He's a talker," I said. "That's for sure."

"We always seem to get our share of them."

"Everybody's getting them," I said. "As long as you're getting teen-agers, you're getting them."

Jim raised his eyebrows and sighed again.

"So," I said. "Something positive."

"Oh all right. . . . You saw the way Daniels was booming punts out there. That was good. We might have the best punter in the district."

Okay, so there was that.

"And he's certainly going to get a lot of work."

I smiled at Jim, who was understandably frustrated after directing some salty offenses over the years. He knew this season would be tricky with our star QB off to Boston College, but our offensive prospects were bleak.

We had a decent offensive line and a hard-nosed running back who was used mostly as a blocker the year before but could probably hold up to running the ball twenty-five times a game. Given that we had no returning receivers and our quarterback would be making his varsity debut, it was good to have that kind of running back. But as willing as Paul Nelson was to jump into battle, and as hard as he worked and as much as we loved him, he would certainly be described as an "athletically limited" running back.

Paul was so smart, so disciplined, so well-liked, and so demanding of himself, I was sure he would be a huge success in the world someday. But only if his success didn't depend on a good time in the 40-yard dash.

Paul would be better served on defense, maybe at linebacker or even as a smallish interior lineman, but our defense was in better shape than the offense.

"So was the Titanic," Jim said.

Did I mention that Jim isn't always the most positive guy?

Again, I couldn't really blame him. Our offense might've been pretty pedestrian if Mickey was still around, and he was headed to Putnam's glamourville. Mickey was finishing the semester at Creekside, but his transfer was basically a done deal, and he wasn't practicing with us. He was working out informally with the Putnam quarterbacks and receivers and making plans to be on their seven-on-seven team in the summer.

With Christine teaching at Putnam and the school offering a university-level computer science program as a reason for the transfer, Mickey's move was going to be smooth. Still, the whole thing was weird, and at times, depressing. But my busy schedule left few moments to question whether Mickey's transfer was the right thing. I just tried to move forward during what already was, and would become, the strangest year of my life.

* * *

Just as predicted by Dave Holgate, my buddy on the school board, Creekside became a trendsetter. Six more school districts in Texas, two of them with high schools the size of Creekside, decided to cut middle school football.

A private school in the Austin area, which had been competitive in football until recent years, cut its football program entirely. The school said participation numbers had dropped to the point where the cost of fielding a team was no longer in the best interests of the overall student body. It was "an inequitable strain on resources."

Most schools that cut middle school football used the same financial rationale as Creekside. But there was also discussion about how football was too dangerous, a topic that was catching fire nationally. Something was always lighting the fuse on the debate. A school was cutting back on football, or a school district or college was getting sued because of an injury, or some former NFL player would talk about the effects of playing the game.

And, you know, those NFL players do get to me. Like when former Packers quarterback Brett Favre said he was having memory problems. God knows that poor guy took a licking during his years in the league. But he's only in his forties, and he talks about gaps in his memory.

That's pretty scary. I never played in the NFL, but there weren't the same concussion protocols in place when I was in college, and I might've played through a concussion. I was thinking of that as I read about a lawsuit by former college football players against the NCAA, claiming that it didn't do enough to protect players while raking in huge profits. All the lawsuits and debates were mixed with heart-wrenching stories about football injuries.

The serious injuries are extremely rare, and I've seen stats that gymnasts and hockey players are more likely to suffer head and neck injuries than football players, but it doesn't matter. More kids play football. A lot more. And when even one suffers a significant injury, the impact is massive. You don't forget a story about a healthy kid walking on to the field and then never walking again.

Everything was changing. Football was being portrayed as some shadowy figure preying on kids, and there were large schools outside of Texas that were completely pulling the plug on football. After ten, twenty, even fifty years of playing, it was over. End of story. End of tradition. A huge part of a school's identity ripped away.

It seemed inconceivable that it could happen, especially given the popularity of college football and the NFL. College powerhouses are so lucrative that their football teams fund the rest of the school's athletic programs, and the NFL is a never-ending gusher of riches. Viewership might not be as high as it once was, but isn't that true with pretty much everything?

The NFL is still huge. Its fans are still nuts about it. The NFL could probably televise hours of players getting their ankles taped, and people would watch.

* * *

"The NFL could televise guys painting the fields," Dave Holgate said, "and people would watch."

I laughed as we walked to our seats at Globe Life Park, home of the Texas Rangers. Dave's accounting firm has a block of season tickets, and he invites me to a baseball game or two each season. It was May, and the weather was perfect as we took our seats and talked a lot of nothing about everything: Donald Trump, vacation plans, the latest Texas drought, and how the new donut place where they put crushed candy bars on top of the frosting is both heavenly and the work of the Devil.

We also talked about the upcoming Springsteen concert—of course, Christine would say with an eye roll—and how spring practice was going. Then we got around to the future of football.

Yeah, the future of football. A pretty deep topic for two former linemen drinking beers and cracking peanuts.

"People still love football," Dave said. "People are still in love with football. Rich, poor, everyone's in. And even with all these players acting like asses."

No doubt about that. The good guys in the league, or at least the ones who seem like good guys to me, are overshadowed by the headline-making behavior of the NFL's slimy outer layer.

"America is addicted to football," Dave said. "People struggling to pay rent fork over cash for NFL tickets. It's in their blood. They can't live without it. And around here . . . you know, people wear NFL jerseys to my church."

"I need to visit your church."

Dave stretched his legs over a seat in the row of front of us, which I did the moment we sat down. Stadium seats are never made to fit even a person of average size.

"Tell you what," Dave said, "If a football church opens, it will be a megachurch in a month. People will be shouting hallelujah."

"I know I'd have less trouble getting Mickey and Andrew on board on Sunday mornings. . . . So would this football church of yours have stained-glass windows with famous football plays?"

"Sure, and the altar would be an end zone, and the pastor would come through an inflatable tunnel, and a marching band would play with the choir."

"Big video screen in there, too?"

"Of course," Dave said. "And be assured, we'd keep things respectful. The cheerleaders would be dressed appropriately."

"Good to know. Lower your voice or someone will steal your idea. Maybe Jerry."

That got a laugh out of Dave, who insisted that the NFL wasn't going away. Things that make money never go away, he said.

But what if fewer kids were playing football? I'd read about participation being down with the really little guys—the pee-wees. That's when kids start falling in love with football. If they're not playing, where are the players of the future?

"I used to think high school football was untouchable," I said. "I mean, how can you have high school without football? But now . . . I can't believe how many schools are considering it."

"Probably going to keep happening," Dave said.

"So what about Creekside?"

Instead of answering, Dave looked down at the infield, where the grounds crew was finishing its work before the game. As the sun started to dip below the top of the stadium behind us, the weather was about as good as it gets in North Texas. Instead of the typical whipping wind, a cool breeze was blending with the warm evening.

It was the kind of setting, even when you're crammed into a plastic stadium seat, that could create some optimism. But there weren't many glimmers of hope.

"High school football isn't getting cut yet," Dave said. "Bashum can't do that. Look at the heat he's taking for cutting middle schools. Calls, letters, emails . . . some nasty stuff."

"How nasty?"

"Nasty enough that the district shared them with the police."

"What?"

"Not death threats or anything like that, but serious. It's not surprising, though. High schools in other states might be able to cut football, but this is football's heart."

"Yeah, but tell me this. Two years ago, even a year ago, would you have believed that middle school football would be cut?"

"Two years ago? No. A year ago . . . I don't know."

"Really? Was Bashum already talking about it then?"

"Nah, I would've said something. But Bashum talked about priorities, and he was interested in what was going on around the country with youth football."

"So does he hate football?"

"I don't know about that. He played."

"Oh yeah?" I responded in surprise, although I had seen the photo in Bashum's office. "You know what position?"

"Not sure. He's never told me any football stories. We're not buddies."

"Thank goodness for that. He's got enough friends on the board."

Our conversation stopped for the national anthem, and as fans rose to their feet below us, I saw a few wearing Cowboys jerseys. It had been four months since the Cowboys' last game, and they wouldn't play one for another three months, but the Cowboys were still front and center.

"Bashum might be on some kind of crusade, but he's not a renegade," Dave said. "It's just that football is in the cross-hairs with all the safety stuff."

"Yeah, I know," I said. "But it's all one-sided. Nobody's talking about the way we instruct the kids now and the added precautions and the way we treat injuries. We know so much more."

"But so do the moms of America," Dave said.

"The all-powerful moms of America?"

"That's right. And what they know is that high school football players get injured. They've heard about the concussions. They've heard of kids dying."

"And it doesn't matter how rare it is," I said.

"When it could be their son, it doesn't matter. What matters is some won't let their kids play football, and when that trickles up to high school, people like Bashum find a reason to cut it."

I knew Dave was right. But I still didn't like hearing him say it.

"So is high school football headed for a slow death?"

"I'm just saying perception is reality, Tuff. High school football is safer now. You've seen the statistics. It doesn't matter."

Yeah, I'd seen the statistics. Back in the sixties and seventies, when there were far fewer football players, about fifteen kids died each year from football-related injuries. Twenty-six once died in a year. Now the average is about five, and yeah, I hate that there are any. It's heartbreaking, you know? I mean, we're talking about kids. But we're also talking about more than a million kids playing football each year.

"You remember what practices were like when we played?" Dave asked. "Full contact every day. Coaches wouldn't let us get water, and we were afraid to ask for it. Unless you got knocked out, you kept playing. We laughed when teammates threw up. I'm not sure we even had a real trainer. Just people with water jugs or hoses. Now we've got trainers, a doctor on the sidelines, an ambulance at the stadium . . ."

Dave stopped to sip from his beer. He took much more than a sip, actually, as he refueled for his rant, and I thought maybe he was disappointed that I wasn't matching his energy as he got worked up. He's the accountant, after all, and I'm the football coach. I should've been leading the charge, but I was worn out by it.

"And think of our equipment," Dave continued. "We have helmet safety ratings now. My team's helmets didn't even match. I'm not sure I even had a helmet that fit. They just gave us each one on the first day of practice. Nobody was paying attention."

"Now everyone pays attention," I said.

"But all it takes is one."

"One injury."

Dave nodded.

"One serious injury and football looks more dangerous than juggling knives. You see a kid leave the field on a stretcher . . . hell yeah, that image is permanent."

Very permanent. I'll never forget when I stood on our football field, surrounded by thousands of eerily quiet fans, looking into the scared eyes of a sixteen-year-old.

CHAPTER 10

IT was the season following our state championship, and although realignment had moved us into a classification with larger schools, we were doing fine. We lost our season opener, but it was against Highland Park, a powerhouse program that churns out a great team each year. I was probably too ambitious when I scheduled that game, but I was the coach of a state champion and hungry to build another.

After the opening loss, we won three straight, including our district opener, and I felt great about the team as October arrived. I felt great about a lot of things at that moment. My sons were still young and innocent, or at least innocent enough to think they would someday be pro football players, and my daughter was toddling around, charming everyone, unintentionally posing for adorable photos that my wife sent out to everyone.

On the football field that year, we had a squared-away defense that could keep us in any game. The offense was improving, with an inexperienced but serviceable quarterback who was helped by a solid offensive line. We had two capable running backs, and the receivers were pretty good. We also had one game-breaker, a guy who could turn a defensive mistake into a big gain and a meat-and-potatoes offense into filet mignon. That was Mosey, and he was worth the trouble.

Trouble isn't the right word, I guess. Mose never really got in trouble. He did well enough in school, although not as well as he could've. He didn't start fights, didn't miss practice, and certainly wasn't disrespectful. His mom and dad made sure of that. I knew Mr. and Mrs. Posey well by then, and they would never let any of that slide with their youngest son. They never call him Mosey, by the way. He has always been Eric to them, and Mosey—or Mose—to just about everyone else.

Mose wasn't trouble, but he was exhausting. He loved to clown around, and he craved attention. When he didn't get it immediately, he turned up the volume—on his music, his personality, his swagger, everything.

Mose mostly played defense as a sophomore, and he was a star cornerback by the end of our championship season. He was rising quickly as a college recruit, and his head was swelling, his ego was soaring, and his volume was rising. He wanted to play offense, too, and I wasn't going to keep him off the field. He was six feet tall and only about 170 pounds, but he saw himself as a giant. He couldn't run anyone over, but he could certainly run by people, and his speed jumped off the screen when you watched his video. As a corner, he could get fooled on a route and then erase the mistake with his closing speed.

When we took the field on that first week in October, the weather was finally turning. Temperatures had reached the high eighties during the week, but after sunset, you could feel the tease of fall. The summer bake was cracking, and the Creekside Knights were heating up.

We were on our way to a fourth straight win late in the first half, leading Richardson Pearce 24–7. Our defense had already forced three punts, and Pearce's offense was getting desperate. Pearce had been an offensive juggernaut in recent years, but its spread offense was struggling with an inexperienced QB.

On third-and-long near midfield, Pearce's quarterback threw a lateral to a receiver, who then set up to throw to another receiver streaking down field. Mose bit on the fake, as he often did because he was so eager to make a big play, and then quickly reversed field and chased the receiver. The pass dropped in over the receiver's shoulder as Mose closed in, stretched out, and reached to get a hand on it. The players collided and fell to the ground, and so did the ball.

Mose bounced up and spread his arms wide to help the officials signal an incomplete pass. Then he ran off the field, gliding, strutting, and of course talking, until he disappeared into an enthusiastic swarm of teammates.

Two minutes later, Mose was on the field again, lined up in the slot, ready to get the ball. It was the same formation we had used earlier for a toss sweep that Mose had taken for about fifteen yards. This time his first option was to pass to a receiver who would fake a run block off the line and then release on a post route. If the safeties bought the play as a run, he'd be open deep.

I might never use the play again because Mosey, for all his athletic gifts, wasn't much of a passer. But connect on the play once, and it would be on video for every future opponent to worry about. That's what I wanted, because it might loosen some things up for us down the line.

Mose took the toss sweep right, and just as in practice, he slowed down and acted like he was looking for an opening and waiting for a block. Then Mose looked downfield, but—kudos to the disciplined safety—the receiver was covered. I should've told Mose to throw it deep even if the receiver was covered. At worst, the pass would be intercepted and Pearce would be deep in its own territory as the half ended.

But Mose wanted to run, and when he saw some room, he took off. A shot at the end zone always juiced him up. The spotlight was like a magnet for Mose, who could never be called a man of steel but had an iron will that belied his easy-breezy personality. He was more than talk and swagger. He was as competitive as anyone.

And on that night, Mose was better than anyone. He was at the height of his football powers, although only sixteen years old and still a Bambi package of skinny legs and big head, literally and figuratively. He saw no need to give up the ball.

Once Mose scooted between a pursuing linebacker and a cornerback near the line of scrimmage, it was showtime. He ran a few yards downfield, then planted his right foot hard and darted left to elude the grasp of two defenders. His path bowed back toward the line of scrimmage, giving up yardage, but as he ran toward our sideline, I knew it would be a touchdown.

One thing that has stuck with me from Mose's last touchdown is the sound. Players and coaches around me were cheering, of course, but I could still hear the cracking and creaking of pads as the defenders changed direction and gave chase. They wore their pads like a set of armadillo plates, and Mose wore his like a track suit. Maybe it was all the noise of the game—and if you've never been on the sidelines, football is a very loud game—but I couldn't hear Mose running. I couldn't hear his pads rubbing, or his cleats digging, or his body straining as he rounded the corner in front of me. He skated by, turned his head to the right, saw one defender to beat, and shifted gears.

The diving defender didn't get within a foot of Mose, who was all alone by the twenty-yard line. He high-stepped the last ten yards, crossed the goal line, spun the ball like a top, and turned toward our stands. He was posing for the crowd, arms folded across his chest, nodding and show-boating, when penalty flags flew like roses from adoring fans.

Unsportsmanlike conduct. It was a fifteen-yard penalty, to be assessed on the kickoff, and he deserved it.

Teammates patted Mose on the helmet as he returned to the side-lines, but when I found him, I pointed to the bench behind the crowd of standing players. I watched our kicker knock the point-after try through the uprights, and then walked toward the bench, trying to stay calm. Even in the heat of whatever burns me, I never blow up a player in front of a crowd. It's not good for him or me.

"What was that shit?"

"Sorry, Coach."

"That's embarrassing!"

"I'm sorry, okay? I'll do the laps."

A fifteen-yard penalty always meant fifteen laps around our practice field the following Monday. Mose knew the path well.

"It's thirty this time."

"Yes sir."

Mose nodded respectfully, but at the same time, he smiled. To him, it was worth it. He set his helmet on the bench and took a water bottle from one of the equipment managers, who moved out quickly when he saw I was pissed.

"Eric, look at me."

Mose looked up, still catching his breath.

"Those kids on the other side are working as hard as you," I said, pointing across the field. "Even harder than you. So don't you disrespect them, you hear me? They don't need your bullshit."

He looked back down.

"Got it?"

"Yes sir."

"If it happens again, that's your last play of the game."

"Yes sir."

"And after the game, you'll be apologizing to the Pearce coach. He shouldn't have to see that crap. Win or lose, we don't do that."

A minute later, leading 31–7, we all jogged off the field. The game was in hand, and I could've held Mose out the rest of the way just to teach him a lesson. But Pearce would be in hurry-up mode in the second half as it tried to get back in the game, and we didn't have a lot of depth in the secondary.

I decided that if we scored a touchdown on our opening possession of the second half, the starting defense would be on the field for only one more drive. But our first two possessions managed a combined three first downs. Pearce didn't do any better when it got the ball, and after our second punt of the third quarter, I thought about pulling the first-team defense. It was 31–7 and four minutes remained in the third quarter.

"Get us another stop," I told the defensive starters as they went back in.

Pearce got two first downs to take the ball near midfield. But then it was third down, and we needed only one play to get the defense off the field. It was third and seven.

It was third down and a long seven. Maybe closer to eight yards. I remember it that well.

Pearce's quarterback tried to find his receiver crossing the middle. He locked in on the slot receiver, and both Mose and linebacker Brian Terry made a play on the ball. Brian and Mose came in from behind the receiver, and I couldn't see who hit the receiver as he was trying to pull in the ball.

Our crowd cheered as the Pearce receiver fell forward and the ball bounced away. He took a big hit, but quickly got to his knees, banged a fist in frustration, and then stood up. Behind him, Brian got to his feet and pulled the collar of his jersey back into place.

Mose was lying on his back behind him.

If ever a moment could stretch into a minute, or just be frozen in time, it was then. People have described it as surreal, but to me, it felt like something more. The way the enthusiastic crowd was instantly smothered. It was like the thousands of fans were suddenly behind some air-tight seal, leaving the stadium so quiet that you could hear a car door shut in the parking lot. It felt supernatural.

Injuries happen, and most of the time, they're not serious. "Most of the time" isn't a good description, actually. Ninety-nine percent of the time, a football player will recover from an injury in a week or two. Ninety-nine-point-nine percent of the time, he'll be able to play football again, and the injury will be long forgotten when he puts his letterman's jacket in storage.

Less than one in every 150,000 high school football players suffers a catastrophic injury. I remember that figure from our coaching convention, where I was sitting in on a discussion about safety protocols. One in every 150,000, the speaker said. He then asked the audience of coaches about the chance of getting struck by lightning in your lifetime.

One in a million, one guy said. One in two million, said another.

It's one in fourteen thousand, apparently. I was shocked by that number, but he said it was from the National Weather Service. The guy at the lectern was obviously trying to put things in perspective.

But you lose all perspective when a player is lying motionless on the ground. You lose everything. Your composure. Your concentration. Your sense of what's going on in the game. Everything just stops.

It's probably a false alarm, probably nothing serious. That's the first thought, and hope, when medical personnel begin assessing an injury. There's an overabundance of caution taken, even when a player says he's okay, and everyone goes through the protocols just in case it's that one freak occurrence.

In more than a decade as a head coach, I've had three players taken off the field on a backboard. One of them played again three weeks later.

Another was injured in the middle of his senior season, and although he was medically cleared, he decided not to play again. He played for our basketball team a few months later.

And then there was Mose. I didn't know how serious it was, but it was different than the others.

When I watched it later on video, it all moved so fast. One player bent down toward Mose to see if he was okay, another walked over, and then the players were waving frantically to the sidelines. That probably took five seconds, and in that five seconds, I remember hearing my breathing, feeling my chest tighten, gripping my headset, and waiting and hoping for it to be a false alarm.

The players voices around me became a jumble of "What?" and "Mose" and "Did you see?" and "I don't know" and then fell off completely. The players kneeled, and I dropped my headset. Our athletic trainer rushed onto the field, followed by our team doctor, whose son had played on the team years before I became coach and was still on the sideline for all our games.

A minute earlier, I had been locked in thought about how our defensive ends needed to get better penetration into the backfield. I was already thinking about changes we could make for the next week. I was looking ahead.

Then I was looking down at Mose, who stared blankly toward the sky. I can't imagine what he was feeling. Terror. Confusion. Shock. Desperation.

911. Ambulance to South Entrance.

I don't know who said it in the sudden flurry of activity. Our assistant principal appeared on the field, clutching a walkie-talkie, and I stepped back to stay out of the way. I directed the players on the field to the sideline.

"Is it bad?" Brian asked with a twinge of panic while still trying to catch his breath from the last play.

"I don't know. They're taking care of him."

"Can he feel . . ."

"I don't know," I said, and my voice cracked. "They're taking care of him."

I moved back toward the circle around Mose, who was still flat on his back.

"Mose, Mose," the athletic trainer said. "I know . . . I need you to stay calm. . . . In my eyes, Mose. Look in my eyes."

I looked over at the Pearce sideline, where all the players were kneeling. Some of their fans were bowing their heads, while others, many of them parents, looked on with hands to the sides of their faces or hands clutched in hopefulness. They all waited for Eric Posey to get to his feet and shake it off.

"Mose," the doctor said. "I know you're scared, but look at me. We're here to take care of you. Don't move. Calm breaths."

Mose's chest rose and fell as he took choppy breaths. The fingers on his right hand fluttered. His face from the sideline, with the wide smile as he celebrated with teammates, had turned tense and distant. The man being chased by boys as he raced toward the end zone looked like a sixteen-year-old again.

He looked younger than sixteen. He looked like one of my boys, scared at the doctor's office, waiting for a shot, waiting for me to help them.

"Mose, hang in there," I said, offering words that were of no help.

I stood there, not sure whether I should stay by Mose, who was being taken care of by people far smarter than me, or walk back to the sideline. I still remember it so clearly: the golf cart in the middle of the field, the walkie-talkie on the ground, the partially untied shoelace of a trainer kneeling next to Mosey. I don't know why I remember such small details, but it's all there, preserved in my mind like a crime scene. I can still hear the players on our sideline, huddled and praying that Mose would be okay.

God, please lift up Mose. Be with him. Protect him . . .

As the wail of the ambulance siren grew stronger, the field remained stone quiet. Mose's parents ran across the field, escorted by our assistant principal. Mose closed his eyes and took a deeper breath. Sweat continued to bead on his forehead as he cooled down from his final moment of football glory.

CHAPTER 11

FALL practice feels nothing like fall when it starts. It's the middle of August, and temperatures often soar to one hundred. Players come in with a combination of excitement, because the opening game is less than three weeks away, and dread, because they know the drudgery that's coming. It's a little bit Christmas morning, a little bit root canal.

When I was a player, we had two practices a day. I remember two-a-days and the beaten feeling after conditioning drills and the stomach-churning sprints at the end of practice. No fun for anyone, but the least fun for linemen like me, who looked like wounded elephants as our legs got heavier and heavier. And I think we got like one water break per hour.

It's different now. Water is always available. Practice time is regulated, too, and there is mandatory recovery time between workouts and limits on contact. Fall practice is still a grind, but it's safer. Softer, some would say, but these are kids, not adults, and they're not pro athletes. Most coaches don't need a reminder of that, but the rules keep any drill sergeant from going medieval.

We made it through our first week of practice, got into pads, and then made our first big decision: quarterback. We went with Cody Shelton as the starter, which seemed like a natural choice because he was a senior and had been backup the season before. But it still wasn't an easy choice. Cody could throw the ball accurately on short routes, but his lack of arm strength showed on other throws, and he didn't move particularly well. That he was the best choice shows how thin we were at the position.

Our former top choice for quarterback was doing pretty well at Putnam. The district executive committee approved Mickey's eligibility without a hitch, and he was becoming a bigger part of the offense as fall practices progressed. At least Mickey felt that way. He thought he would get lots of balls thrown his way as defenses focused on receiver Kingsley

Savage, the monster recruit. Mickey also expected to take some snaps as a wildcat QB.

All I had heard from Coach Greer was that he loved having Mickey on the team and that "Mick"—I never call him that—was doing great. I knew Mickey would fit in well over at Putnam. He knew a lot of the football players from camps and other sports, and Mickey's outgoing personality, which he got from his mom, seemed to work in every environment.

That's probably why he had his first girlfriend, along with stern warnings from me, at age fifteen. Now he was seeing Kirsten, a Putnam High volleyball player. Volleyball teams begin playing matches a few weeks before school begins, and Mickey had been going to her games. Well, I'm glad he's happy.

I had enough to worry about with my Creekside squad, but it was in better shape than I expected. We were certainly thin in places, such as the aforementioned QB, and yeah, that's a big deal. But, going "glass half full" here, it could've been much worse. By my count, the cutting of middle school football had cost us at least eight players who I expected to get varsity playing time. The sophomore class, a solid bunch that won eight games and lost only two as freshmen, was hit hardest.

The kids who transferred needed me to sign their Previous Athletic Participation Form, and there's a box I can mark if I believe a student is changing schools for athletic purposes. But their parents were seeking the best situation for the kids, and when they moved into the Creekside attendance zone, they had no idea that the school district was going to start lopping off parts of the athletic program. I let all the kids go and wished them well.

I was realistic but also determined to keep our team competitive. I knew our defense could keep us in games, and we had decent size along our offensive line. With that line and our workhorse running back Paul Nelson, we could grind out some first downs. Our passing game was going to be modest as we worked in a new quarterback and an inexperienced group of receivers, but if we kept things simple and leaned on the big boys up front, we could win some games. Three, I'd say. Maybe four.

Of course, a three- or four-win season wouldn't do wonders for the program. Fans might lose interest, ticket revenue would drop, and Bashum would have another bullet in the chamber as he took aim at football. But considering the situation . . .

Well, I didn't want to consider the situation. I didn't want excuses, although plenty of them were around me. What I wanted was to find some offense.

"Bring on the smoke and mirrors," Jim Hartline said as we talked in my office. "I'm also open to any magic tricks. Black magic. Voodoo. Whatever."

"Wish I had some magic for you," said Reggie Glover, my new defensive coordinator. Reggie's a former defensive lineman at Hampton University and looks like he could still play. He's six-foot-two and, I'm guessing, about 270. He shaves his head, and when he furrows his brow, he has that intimidating look of actor Ving Rhames. When Reggie smiles, he cracks into something like George Foreman in a commercial for the Lean, Mean, Grilling Machine.

It was a blow to the staff when our defensive coordinator left in February, but at least it allowed me to hang on to Reggie, who had been working with the defensive line and linebackers for three seasons. Despite the uncertain future created by the football cutbacks, I convinced him to stay by promoting him to coordinator. Coach G certainly deserved the opportunity, and his enthusiasm was something every staff needs.

Unfortunately, Jim and I were about to dampen that enthusiasm.

"Coach, the defense is really doing some good things," I said to Reggie. "Back when I was a DC, I didn't have many defenses come along this quickly. The players are really responding. Thanks for all your work."

"Thanks, Coach," Reggie said.

He nodded and waited for what was next, and looking back, I think he knew what it was. All the coaches agreed that the offense needed some juice. The defense could keep us in games, but not if our offense couldn't stay on the field. Our defense would be dead tired by the third quarter.

"You know how we've been looking for something on offense, and although I love how our defense looks . . ."

"You want Tyreke," Reggie said.

I smiled. Yeah, he knew.

"We need him," I said.

"The first time you tried him at QB, I knew it was going to happen. But he can play some both ways, right?"

"Yeah," I said, "but next week I'm going to run him almost exclusively with the offense. He needs a lot of reps so I can see what he can do. I know it's late in the game to be experimenting, but you've seen where we're at."

"Does Cody know what's going on?"

"I told him we're going to mix some things up," Jim said, "which is what we're doing. Cody's still the starting QB."

"But Cody's pissed, right?" Reggie said.

"Does Cody ever get pissed about anything?" I said.

"That's part of the problem," Jim said. "Too laid back. No intensity. He's just . . . there."

"Too nice," Reggie said.

I waved off the conversation.

"Doesn't matter. We just need to talk about Tyreke right now."

"So what's the deal with Tyreke?" Reggie said.

"The offensive line and Paul are the thunder," I said. "Tyreke's our lightning."

"At QB?"

"Tyreke's going to be everything. He'll take snaps as QB, line up wide, line up next to Paul, whatever works, because not much is working with our offense right now. He'll be in on most snaps, so I'm not sure how many defensive series he'll play, but he's too talented to keep off the field for long. We'll have to pick our spots or we'll burn him up."

Reggie nodded. He was frustrated that his defense was taking a hit, but he'd seen our offense. Desperate times, desperate measures.

"You think KT is ready to step up?" I said, asking about one of our backup cornerbacks.

"He'll have to be," Reggie said. "If not KT, maybe Isaac. The second corner could be a little scary. But we've got some time."

Not really. There's never enough time to prep for the first game. Things always get missed, and you usually find out in a painful moment in the season opener, like when you have ten kids on the field on your first punt.

"Sorry we're making your job tougher," I said.

Reggie smiled.

"Maybe it's your job that just got a little tougher. Tyreke . . . We're talking about a sophomore who thinks he knows a lot more than he does."

"Yeah, I know," I said with a laugh. "It's a year of experiments. Maybe that's what I should tell the reporter when he comes by today."

"Tell him we're switching back to the Wing-T and ordering throwback jerseys," Jim said, "so we can remember the days when football was respected at this school and superintendents stuck to what they know."

"Yeah, but remember, Bashum played football," Reggie said.

That was the running joke in the office. Every time we talked about Bashum's assault on the football program, we'd point out that he was once a player. Everybody knew about the photo in his office, but we still didn't know what position he played, or how much he played, or even about his high school.

"Speaking of Bashum," I said as Reggie got up to leave, "if you guys hear anything from the players about sending something to him, please let me know. I don't know where the stuff is coming from, but eventually, the emails and letters are going to get someone in trouble."

"Got it," Reggie said. "Anything else?"

"Just a reminder to keep the stuff about threatening letters to yourself. No other coaches. I've still only told you guys."

"Yup," Reggie said.

Reggie's wide shoulders barely cleared the doorway as he left my office and walked into the large adjoining room for assistant coaches. That room is kind of a catch-all for everything, with football equipment scattered around, along with sports bags, notebooks, and other stuff that gets tossed near the long tables and computers. At the far end of the room, a large dry-erase board always has notes, plays, thoughts, diagrams, sayings and that sort of stuff. It also has "FAMILY" written in all caps at the top. That started out as a motto for us one season, but then we never wanted to take it down. Family isn't really a motto, anyway. It's just what we are as a football team.

You always defend your family, which is why I thought the threatening letters might be coming from someone inside the program. I worried that it might escalate into something worse, and I didn't want a kid getting in trouble for having his heart in the right and his brain in the wrong.

"Could it be a parent?" asked Jim, who was still sitting across from me. "I'd say we have a few red-flag parents."

"I've only seen a couple of the letters," I said, "but it has a kid feel."

"What's Bashum going to do? Hire a private investigator or something?"

"I doubt it, but I don't know what they're going to do. They're not death threats. They're just kind of vile, juvenile, you know. Threatening, I guess, but I don't think the police are involved. I'm sure Bashum doesn't want the public to know because it would be embarrassing."

"How many have there been?"

"Three I know of."

"So what do they want you to do?"

I didn't really want to get into a long conversation about the letters, but I should've known Jim would pepper me with questions. I closed the door to my office and sat back down.

"They're just keeping me informed," I said. "I'm supposed to let them know if I hear of anything or suspect anyone."

"You think it's a player?"

"I don't know if it's a player, but I think it's a kid. Some kid, maybe thinking he's being a hero, could get in a lot of trouble."

"There won't be trouble if Bashum backs off," Jim said, crossing his arms and leaning back in his chair.

"He's not going to bring back middle school football," I said. "It's done."

"But he's not done. He's planning more. It's some kind of vendetta."

"You and Alex think the same. He says it's a vendetta."

"Great minds think alike," Jim said.

Jim leaned back in his chair and put his hands behind his head.

"So how's Alex doing? How's Boston?"

"A lot different than Texas," I said. "I think he's a little homesick."

"Of course he is. He's two thousand miles from home."

"He'll get over it. But I think he's going to redshirt. I told him that might be for the best. Give him some time to get settled, soak up everything."

"But he wants to play now."

"You know Alex. He's a competitor. He goes hard at everything."

As we talked, Mosey rolled into the room behind Jim and exchanged fist bumps with Reggie. Mosey had on bright white Nike shoes with orange swooshes and matching laces. His cap of the day was black with orange trim and the Texas Longhorns logo on the front. Stitched on the back was "#HisHands," the Twitter hashtag Mosey sent out with his inspirational tweets about God and faith. I always thought Mosey, with his style and sincerity, would make a great preacher or pitch man. Whether he was speaking the words of God or words about some gadget on a late-night infomercial, people would be sold on Mose.

"Hey Mose," I called into the room.

Mose said a few more words to Reggie, then spun his wheelchair and came our way.

"Full Longhorns mode today?" Jim said.

"It's Longhorns day," Mose said. "You know, whatever team I'm going with, I fully commit."

"So Mose, what you got going on today?" I said.

"Video cuts for recruiting, unless there's something else you need."

"Yeah. Before the video, I need you to look over a few pages in the game program. It goes to the printer next week, so another set of eyes would be good."

"Okay," Mose said with a confused look. Proofreading wasn't something he wanted to spend time on. He volunteers his time, so I basically let him choose how to help, and I think he's proud to be our video and tech guru. He puts together great video packages each year for the graduating seniors, using music and all kinds of graphic flourishes.

"Just a few pages," I said, sensing his disappointment. "There's a stack over there on Booker's desk. Start with page thirty-one. That's the one that really needs to be checked."

Mose turned and headed for the desk, and I motioned to Jim to watch. Jim turned in his chair as Mose approached the stack of papers, shuffled them to find page thirty-one, and then froze. His mouth dropped slightly as he stared down, and then a smile started to break out. He raised his arm to cover his mouth with the back of his hand, as he often did when he broke into a big smile. I think he developed that habit back when he thought of a smile as a crack in the tough-guy armor.

Mose looked over at Reggie, who was smiling, and then looked over at us.

"Coach?"

I pointed at him and smiled.

"What?"

"Coach . . . what's going on?"

Mose, with a smile so big it was impossible to cover, looked over toward me. Then he looked back at page thirty-one. It was a full-page advertisement for The Groove, and specifically, Mose's show on Saturday nights. He had been moved from Thursday to Saturday and now had two hours instead of one. That meant twice as many songs that I didn't want to hear, but I still tuned in from time to time to hear Mose. He also sent me a digital file of each week's show. Sometimes I felt like he was going to quiz me on it.

"Make sure everything's okay on there. Once it goes to the printer, it's gone."

Mose looked back down at the page, which was anchored by a photo of him in the radio studio, with headphones on, surrounded by computer screens, knobs, and switches. The photo captured him in the middle of some statement that was important, or at least important to him, because Mose's brow was furrowed and his eyes were serious. He looked so mature, so professional.

Above the photo, *The Mosey Show* arched across the page in a splash of silver and gold. One of the football players, a backup defensive lineman who was better at graphic design than making tackles, put the whole thing together. The only design tip I gave him was to make it look good, and he did. "I'm going to use Copperplate Gothic bold for the font," he said, as if that meant something to me.

I gave him the words to write below the photo:

Tune into 93.7 The Groove every Saturday night from 7 to 9
The Mosey Show

Featuring Creekside football legend and assistant coach
Eric "Mosey" Posey

"So what do you think?" I asked as Mose looked down at the page.

"Coach . . . this is crazy . . . who took this photo?"

"The station sent it over. You don't remember them taking it?"

"Nope."

"Well, the stations always need photos of their stars. Something to give out to all your adoring fans."

Mose looked up, smirked, and shook his head. I'm sure he was embarrassed by the attention. He's by no means shy, but he's also not emotional. Or I guess he doesn't like to show much emotion.

"So does everything look okay? Anything we need to change?"

Mose looked over at Reggie, and then over at Jim and me.

"Who did this?"

Reggie pointed at me.

"Keaton Banks designed it," I said. "You wouldn't want me putting that together."

"But it was Coach's idea," Jim said, also pointing at me.

I shrugged.

"We've got a celebrity on our staff," I said. "Obviously, we need to take full advantage."

Mose shook his head some more, and once again, his smile cracked wide.

"So it's okay?" I said. "We've got to get those pages to the printer."

"Yeah," Mose said. "Thanks Coach."

"You're welcome. So now, can you maybe, you know, mix in a little Springsteen?"

Mose dropped his head in mock exasperation and began to laugh. He had tears in his eyes, which I'm sure he would say were from laughing so hard at my old-man music.

Chapter 12

ON the first Friday of the new school year, Creekside students filed into the gymnasium. I'm always stunned to see the new freshmen, who appear to be getting younger as I get older. I know it's more me than the freshmen, because occasionally I'll see a kid driving a car who I'd swear was twelve years old. He'll look barely past his Tonka truck days and he's driving some big ol' SUV.

On that first Friday, Creekside students filled up the gym bleachers for the annual "School Spirit Launch Event." The principal offered some words of inspiration before the new members of the student council spoke, the band played, and the cheerleaders and dance line combined for a performance. The volleyball and cross-country teams were introduced, and then, as the band started the school fight song, the football team walked onto the floor.

They gathered in the middle of the gym, most wearing jeans, all wearing their jerseys. They looked awkward as they folded their arms and tucked their hands into their pockets. You could see the strain on the faces of the guys trying to flex their muscles without anyone knowing it. They all wanted to look tough and serious as the four senior captains—running back Paul Nelson, quarterback Cody Shelton, defensive lineman Mason Gaines, and safety Elijah Lawal—stood in front and waited for the microphone.

"We just wanted to say that we really need your support tonight," Paul said. "We want to start off with a win, and the fans can really help us."

Not the most riveting stuff. But cheers followed each captain's speech, along with a short burst of music by the band. A pair of cheerleaders did back handsprings across the court, and our Knight mascot pretended to run for a touchdown, then spiked the mini football and started a celebration dance. It was a big, hokey production, which is kind of the tradition.

As it was going on, I looked up at the gymnasium walls, where the school posts banners for athletic accomplishments. Banners hang for regional championships in basketball and district titles in soccer. A banner for the volleyball team has a line for each successful season, plus an extra one for the state semifinalist a few years ago.

Out in the gym hallway, a trophy case displays all the hardware from over the years. The football state title trophy is in there, along with a football from the championship game and a huge nylon banner with a team photo and everyone's signature. I admit that I stop by the trophy case once in a while just to look at the photo of that unbelievable day. I love looking at the faces of the kids and seeing them as I'll always remember them, even when they're going to college, getting married, and sending me photos of their kids. They're forever young to me.

At every school, the banners and trophies are a pride thing. Look everyone, here's what we did. Look everyone, here's our history. Look everyone, these are the people that came before us, set the standard, started the traditions. The number-one priority of our high school is to get kids ready for college or whatever is the next step in their lives, but the number-one thing that unifies a school is sports. And the number-one sport, at least in that sense, is football. It's not even close.

It's no coincidence that the "School Spirit Launch Event" is always on the day of our season opener. On the occasional years when we open on a Thursday night, the pep rally gets moved up a day. The rally isn't all about football, obviously, but it wouldn't be the same without the excitement and anticipation of a game.

A game night still pulls the school and community together in our fragmented world. Everyone is going in different directions, interested in different things, and attention spans are zippo, but football nights remain community events. I had thought it would always be that way, but more schools in Texas were considering cutting back on their football programs. It wasn't like what was happening in other states, where dozens of districts had dropped football completely, but some Texas districts were talking about it. There was a lot of resistance, of course, but I think Creekside's decision created some momentum, or bravery, for opponents of football.

The media drumbeat of "football is too dangerous" was also part of it. A cover of *TIME* magazine had the headline "Is Football Worth It?" and a picture of a sixteen-year-old player who died. Inside, the story talked about the tragic risks of an "American obsession." Yes, football is an American obsession. But so is driving a car, and if you're talking about tragic risks, a teenager behind a wheel tops them all.

Every football injury was being magnified. Every serious injury was being dissected. Someone needed to be blamed, and in some cases, sued. A football player in Illinois filed a class-action suit against his state's high school association, saying that he suffered multiple concussions and wasn't warned of the risks. A player in California sued his high school, the high school coaches, and the school principal, and a player in Iowa was awarded nearly a million dollars after suffering a head injury in practice.

Fortunately, I hadn't heard anything new about the lawsuit for Chris Dozier, the player who was injured when he was in eighth grade. No news on that, I figured, was good news. The lawsuit might not be going forward. Maybe the district's sovereign immunity stopped it, or maybe the parents had second thoughts.

Still, I kept hearing people talk about the dominoes falling. I would've recognized it more, and been more upset, but a football season was starting. The greatest distraction from the attack on football was football—and the all-consuming job of getting ready for the first game.

As the captains stumbled through their speeches at the pep rally, I thought about Mickey. He would've given a speech that day at Creekside, grabbing the microphone as a senior captain and the new starting quarterback. But Mickey was at Putnam, somewhere in the ocean of six thousand students, getting ready for his first game with a state contender.

I thought about all the times I had coached Mickey, who played half a dozen sports growing up. Before trimming his sports to football and baseball in high school, Mickey played basketball and soccer, was on a swim team in the summer, and even got interested in tennis for a while. My football duties sometimes kept me from being head coach on his teams, but I was always some kind of assistant. One time when Mickey was seven years old and playing for a coach-pitch baseball team, I had to fill in as the pitcher because two other coaches couldn't make it. I remember trying to throw pitches to Mickey, who looked like a miniature pro with his eye black and batting gloves. I struggled to find the strike zone, and I even hit Mickey in the leg once. The parents in the stands jokingly yelled, "Charge the mound!"

As Mickey got older, I tried hard not to put pressure on him. I didn't want to become the sad cliché of the parent living his sports dreams through his kid. But I know most parents do it in some regard, and it's just the level of unhealthiness that varies. I've dealt with some parents who are off-the-charts delusional about their kid's athletic abilities. But when the delusion grows out of love, I understand it. I certainly understood it as I leaned against the gym wall, watching the pep rally and wishing that Mickey was standing with his former teammates.

Of course I wished he was there. But Mickey deserved the opportunity to spend his last season of football in an environment like that at Putnam. Mickey talked excitedly about it with Andrew two nights earlier when I took them out to dinner. It was kind of a boys' night out while my wife took our daughter to a Wednesday night double-shot of dance classes. Emma was already very serious about it all. Jazz, hip hop—something else I can't remember.

Andrew was a day away from his first game as quarterback for what was expected to be Bevell Middle School's last eighth grade team ever. Andrew had already been part of the last seventh grade team, which was cut after the previous season. He still expected to attend Creekside the following year, but nothing was certain. The family game plan was pretty much on hold until we knew more of Bashum's playbook.

Andrew was nervous and excited, but Mickey just seemed excited. I wished I could see his first game at Putnam, and I looked forward to the following week, when Creekside would play on Friday and Putnam on Saturday. There were four weeks during the season when the schedule would allow me to see Mickey play.

I felt strange as the pep rally continued. The buzz from the start of the season was still there, but as the cheerleaders danced and the band played, I felt a heaviness. Some of it, no doubt, was from the sudden, swirling uncertainty in my life. Football was still the undisputed king of sports, and high school football was still as ingrained in Texas culture as anything else, but the impossible now seemed possible. Football was mortal. The sea change in the perception of football could eventually, unbelievably, drown the sport in fears and lawsuits.

But as the pep rally continued, I think the weight I felt on my shoulders, and in my heart, was for Mickey. He was my first child, my first real introduction to adulthood, and now, my first lesson in letting go.

My phone buzzed, and I pulled it from my pocket and saw a text from Mickey.

Hows the rally? Best speech?

I texted back, starting a typical back and forth between Mickey, a texting master, and me, who still prefers spoken conversation.

Nelson maybe. What are you doing?
No rally here. Team meal from booster club later
Steak and lobster?
Sandwiches gatorade
You're at Putnam. Should be catered, have dj
I think they hired springsteen. Come over

I grinned and looked up as the cheerleaders did a final routine and the band played the fight song that has been part of Creekside football games for more than forty years. The Creekside mascot, with a big cartoonish Knight head and a costume puffed with muscles, stomped across the court, trying to look menacing.

My phone buzzed again.

Good luck Dad
Same to you. Talk tomorrow

How could I not feel a twinge of sadness?

Yeah, I felt it. But I was still feeling a rush of adrenaline. It's inescapable on the opening weekend of Texas high school football, which remains a spectacle that most people from outside the state will never understand. If you haven't experienced it, you won't understand it; if you have experienced it, you'll understand why it's inconceivable that it will ever go away.

After the pep rally ended, students headed home for the day, and the football players headed to the locker room. For many of the players, this would be their last season of organized football. Good or bad, this would be the season they remembered most and the season they told their kids and grandkids about. That was annual motivation for me, even before a season I knew would be more challenging than any other.

Kickoff was five hours away.

* * *

With our home crowd cheering, quarterback Cody Shelton took the first snap of the season, took two steps back, and handed the ball off to Paul Nelson, who slammed forward for three yards. Two hours later, fans at Creekside ISD Stadium would undoubtedly wonder how many times we ran that play.

A season after watching star QB Alex Cason throw the ball thirty times a game, our fans probably thought they were watching a different sport. But a team needs to play to its strengths, and in our season opener, we needed to grind. We were playing Royse City, a program that, although it had hit some high marks in recent years, was now rebuilding. Some newspaper and online football previews had described Creekside the same way, but we weren't rebuilding as much as we were being disassembled. Some key pieces to our team were now playing for other schools.

For the last two weeks of fall practice, we worked Tyreke Abrams in at QB. As expected, his running ability added an exciting dynamic. But we were cautious with what Jim began calling "Project Lightning." Tyreke had only played one year of quarterback ever, and that was on his first youth team in sixth grade.

"I mostly just took snaps and ran with the ball," he said.

That's pretty much what we had him do in his varsity QB debut. Tyreke's first snap came early in the second quarter, when he took over for Cody, who had expected to be out of the game for one series in each half. On Tyreke's first play as QB, he juggled the shotgun snap, and in the second it took him to collect the ball, the Royse City defensive front pushed into the backfield. But Tyreke stepped back to elude one tackler, and then ran right and was quick enough to get around an edge rusher and to the sideline. He tiptoed along the edge, and a play that could've been a disaster turned into a seven-yard gain.

Tyreke took twelve snaps in the game, handed off four times, ran seven times and attempted one pass that wasn't terrible. It came on a sweep to the right in which he had the option to throw a pass to tight end Gregory Wallis in the middle of the field. Wallis dropped the pass, possibly because he was stunned that it got to him fifteen yards downfield.

The second of Tyreke's QB drives ended with a two-yard TD run by Paul Nelson, giving us a 17–10 lead early in the fourth quarter. When our defense forced a punt on Royse City's next possession, I knew we could close it out. Royse City's defense was tired from spending so much time on the field, so it was a time to keep things simple. We ran the ball six straight times, going full vanilla with our plays against Royse City's exhausted front seven. Most of the handoffs were to Paul, who may never run away from anyone but is willing to run over everyone. Even in the fourth quarter, after twenty-five carries, he seemed to seek out collisions.

We drove past midfield on a seven-yard run that set up second and short. With Royse City's defense bunching more and more together, desperate to stop our energy-sapping, time-draining runs, we decided to go with a short, safe, swing pass that could get Tyreke in the open field.

Against a tired defense, the star of Project Lightning looked even more electric. Cody took the snap, faked a handoff to Paul, and threw to the right to Tyreke, who caught the ball a couple of yards behind the line of scrimmage. Tyreke beat one defender by leaning left and then bolting right, a move that drew an *ooooooh* from the crowd. The cheer grew as Tyreke beat the safety to the sideline, stepped out of a diving tackle attempt, and then sprinted forty yards for the touchdown.

"Yessir! Yessir!" Jim yelled into the headset. "Tuff, that's what I'm talking about. That, right there. . . . That's our lightning!"

Yeah, we had some lightning there. We also had nearly three quarters of pedestrian offense, and if not for the play of our defense, we could've been in trouble. The exuberant feeling of winning would be much more subdued when we saw the video and realized all the things we needed to improve. We had won a game that I expected to win, and we certainly didn't dominate.

But it was a win, and before that Friday, half our team had never played a down of varsity football. They had watched teammates transfer to other schools and had heard about how cutting middle school football would eventually kill our high school program. There was a lot of gloom and doom, and as they strained and struggled through fall practice, they needed a reward. They needed something to convince them that what the coaches were saying, in our strategically overenthusiastic way, wasn't a load of crap.

Some of it was, of course. Our team, thin in numbers and fragile in psyche, needed some early-season unicorns and rainbows. The players got it in the first week, and I soaked up the happiness with them as we stood in front of our stands and listened to our band play our fight song.

The players, along with students and fans still in the stands, pumped a fist in the air as the song finished with "Fight! Fight! For a win we'll fight! . . . forever, we're Creekside Knights." The players were exhausted, and even the guys who never made it on the field looked drenched with sweat on the steamy August evening.

"Yeah, baaaaaybeeee," one of the players yelled as we began walking off the field. "First step to state."

I laughed with Coach Glover, appreciating the blissful ignorance of youth. We knew we didn't have a state contender. But we also knew to enjoy the moments while we could.

"Reggie, your defense was great," I told Coach G as I slapped him on the back. "Absolutely kept us in it."

"Still need to force some turnovers," he said. "But we did keep them off the field."

We watched as Reggie's six-year-old son, Mychal, ran down the field with a miniature football, heading for the end zone.

"We could use some of that speed," I said.

Reggie laughed and then yelled for Mychal to run back our way. Mychal did, although not in a straight line. He zigged and zagged, stiff-armed imaginary defenders and then spiked the ball when he got near us. It reminded me of Mickey and Andrew, from a time that didn't seem that long ago. It was hard to drag them off the field as they reveled in the chance to emulate their heroes.

But on this night, none of my family members were at the game. They were ten miles away, watching the end of Putnam's lopsided victory in its season opener. According to the stats I could pull up from the internet, Mickey caught five passes for fifty-three yards. He was fitting in just fine.

CHAPTER 13

"WHAT are you trying to do to us?" I said, smiling.

Lee Fountain was sitting across from me in my office with a notebook on his lap and a confused look on his face.

"What did I do?"

"This week's rankings."

Lee smiled.

"Yeah, well, we need to find twenty teams each week that we can jinx. And your team won a playoff game last year, and then you won your opener. That got you on our list of victims. You guys don't belong in the rankings?"

"No, we don't. But I'm just giving you a hard time. So what do you want to talk about?"

"As the top to my football notebook, it seems like a no-brainer. Coach wins at one school, son wins at another."

"Ah . . . well, yeah, it was a good week for the family. Andrew's team won, too."

"Is Andrew playing QB?"

"At least for now. I think he likes receiver better. He wants to be like Mickey."

"Looks up to the older brother, huh?"

"Definitely. But he'll be looking down at him in a year or two. Andrew got the tall genes in the family."

"How tall?"

"Like me, maybe six-two, six-three."

"Sounds like prototypical QB size to me. I better call my Longhorns."

"We might need you to call everybody," I said, laughing. "I don't know. I'm not sure Andrew has the same drive as Mickey. At least not for football. Maybe it'll come later. He really likes baseball."

"Oh that's right. He's on some great select team."

"NTX Heat . . . I don't know about great. Pretty good, I guess. They should be with as much as they practice."

Lee flipped open his notebook. That was the sign that we were on the record and not just shooting the bull, at least officially. I always felt like we were kind of just talking. In the few times I've said anything that might be a lightning rod, or get me in trouble, Lee has run it by me before using it. I'd like to say it's because we're friends, but it could be as much that Lee doesn't want to mess up our relationship. I've helped him out with some things over the years, and he's done the same for me.

"I'd like to do a lead on you and Mickey," Lee said.

"Don't make a big deal out of us, Lee."

"Not a big deal. But coach and son on different teams is a good story."

"I just don't want to bring more attention to what's going on here and the talk of cutting middle school football. That wiped me out in the spring."

"I know, and I appreciate what you gave me then. I know with the superintendent and everything that it's dicey. Strictly softballs today, promise."

"Okay," I said, leaning back in my chair.

"So did it feel strange not seeing Mickey out there?"

"Oh sure. It was strange just missing one of his games. I was focused on my team during the game, but at halftime, I was tempted to pull out my phone and read the texts I was getting from my wife."

"She was sending them during the game?"

"Yeah, she and Andrew were sending them. But they knew I wouldn't look at them till after the game."

"Avoiding looking at those . . . that's got to be tough for a dad."

"Definitely. But I prepared for it when Mickey decided to go to Putnam."

"Speaking of that," Lee said, "I know the editors will want me to explain the transfer. I asked you about it before when we did something in the summer. I'm just going to use the same reason unless you want to say something else now."

"Nope. Same thing. Mickey's smart as hell and he wanted to be part of the specialized curriculum that Putnam offers, and his mom works at the school. Off the record, his girlfriend is over there, too. "

"So . . . transferring for romantic purposes?"

"I don't like thinking about that," I said.

"Know what you mean. I've got two daughters who will be teenagers in a few years."

"You're in my thoughts and prayers."

We talked for a few more minutes about the first week of the season and how the summer had been so brutally hot. Then we hit on weighty topics such as door-to-door roof salesmen and the Whataburger sweet-and-spicy bacon burger. Our conversations tended to go that way, and at some point, Lee would close his notebook to signal everything was off the record. On that day, he flipped his notebook closed in a very obvious way, making sure I noticed.

"So . . ." Lee said.

"So what?"

"So what's going on . . . with everything? What's up with Bashum? Is there anything I should be looking out for?"

"I should ask you the same thing."

"Fair enough, and yeah, there is something I wanted to tell you. Just between us, just like always."

"What is it?"

"Creekside is going to be part of a story about the state of football."

"The state of football?"

"Something like that. I don't exactly know. But it's top down from the NFL, college, everything. With the lawsuits regarding the NFL and the NCAA, football is a hot topic. The editors are really pushing the idea."

I sighed and leaned back, and then rubbed my eyes for a few seconds, trying to rub the moment away. I wasn't living in fantasyland. I knew what was going on at Creekside and what I was up against. But I didn't want more attention. I didn't need someone screaming it through a megaphone.

"I really can't talk about it," I said.

"Just wanted to give you a heads-up. I know you're in a tough position, and although I'd like to talk with you for a story, I know you don't want to talk about it during the season. But either way, there's going to be a story. Or stories."

"How soon?"

"Not sure. But if someone contacted you, I didn't want it to be out of the blue. Also . . . I'm going to be talking with your favorite person in a couple of weeks."

"Oh no . . ."

Lee nodded.

"Bashum?"

"Yeah. Our education reporter helped me set up an interview. She did a profile on him when he was hired. She's talked to him a few times."

"Good luck with Bashum," I said. "I don't talk with him much, but even when I do, I don't get much from it. I hope he gives you whatever you're looking for."

"I'm not looking for anything. Just asking questions, trying to figure out things. I don't have any relationship with Bashum, but he didn't have to do the interview. I'll let you know how it goes."

"Thanks. Depending on what Bashum says, I might have something to say. So when will the story will come out?"

"No idea, but probably not for a while. I'll tell the editors you're not talking right now so nobody calls you . . . at least from us. Are you still getting a lot of calls?"

"It's slowed down. I'd like to say that's a good thing, but I think it's because other school districts are making cuts in football or considering it. More people to talk to."

"Definitely true," Lee said.

"Have you talked with that doctor who spoke at our board meeting? The guy who's giving all the speeches?"

"No, but I know who you're talking about."

Anyone who followed football would know who I was talking about. There was this doctor talking up a storm, telling everyone that football was ruining lives. He was from California, and that's where he did most of his talking, but then he showed up at one of our board meetings. Maybe Bashum invited him.

"Also . . ." Lee said, "you know of that Intensity team, right? The one with the home-school kids?"

"Yeah. Why?"

"I'm going to talk with the coach."

I couldn't suppress a groan.

"I figured you knew him."

"I don't really," I said. "Hell, I don't even know his name. But I know of him. And I know what he represents."

"Which is?"

"A scary future for football."

"I was trying to explain that to my editor," Lee said, gaining enthusiasm. "I think that's what people need to know about . . . and that's what I'd like to talk with you and other coaches about."

"Talk to Bashum first, and then I'll see."

"I'll find some coaches. I'm not trying to put it all on you. But some of the other coaches are skittish about talking, and even with some other schools considering cutting middle school football, you're the highest-profile program that has pulled the trigger."

"Pulled the trigger. Good way of putting it."

"Sorry," Lee said. "The way this is all going down with football, with teams getting cut, and some schools cutting football completely . . . it's pretty crazy to me. I can only imagine what it's like for you."

I shrugged. My natural instinct, because I don't like a lot of attention, is to downplay everything. Even keel. Not too high, not too low, safe in the middle.

"I don't need a pity party," I said, again leaning back in my chair.

My phone buzzed. Another text. I was getting so many

messages—showing support, asking questions, offering advice—that I was thinking about changing my number. I had no idea how many people could reach me.

I sighed and shook my head.

"You know, I'd be sad if I couldn't coach anymore, but really, I don't think about me that much. If I did, I probably would've left for Putnam to be the offensive coordinator. That would've been a good, safe job."

Lee nodded.

"I think about the kids," I continued, "and here's what I can tell you, off the record. It's the same thing I've said to other high school coaches, and what I've heard from other coaches."

I've talked with enough reporters over the years to know when their minds begin clicking away on some story angle, and I could tell Lee wished he could use this for a story. I didn't want more attention, and I certainly didn't want people to think I had all the answers. But I'd been thinking a lot about the future of football. I'd been thinking about it too much, really. Worrying about something I couldn't control.

"Football," I said, tapping my hands on the desk, "is not going away."

"You're sure?"

"One hundred percent sure. Football is not going away. It's too huge. It's too much a part of everything. Too American. Too everything for so many people. And there's all the money, you know. But . . ."

I rubbed my temple and closed my eyes for a second. I wasn't sure that I should talk about it, but I really wanted to.

"High school football could go away."

"You think so?" Lee said, sitting up and scooting toward my desk.

"Still off the record . . ."

"Of course."

"School districts play follow the leader. Nobody wants to be the guinea pig on anything. Nobody wants to stick their neck out or be the one that makes a wrong move. But when something happens, or when someone starts something, they fall in line with each other."

"So you think more schools are going to cut football?"

"It's terrible, but yeah. I used to think it would come from lawsuits, like in the NFL and college, but it might just be more gradual, with a kind of hysteria that leads to parents pulling their kids out of football. Fewer players means fewer reasons for school districts to support football . . . and more reasons to cut when it's time to cut something. And for a lot of schools, especially the ones that can't pull in big crowds and find ways to make money, football is expensive."

"But it's such a huge move for a school."

"Enormous. What would be bigger, you know? . . . But if more schools start doing it across the country, I don't know . . . there's a weird momentum out there."

Lee didn't look convinced.

"I can't imagine not having high school football," he said. "Such a void."

"But there will always be football," I said. "There just might not be high school football."

"So the high schools could pull out?"

"The school districts."

"Right. So then what happens?"

"That's what scares me," I said.

It was scary because it suddenly seemed so possible. I had talked with other guys about it at the state coaching convention, and it had crossed their minds, too. What would happen if schools stopped sponsoring football? Nobody was sure. But we were sure that it wouldn't stop football.

There's just too much money in the NFL and college football. And with the glamour of football and its place in our culture, kids aren't going to stop wanting to play football. The sport would continue on without middle school and high school involvement. Club football teams would spring up like those select squads in basketball, baseball, soccer, and other sports. They'd try to fill the huge void left without high school football.

It would be different in a lot of ways, but the coaches of these teams are what I think about. They wouldn't have years of training and experience, wouldn't be certified teachers, and would be working with the same vulnerable kids.

If you want to be a high school football coach in Texas, you need to get a college degree, go through years of training, work your way through the lower grades, work as an assistant, and then eventually you can become a head coach. And that's oversimplifying the process.

What do you need to coach some youth football team?

A whistle, basically.

Some youth sports organizations have background checks and a few safety courses. But most of those coaches are Monday morning quarterbacks, dads of the players, well-meaning guys who are as out of place as me coaching the Creekside Debate Team. I can live with that when the kids are young, and they'll eventually have middle school and high school coaches who make sure they're doing things the proper way.

And that's not the worst of it. Not even close.

"Football will go on," I told Lee, "but if the high schools aren't involved, you'll put kids in the hands of the Intensity, or the Extreme, or those other club teams. Those clubs are already sprouting, and if high school football steps back, the clubs will grow like weeds. That's where football will go. It'll be like those traveling AAU club teams in basketball with all the shady characters."

"There definitely are some vultures there," Lee said.

"Hey, there's money there. You've got guys trying to act as agents for kids, and look at basketball with all the transferring and recruiting. And now all these agents or whatever they call themselves—mentors, handlers—are getting involved with seven-on-seven. These all-star, traveling teams. When high school coaches aren't involved, it's open season on the kids."

Lee nodded, happily allowing me to keep babbling, hoping, I'm sure, I would eventually talk on the record. It felt good to talk about it. I just couldn't offer any solutions.

"But look at what's invested in football," Lee said. "Putnam's stadium is only a few years old, Allen's got that sixty-million-dollar palace, McKinney built one like it, and so many schools just spent millions on practice facilities."

"Yeah, but most places aren't like here. That's where the dominoes can fall."

I had been thinking about that more and more. How many dominoes needed to fall for Texas to feel it? Would there be more superintendents like Bashum ready to challenge football?

I had been talking with Lee for half an hour.

"See what happens when you get me started?" I said.

"I don't mind a bit," Lee said, "and if you ever want to be quoted . . ."

"I've already got enough going on without creating more problems. All this stuff I'm talking with you about is what I spend my time thinking about, and I should be thinking about trying to beat Summit."

"Tough opponent."

"It's a huge step up, and it won't get easier after that with Lovejoy. We'll have to play well just to hang in there. And then we jump into district with North Forney, which won ten games last season."

"You need to schedule some creampuffs."

"Yeah, I guess so," I said, chuckling. "Usually my thought is, schedule creampuffs and you become one. But right now, I'm a little worried about getting creamed."

CHAPTER 14

MANSFIELD Summit was a gracious host in our first road game of the season. Graciously merciful.

Summit was up 35–0 by midway through the third quarter, and then the Stallions pretty much cut the engines. We scored a touchdown early in the fourth quarter when Paul Nelson plowed into the end zone from three yards out, but that was after Summit pulled its starters. Our team's fragile confidence had been shattered long before then. The 38–13 final score could've been more lopsided, and week two of the season was either a step backward or a step toward reality.

I knew our opening-night win had masked a lot of deficiencies, and Summit exposed them all. Our lack of team speed was magnified by one of the most athletic teams in the Dallas area. Our secondary struggled to keep up with the receivers in all sorts of coverages, and our linebackers showed their limitations when pursuing plays to the sidelines. It certainly would've helped to have Tyreke Abrams at cornerback more, but he couldn't play the entire game, and we needed him for our sputtering offense.

The defense played better the following week, and we trailed Lovejoy by only a touchdown until the game got away in the fourth quarter. But in the 28–7 loss, we had the same problem: our offense just couldn't move the ball. We hadn't moved the ball well in any of our three games, so I was thankful to have the one victory.

The day after our loss to Lovejoy, I got my first chance to see Mickey play for Putnam, which was facing a team from Arkansas as part of a Saturday doubleheader at Southern Methodist University's Ford Stadium in Dallas. The heat was still fierce two weeks into September, so thankfully, Putnam played in the evening game.

Mickey caught three passes for thirty-eight yards, and he also had one run for nine yards on a reverse. Not a standout performance by any means, but Mickey was a contributor, just as I knew he would be. At Creekside, Mickey would've been the star on a team I was trying to push past mediocre, but Mickey was never drawn to the spotlight. What he wanted was the chance to prove himself at another level. He didn't mind playing in the shadow of the megastar receiver lined up a few yards away.

Kingsley Savage. Wow, what a player. His nicknames, "King" and Beast," were pretty cliché, but pretty dead on. You've probably heard football and basketball players talk about going into "beast mode" in the typical bluster of cocky teenagers. But beast mode was the only mode Kingsley played in.

Kingsley was fast, but it was his imposing physique, combined with an acrobatic athleticism, that was astounding for someone who had just turned eighteen. In Putnam's win over the Arkansas team, Kingsley caught a touchdown pass by soaring above two defenders on what was essentially a jump ball thrown into the end zone.

The other touchdown was even more impressive. Set up wide right, Kingsley sprinted off the line of scrimmage toward the middle of the field. About ten yards downfield, he cut back toward the sideline, and although that dropped one of the two defenders on him, he was still tightly covered. The quarterback threw it anyway.

Kingsley bounced softly into the air, soaring with an ease that seemed to turn live action into slow motion, and at the peak of his jump cupped the ball in his right hand. He used his left hand to help secure the ball and then kept his balance while landing with a defender hooked around his waist. The falling defender slid down the back of Kingsley's legs and managed to get a grip on a leg, but "Beast" kicked him off like an old slipper. He stiff-armed another defender and skated sixty yards to the end zone.

* * *

"He's a total freak," Mickey said. "It's like I'm playing next to Julio Jones."

I laughed at the ridiculousness of comparing a high school kid with an NFL star, but Mickey was going on and on about him. We were out on our backyard patio, along with the rest of the family, enjoying some rare time together during the season. It was Sunday evening, and with the next Creekside game twelve days away because of our scheduled bye week, it was a family day. With eighty-hour work weeks common during the football season, I squeeze in family time any way I can.

I'm serious about working eighty hours a week during the season, which runs from August through November—and through December if you make a deep playoff run. Some coaches say they work even more than that. The hours are gobbled up by practice time, work in the weight room, watching hours of practice and game film of your team, breaking down film of the opponent, game planning with the staff, responding to parents, reassuring parents, and sometimes being a parent for one of your players. You're a fund-raiser, a mediator, the equipment guy—all that. Sometimes you're trying to help a kid straighten out his academics, other times you're trying to get him recruited, and once in a while you're just trying to get him home safe.

You have to love it, and I do. But I also know the sacrifices that come with the job. It will affect your family, and I didn't always handle it well when I was younger and feeling more pressure to win, prove myself, and stay in front of whoever was chasing me. Back then, even entering a bye week, I probably wouldn't have been on the patio hanging out with the family.

"Daddy," Emma called out from the pool, where she was floating on an inflatable alligator, "did Mom tell you Gabby's getting her ears pierced?"

"What?"

I looked over at my wife, who smiled and looked away. I wasn't going to get any help on this one. I was the one who said Emma couldn't get her ears pierced until she was ten, so I was the one who had to fight the battle. Christine supported my decision, but she didn't feel as strongly as me. She gave me a "good luck, buddy" pat on the shoulder and walked into the house.

I'm not sure why I picked ten as the age when Emma could get her ears pierced. I think when Emma first asked two years earlier, age ten just seemed far enough away to ease the twinges of panic that my girl was growing up too fast.

Yeah, I'm overprotective. But if you have a daughter, you know what I'm talking about. If you've seen how our culture tries to fast-forward a girl's trip from innocence to adolescence, you know what I mean.

"Gabby's getting her ears pierced Saturday for her birthday," Emma said. She paddled the alligator toward the shallow end of the pool while Andrew did pull-ups on the end of the diving board.

"Huh," I said, basically just making some noise so she knew I was listening (sort of).

"And I'm older than her."

I nodded.

"So?" Emma said.

"That sounds like it could be a good birthday present for you . . . when you're ten."

"Daddy!"

"We've been over this, Em."

"But Daddy, that's so far away."

"I know that. I've been keeping track of your age since you were born."

Emma flopped her head down on the alligator in exasperation. "But Tasha and Kylie . . ."

Emma's argument was cut short by an underwater attack. Andrew swam under her, overturned the alligator and sent Emma into the water.

"Drew!" Emma yelled as she surfaced and brushed soppy blonde hair from her face. Andrew splashed water at Emma as he climbed the pool steps, then stopped, turned toward her, and flexed a modest amount of muscle as she swung the alligator at him.

"When you're ten, I'll be sixteen," Andrew said, sitting down in one of the patio chairs. "I'll take you to get your ears pierced. I'm going to get my ears pierced, too . . . and my nose and lip."

Andrew is also the comedian of the family, or at least he thinks so.

"Just get a face tattoo," Mickey said as he sat down with a second plate of food.

"Yes!" Andrew said, punching his fist into his palm. He dried off and walked into the house, stopping for a moment to nudge the back of Mickey's head so that the bill of his cap fell in front of his face.

I looked over at Mickey and was astounded again by how much food he could put away.

"Are you still at receiver this week, or are you moving to lineman?"

Mickey looked up with his familiar smirk-smile.

"I have to eat a lot," he said. "I'm working hard in life. Grinding."

Yeah, okay.

Mickey finished off the chicken and left a few bites of potato salad before sitting back and taking a deep breath. I think it was a workout for him to eat at that pace.

"So . . ." I said, "how you guys gonna beat DeSoto?"

"We'll need to keep on scoring," Mickey said with a nod to himself, like he'd been thinking about it. "I'm not sure we can stop DeSoto. That offense is crazy."

"To have that many weapons is almost unfair," I said. "Makes me happy I didn't take the Putnam DC position. Long nights getting ready for that."

"Yeah," Mickey said.

He was quiet for a few seconds, and I looked back at Emma, who was now working on dance moves. It looked like I had survived another discussion about getting ears pierced.

"I wish you were there, though," Mickey said.

"What?"

"I wish you had come to Putnam," he said. "You'd get a chance to win another state title."

"You saying Creekside can't win state?"

I acted like I was offended.

"I'm not saying anything," Mickey said, smiling. He put his hands behind his head to ease the full feeling from his pre-apocalypse gorging. "So then, Coach . . . what's your plan for North Forney?"

"I'm more about working on a plan for the rest of the season. North

Forney's the best team in our district right now, and it's not even close. I'm just trying to get us in position to beat the other fish our size."

"So how do you do that?"

"Well, it's the off week, so it's kind of the last good chance to make any big changes. I'm thinkin' about a few things."

"Cody?"

"Yeah, I think so. Feel bad about it, but it's best for the team."

Mickey nodded. "Sucks for him."

"Has Cody mentioned it?"

"No," Mickey said. "We don't talk about football."

I had already talked about it with Cody. I didn't talk about his performance, just that Tyreke needed more chances. I could see the disappointment in Cody's eyes, but I don't think he was shocked. Maybe he was even a little relieved, because he was undoubtedly trying his hardest and frustrated by the lack of results. Cody's a great kid, and I told him that, although I'm not sure those words meant much in the wake of a demotion.

"Tough following in the footsteps of a big-timer," Mickey said.

No doubt. Alex Cason was the best quarterback ever at Creekside.

"I haven't talked with Alex in a few weeks," I said. "Guess everything's going all right, or still the same."

"I know he's bored," Mickey said. "Lots of studying, no real football. Sucks after being the guy for so long."

"So I guess he's just grinding like you?"

He gave me another smile-smirk.

Alex had hoped to get some playing time as a freshman, especially after enrolling early. But he was third on the depth chart at quarterback, and unless there was an injury, he wasn't getting on the field. The coaches planned to have Alex redshirt so he could keep four years of eligibility. It could be good for him in the long run, but I'm sure it made it harder to feel at home in Boston.

"Is he homesick?"

Mickey shrugged.

"Maybe. He asks a lot about what's going on with Creekside."

"If he's seen the scores, he knows."

"He actually asks a lot about what's going on with the whole program."

I didn't say anything, trying to avoid playing into the victim role. I don't like to make excuses and blame others, and I don't want my kids to fall into that. It's too easy to be a whiner.

So I changed the topic.

"Everything's good over at Putnam?"

"Yeah," Mickey said. "Why?"

"Just asking. We don't get to talk as much now."

"Everything's fine."

"Coach Greer's treating you well."

"Sure."

"Julio Jones is a good teammate?"

"Yeah," Mickey laughed. "This is a lot of questions, coming from you. I only expect it from Mom."

"You won't be around a year from now. I've got to get 'em in now."

Mickey was still chuckling, and I'm sure he was kind of laughing at me. He could probably sense his old man getting a little sappy. I missed him. I missed having him in my sight most of the day, having him in the office after practice, having talks with him about the next opponent. I missed him making fun of my music, and the way he and Mosey had tag-team conversations about how I didn't know anything about pop culture.

"I know that it wasn't always easy to play for me."

"Dad," Mickey said, shaking his head and trying to wave off the conversation. "What are you talking about?"

"I always worried, and I worry now, that I put too much pressure on you. Coach's son . . . you had to do everything right, had to be perfect, had to be on top of everything. I thought maybe that made it easy for you to go over to Putnam."

"You wanted me to go."

"I didn't want you to go. I wanted what was best for you."

"Right," Mickey said, a little agitated. "So what are you talking about?"

"So I didn't put too much pressure on you?"

Mickey frowned and shook his head.

"Yeah, there was pressure. But there's always pressure. I wanted to do well. I wanted to win. But if you're wondering, like, did I ever think that if I did something wrong, or I failed at something . . ."

He stopped mid-sentence.

"It was great playing at Creekside."

I'm not sure I was convinced, but I was happy to hear it. I didn't need to torture Mickey any more with my sudden onset of a midlife coaching crisis. Mickey changed the subject, anyway.

"Have you seen the new uniforms for that Intensity team?"

"No, I haven't seen Intensity at all. Let me guess . . . flashy, neon, something that looks like a space suit?"

"Pretty much."

The North Texas Intensity had been around for several years as a select football program, and it now had five or six teams for various age groups. Some dads started it to create a sort of all-star team for their kids, and as they attracted more players, they added teams. This was the second year that Intensity had a high school team, or more accurately, a team of high school-age players, and they cobbled together a schedule against some small private schools and other teams from all over the place.

"Yeah, the jerseys are flashy. They're actually pretty nice," Mickey said. "They look a lot like Oregon, but with blue. They have diamond patterns on them and the numbers have some color-shift thing that makes them change colors."

"Color shift?"

"I haven't seen it. A couple guys had shots on their phone. Colors change when the fabric expands. Something like that."

"Sounds ridiculous, which means it's probably true," I said. "Wonder how much parents are paying for those jerseys?"

"Intensity has an equipment deal with Under Armour."

"How do you know all this?"

"Putnam guys. And it's on flyers that are getting posted around because they're looking for more players."

"I'm sure they're always looking for more players."

I didn't really know much about the team, but it was time to find out more.

Chapter 15

HAVING a week off from games didn't decrease the coaching workload, especially with the problems we needed to address before district play. The good news was that our biggest problems were limited to one side of the ball, and so we decided to sacrifice some defense to get some more offense. We hoped we'd get some more offense, anyway, as Tyreke took more snaps.

I still expected we'd plug Tyreke in on defense occasionally, but he was the new number-one quarterback and Cody moved to backup. I had a talk with Cody about what was going on, and that was tough. It's always painful, for both the coach and the kid, when you have to get real about what isn't working. I'm no master at breaking the news, but I like to think my heart's at least in the right place. I was the kid in Cody's place, after all, and more than once.

I know Cody's pride was hurt, but he handled it well. I've had some kids quit the team when they were pulled as starters or moved to other positions. It can be a crushing deal for them, I know that. But when things don't go right for you, for whatever reason . . . there might not be a better lesson football can teach than how to deal with that. Sixteen or sixty, it's a good lesson. It sucks, though, and it can stick with you. I'm still a bit haunted by those moments of adolescence when I learned of my, uh, limitations—in football and whatever else.

And don't get me wrong about Cody. He wasn't a total "good soldier" type about the move. He told me he needed more time with the receivers, and while there was no doubt about that, I told him that we needed to try some new things. I also told him how much the team still needed him, both as a player and a leader. The team needed him to be ready.

Cody was a little sulky at the next few practices, but hey, I'll give any kid that. He continued to practice as quarterback, and we also worked him in as an inside receiver. I wanted to get him on the field somehow.

While Cody handled it well, his dad was a bit different. He told me that I was betraying his son, failing him as a coach, and not appreciating all his hard work. That might sound harsh, but coaches hear that kind of stuff all the time. Every year, we're the ones telling kids that they won't be starters or they won't get to play. We're the dream killers, you know?

In my experience with upset parents, I've found it best to let them vent, no matter how unreasonable or emotional they get, and then douse the fire with kindness. You might feel you're right and the parents are just blind to reality, but it's best not to stir the hot coals. One of my coaching mentors taught me long ago that the biggest threats to your program come from within. Before you win games, you must win the parents.

When Mr. Shelton called me, I didn't mention that Cody was completing less than forty percent of his passes and had four interceptions to just three touchdowns. And I didn't mention that, had Mickey not transferred, Cody never would've been the starter. What I did tell Mr. Shelton was that he had a great son, that I appreciated all of Cody's hard work, and that he was still a big part of the team. I told him that if he wanted to talk more, we could meet at my office. He said he would get back to me, but I knew he wouldn't. He vented, I listened—we were done. He wasn't happy, but I think he was closer to satisfied.

Our practices on Monday, Tuesday, and Wednesday were pretty good, but I could tell the players were feeling the weight of the back-to-back blowout losses. They also had no game to look forward to that week, and that probably magnified the drudgery of each day's workout. By Wednesday afternoon, an unusually hot one in mid-September, the kids were really dragging.

On Thursday, I cut practice a half hour short. I called the players together in the middle of the field, and as they knelt in a semicircle in front of me, I told them about my high school team.

"My final year in high school, we lost our first three games, and we lost them ugly . . ."

In reality, my high school team had been blown out in only one of the three games, and the first of the three straight losses was a preseason scrimmage. But I needed to add some drama. My Creekside kids needed an underdog story.

"I remember my coaches telling us to hang in there, believe in what we were doing, and the results would come. But, I'm telling ya, there were times when I didn't believe them. We were doing all this work, and for what? Was it really worth it? I was even thinking, seriously, was football really worth it?"

I had the players' attention, but I didn't know for how long. They looked tired. Tired of practice, tired of losing, probably tired of listening to me. Everyone is tired of listening to the coach after a while.

"I seriously thought that maybe football wasn't worth it," I continued. "There were other ways to spend my time. You know . . . I was a pretty good-lookin' guy back then."

I pulled off my hat and rubbed my head, which now only offers a graying, thinning version of the brown hair I had years ago. The kids laughed, so maybe I had their attention. It was just in time, because the pickup truck was pulling into the parking lot next to our practice field.

"But my teammates and I didn't want to be quitters. We didn't want our last high school season to be a washout. Even if we didn't win another game, we wanted it to be our best effort. We didn't want to have regrets, you guys understand?"

"Yes sir," the players replied in a tired monotone.

"Do you really understand?"

"Yes sir." There was a little more energy this time. Forced enthusiasm for the coach.

"And we ended up turning it around," I said. "There were ups, there were downs, but we made the playoffs. We turned it around, and you know how we did it?"

A couple of our student trainers were teaming up to pull a cooler from the back of the pickup. One of the assistant coaches, standing behind the players as I finished my story, waved the trainers over.

"We turned it around with hard work. My coaches said we might not have as much talent as some other teams, but we wouldn't be outworked. We would do one more drill than everyone else, we would do one more rep in the weight room, we would outwork everyone."

The players looked at me, starting to dread where this was going.

"My coach back then, I mean he was Old School. Even when I was playing, he was Old School. When things got tough, when things went wrong, the answer was to work harder. *Ooooooooold* School."

"So captains, what do you think? Nelly?"

"We work harder," said Paul Nelson.

"Whatever it takes, Coach," added Mason Gaines.

"Grind," said Elijah Lawal.

"What about the rest of you? You ready for whatever it takes?"

"Yes sir."

"All right," I said. "I want you guys to know that I appreciate all the work you're doing, but I also want you to appreciate all the work you're doing. Be proud of yourselves. Be proud that you're part of something special here, no matter what our record is now or will be at the end of the season. Understand?"

"Yes sir."

"We're all in this together. We'll be the nasty underdogs and maximize everything we've got. We'll give maximum effort, we'll make sure every other team gets our best, we'll be Old School."

"Yes sir."

"And one other thing, guys. . . . I know you might think I'm older than dirt. That maybe I once dodged dinosaurs at practice. But I'm a little more New School than you think. You know, Mose's even got me listening to some hip hop."

The players laughed again.

"What? Am I not cool enough?"

I waited for the snickers to stop and for the trainers to get ready.

"All right, all right . . . so here's the deal. Wins aren't guarantees, but effort can be, and success comes through perseverance. So the turnaround starts now."

"Understand?"

"Yes sir."

They kept looking at me, and I let a few seconds pass.

"No, I mean you can turn around now."

I pointed behind them, and the players turned around as three ice chests were opened to reveal boxes of ice cream sandwiches. The players broke into hollers and cheers, and a few jumped to their feet and started dancing.

"Get in line, guys," I said. "Two each, and let the trainers get theirs first. You guys will eat everything, including the coolers, before anyone gets a hand in there."

The players started laughing again. You could feel the energy level rise as they realized they would be eating ice cream sandwiches instead of running sprints.

Fifty bucks well spent, I'd say.

CHAPTER 16

I left the practice quickly, ice cream sandwich in hand, and headed to a practice for the North Texas Intensity. It's actually the North Texas INTENSITY!—all caps, with an exclamation point, like it's some kind of energy drink. That's how it was written on the flyer I found pinned to the community bulletin board at the Creekside library.

The flyer said Intensity was looking for players from third grade through high school. A huge logo for Under Armour, like a stamp of approval, was at the top. The handout included an email address for the head coach, Driphus Coleman, so I contacted him and told him I'd like to come out to a practice. I didn't want to show up unannounced and seem like I was spying.

Intensity practices on the football field of Knoll Christian, a small private school that's a fifteen-minute drive from Creekside. I don't know if the team rents the field, or the coach knows somebody, or what the deal is. The private school is actually closer to Putnam than Creekside, and Mickey said a couple of Putnam students play for Intensity. I asked Putnam's coach about it, and he didn't seem concerned. They were kids who didn't get much playing time at Putnam, and his team has plenty of depth. A school with six thousand kids can stand to lose a few.

It's hard to get on the field at a competitive program like Putnam, so I can see kids, and their families, seeking out greener grass. But what a change. Play for Putnam and you take the field in front of fifteen thousand fans every week, and in a state-of-the-art stadium, and with your high school classmates. Join up with Intensity, and you'll play nothing but road games at small schools and in whatever rag-tag scrimmages the coaches put together.

You get to play in some sharp-looking uniforms, but who's going to see you? Even the official games are like glorified practices. There's no band, no crowd, no atmosphere, no adrenaline. The younger teams, before middle school . . . yeah, I get the attraction for the kids. But who wants to go play scrub ball when they can be a part of the best of the best, Texas high school football?

I walked across the weathered six-lane track that surrounded the field and stood on the sideline. The team was on the field, split into offensive and defensive groups, and there weren't more than thirty players out there total. The sideline opposite me was littered with football equipment, water bottles, coolers, and a few tackling dummies. I saw four coaches, each of which was wearing the same blue-and-green workout shirt, along with matching shorts and hats. Three boys, around ten years old or so, were filling up water bottles. Two of them were, anyway. The third was squirting the other two with a water bottle. All three boys were wearing high school size Intensity jerseys that draped close to their knees.

A coach waved to me and I waved back. He jogged over, shook my hand, and I told him I was looking for Coach Coleman. He pointed to a truck parked next to the field, where a player was sitting on the lowered tailgate, getting his ankle taped. The head coach was taping an ankle during practice?

No, that wasn't him. Coach Coleman emerged from behind the truck, with a phone to his ear as he walked toward the field. He looked up, saw me, and started walking my way as he talked. He was wearing the green-and-blue coaching garb that included a block "I" and Under Armour logo.

"Coach Nehls?" he said, extending his hand.

"Yes sir. Nice to meet you."

We shook hands and turned toward the practice field. The players certainly had a dazzling look. Their uniforms—and these were for practice—looked straight from the test lab. The blue tops had white numbers outlined with green and gold. The blue pants had sunbursts of gold near the hip that streaked down the leg like an electric current. Most had matching black shoes with golden laces. It was weird to see the bustle of cutting-edge uniforms on a worn field.

"Sorry," Coach Coleman said as he pulled the phone away from his ear. "Trying to lock down another game."

"Oh," I nodded. "How many are you playing?"

"This would give us six. I'm trying to get to eight."

"Tough deal having to schedule games in the middle of the season."

"Yeah . . . but you know, it's coming around."

We looked out at the field as the offensive and defensive groups came together. I could see that Intensity had a lot of skill guys—backs and receivers—but not much size.

"Ten plays," Coach Coleman yelled out, "and then special teams."

An assistant coach nodded, and Coach Coleman turned back toward me.

"So what can I do for you?" he said.

"I just wanted to come see what you guys were doing. Second year of the team, right?"

"That's right. Trying to grow a little each year, and get better each week . . . and try not to go crazy working with teenagers."

He smiled.

"You know how it is."

"Yeah, it's a challenge," I said. "But a good one."

"Oh absolutely, Coach. That's why I'm out here. It's for these kids, you know. Football just means so much to them."

I nodded again as we watched a tailback run a wheel route to the right side and stretch out to make a catch in the end zone. It was nice, and the players let him know it. They cheered as he got to his feet, pulled off his helmet and jogged backed to them, taking his time like it was a home run trot.

"Quite a grab," I said.

"Vincent Beal," Coleman said. "He's going to be big time."

"What year is he?"

"Sophomore. Most of these guys are freshmen or sophomores. We've got a few juniors, but most of these kids were just getting into high school when we started the team."

"So . . . if you don't mind me asking . . . why a high school team?"

"Saw a need," he said with a shrug.

"A need for another high school football team?"

"Yeah. And, I mean, there was also one personal reason . . . my son Kendrick. I've coached him since he was six and I wanted to keep coaching him. The assistant coaches also have sons on the team. But basically, what it was, I just saw a need."

"How so?"

"Some of these guys are home schooled. It was us or nothing, because youth leagues pretty much end when you get to junior high."

"How many are home schoolers?"

"Five or six. Not sure about a couple," he said with a smile.

"And the other guys?"

"They go to high schools all around but wanted a better opportunity here."

"Better opportunity for what?" I said, and as I said it, I realized I needed to tread lightly. "I just mean, how is this better than playing for their high school?"

"More chance to play. More exposure. More chance to get a college scholarship. I want to get all these kids to college if I can. That's why I'm out here. It's for these kids."

"But Coach," I said, again trying to be respectful. "No offense, but you guys aren't playing high-level teams. It's hard to find teams to play."

"Remember, it's just starting, Coach. These are freshmen and sophomores. And here's the thing that's great for this team. We don't have a league limiting the time we can practice, or telling us what we can and can't do. I can do everything for these kids. We can practice year-round, play in seven-on-seven tournaments, or travel to recruiting showcases. And we've also got some sponsors to help with costs."

"And you can recruit," I said.

"I'm not recruiting your kids, Coach."

"I saw the flyer at the library."

"Yeah, but that's not going after your kids. Sure, I have to recruit in a way. I don't have a high school. We're not a school. We're a team."

I started to say something else, but Coach Coleman looked over at his players and blew his whistle.

"Kyle, that cut needs to be sharp! Don't be rounding that thing off. Dig hard, then bam!" he said, smacking his hands together. "Coach Sands . . . show him."

"Sorry," Coach Coleman said, turning back toward me.

"No need, I'm at your practice," I said with a smile. "But if you're not going after my kids, who are those flyers for?"

"We've put them up at a lot of places. It's for kids who aren't playing football and wanna get into it."

"So you have kids joining in the middle of the season?"

"We take kids all the time. Like I said, Coach, I have to find players. I don't have a school."

"So the kids who aren't home schooled, where are these guys from?"

"Just a second," Coach Coleman said before jogging a few steps onto the field and yelling to the coaches to run kickoff right and left. I started to feel like I was getting in the way, but I wasn't ready to leave.

The players shifted into position for a kickoff as Coach Coleman walked back toward me.

"Coach, I don't know what schools all the kids go to. But I know none are Creekside. We have a couple kids from Creekside on the seventh grade team, but you cut seventh grade football. That's what I'm talking about, you know. There's a need."

"But we're not cutting high school football."

"Yeah, well some schools are."

He was right about that. Dozens of districts across the nation had announced they were cutting their entire football programs—middle school and high school. Whenever I thought the trend might lose some momentum, something would fan the flames of the "football is too dangerous" debate. And then the NFL came out and acknowledged that chronic traumatic encephalopathy, the brain disease some former players were suffering from, might be linked to football. Doctor Wellington, the anti-football doc, seemed to be on speed dial for every TV station, newspaper, and website.

"Only a few Texas high schools have cut football," I said. "And Creekside isn't going to."

Coach Coleman shook his head. "I hope not. Football's good for kids."

He looked back out at the field and pointed.

"You see these kids . . . these kids right here . . . they need football."

I nodded. I didn't have much left to say but still had a ton of questions.

"You said you want the program to grow. Are you adding more high school teams?"

"I'd like a team for every grade. Eventually I mean. We've got a long way to go, but I want Intensity to be national. I want to be something like IMG Academy."

IMG is a sports academy well known as a training destination for athletes in sports such as tennis and soccer. Then it branched out into football and began attracting players—and going after them. Recruiting exposure is the big draw for the kids, I guess, but a lot of them are big-time college recruits before they move to Florida to play for something like an all-star team. It's not a high school. It's a training camp.

"IMG, huh? Lofty goals."

"The first step toward achieving a goal," Coach Coleman said, "is setting it."

I'm sure that's from one of his motivational speeches. I was in no mood for instruction, so I decided it was time to go.

"Well, I'll let you get back to your team. Good luck with the scheduling."

"Okay . . . thanks Coach. Once I get through this fall, it'll be better. A couple more teams are adding high school kids."

I stopped and turned back.

"More high school teams are starting?"

"Two I know of. Dallas Force has some freshmen, and we scrimmaged them, just with our younger guys. And looks like Grand Prairie Impact will have a high school team next year."

Grand Prairie Impact. What a name. I wondered if it was in all caps and had an exclamation point.

"I'm telling you," Coach Coleman said, "where there's a need, there's a team. And there's a need. I've seen people say maybe someday school districts won't have teams and it will be all private club teams, like youth sports over in Europe."

He turned toward me and extended his hand.

"Coach, it was nice meeting you."

"Likewise," I said, gripping his hand, "but let me ask you one more thing . . ."

"What's that?"

"When a player gets injured, what's the procedure?"

"What do you mean?"

"I mean . . ." I said, struggling to not sound condescending, "when a kid gets injured out here, what's the procedure?"

"Well, that depends on the injury," he said.

"What if it's serious? How do you handle it? Have you and your staff done safety training? Do you know C.P.R.? Do you have procedures for dealing with serious injuries and concussions?"

"Coach, Coach, come on. If it's serious, we call an ambulance, just like anyone. We're not doctors."

"Is that your trainer over there?" I said, pointing to the man who was taping an ankle.

"That's right."

"Is he the only trainer?"

"We have two who work with the team, and one is usually at practice. Sometimes both. And then we have some young guys who help out."

"Certified Athletic Trainers?"

"They know what they're doing, Coach."

"But do they have training in dealing with serious injuries, emergencies, the things that can happen? Are these certified guys or just guys from the gym?"

Coach Coleman gave an annoyed sigh.

"They know what they're doing, Coach," he said, raising his voice as he began backpedaling toward his players on the field. "I need to get back to my team. Good luck the rest of the season."

CHAPTER 17

PUTNAM'S game against DeSoto was ugly almost from the start. The Putnam offense didn't get going until midway through the second quarter, and by then, DeSoto was out of reach. That DeSoto team was ridiculous. There were a dozen or so guys with sprinter speed, and that was just on offense. DeSoto's defensive backs had no trouble sticking with the Putnam receivers, and they doubled up on Kingsley Savage.

Kingsley still caught two touchdown passes, but Mickey looked like he was in slow motion as he tried to evade defenders. He ended up with two catches for twenty-one yards and was disappointed with his performance. I'm sure he would've been more disappointed had I told him what I really thought, which was that he actually played well.

Sometimes you work as hard as you can, try as hard as you can, want it more than anyone, and still it doesn't work out. It's not a popular coaching spiel, but it's the truth. Sometimes the talent gap trumps effort, grit, determination, and the other characteristics we so value in our players.

"We'll be a different team come playoff time," Mickey said after the 45–24 loss ended Putnam's perfect start.

I hoped for the same with my Creekside team—that we would be a different team come playoff time. But I knew our season would probably end before the playoffs began. After our week off, we lost to North Forney, giving us a third straight loss. I know it's hard to pretty up a lousy record, but I wasn't disappointed after the loss. We didn't give North Forney a scare, but we hung around with the team I expected to be the district champion before losing 35–17.

"Project Lightning"—yeah, Coach Hartline was still calling it that—showed some promise. With Tyreke Abrams at quarterback, our offense sometimes looked like a rough draft in constant revision. It essentially was a cut-and-paste job, with a lot of "let's just see what happens" every time he took the snap. That's not a good place to be in your fourth game of the season, but at least we were moving forward.

Tyreke ran for one long touchdown and got dropped for losses on six of his nineteen runs. He was an all-or-nothing kind of guy who was still learning that sometimes a one- or two-yard gain was fine and that he couldn't turn everything into an ESPN highlight.

Tyreke also passed for a touchdown, and he led us on a long drive that ended with a short touchdown run by Paul Nelson. It was our best drive of the year, with seven runs and four passes, and I didn't care that it came after North Forney began pulling its starters. It showed what we could do, and what I hoped we could do, the rest of the season.

I was also happy that Cody Shelton, our former starting quarterback, was still able to contribute. He took about a quarter of the snaps, and he also worked in at receiver. After he caught a pass in the third quarter, I saw him smiling on the sidelines and talking with Paul. That didn't mean all was well with him—and his dad—but it was something.

Cody is a lot like Alex Cason. Both of those guys are so rock solid, so loyal, so everything you want your son to be. Alex just happened to be the Jolly Green Giant with a cannon for an arm, while Cody has the head and heart of a champion and the legs and arms for trying really hard. It's impossible not to love Cody. That's probably why I so badly wanted him to come up big at quarterback.

Wishful thinking, I guess, which is how I felt about our playoff chances before the season. But even after three straight losses, I knew we had a chance. We had only one district loss, and there would be four playoff teams in our eight-team district. We just needed to keep moving forward, no matter how slowly.

✳ ✳ ✳

But it was easy to lose focus. I was still irritated by my meeting with Coach Coleman at the Intensity practice, and I was still wasting time worrying about Superintendent Bashum, about more cuts to come, about other schools making cuts, about things I couldn't control.

And then Lee Fountain called to tell me about his meeting with superintendent Bashum.

"He's not against football," Lee said.

I laughed and almost dropped my phone. I remember that's how Bashum started a conversation with me a few months earlier. "Honestly, I'm not against football," he said to me, and the way he said it actually convinced me he was against football.

Honestly.

"I guess I expected him to say that," Lee said. "But he thinks school districts should explore whether the cost of football takes away from its aim to serve all students."

"Bashum's been saying that for almost a year," I said. "I'm just not sure what he means by it, like what he's planning."

"He was generic, either on purpose or because he's boring. But he wanted to know more about what we were doing for the paper. I just told him it's a look at football at all levels, which is about all I know. I'm not sure what form it's going to take."

"Still no idea when it's going to run?"

"No, but I'll give you a heads up. Ready yet to talk on the record?"

"No. Too much going on right now. Anything else to share from the superintendent?"

"Has he said anything about a community forum?"

"No. Nothing."

"Huh. Bashum mentioned there was going to be a night of football discussion. Like what they had in San Antonio last week."

The discussion Lee was talking about was kind of a joke, according to coaches from down that way. They told me it was mostly bitter parents with an axe to grind.

"That San Antonio meeting sounded like there was a lot of support for football," I said. "Folks were ready to march with torches when there was talk of cutting high school football."

"But there were some people saying why schools should not be involved with football, and that was surprising," Lee said. "Who in Texas had taken that stance before? Nobody I know."

"That's because it's crazy."

"Certainly seemed that way not long ago."

"You think that's changing?" I said. "Even in Texas?"

"Something's changing. I love football, and I feel for you, Coach, that your superintendent seems to be all out in front. But it's hard to deny the wave that's going on across the country."

"But it's misinformed."

"Yeah, but it's a tidal wave out there," Lee said. "Did you know there's a website tracking which school districts drop football?"

"A website is keeping track?"

"Yeah. I'll send you a link."

"Thanks . . . I guess. Is there anything else I should know—I mean from Bashum?"

"He mentioned there's a group of superintendents from around the country, some association or organization, talking about feasibility studies for football. That might not be news to you."

"I know he's meeting with a lot of people, trying to build support."

"Or maybe he's trying to build connections to other districts. I mean, think about it, Coach. The way Bashum is sticking his neck out on this, I'm sure he knows the backlash. Could it be he's planning to leave the district?"

I chuckled.

"Man, I barely have enough time to think about my team right now, let alone think about some sinister superintendent plot. But I like the end of your theory, where he leaves."

"Oh yeah, I'm sure. But it probably won't . . ."

The frantic barks of a dog drowned out Lee's voice.

"Oh hang on . . ."

"Working from home, or has the newsroom added some new staff?"

"Ha . . . yeah, my fearless house defender saw a squirrel. Anyway . . . how are Mickey and Andrew doing? Looks like Putnam bounced back nicely after that loss to DeSoto."

"Yeah. Mickey really likes it over there."

"I'm glad. I think Putnam can make a nice run. Shouldn't lose another game before the playoffs."

"That's what Mickey says."

"And you guys should get back in the 'W' column this week."

"Yeah, well . . . I sure hope so."

We did get back in the win column that Friday. But that didn't mean we took a huge step forward. The win was against a school we hadn't lost to in six years and the closest thing to a sure win in our district.

Tyreke ran crazy for us, taking snaps and then basically taking off in whatever direction. When we were safely up 28–7 at halftime, we tried to work on some things, and Tyreke threw his first legitimate touchdown pass. He rolled to his right, stopped, and then threw a nice strike for a twenty-yard touchdown. Who knows if he would ever throw a pass like that again, but for at least one moment, he looked like a quarterback.

As we walked off the field, our regular season was half over. We had a losing record, two wins and three losses, but we also had some direction. We were going to play tough defense, try to stay in games, and then hope Tyreke could create enough offense to get us over the top. I would never tell Tyreke that, of course. It would be unfair to lay that much on the shoulders of anyone, even the swaggering shoulders of a kid who thought he could win a game by himself.

Because Putnam had its bye week, Mickey was able to be on the sidelines for our win over Memorial. He enjoyed seeing his buddies, although they of course gave him a hard time about transferring. It was good natured. They also razzed him about how his girlfriend was a better athlete than him. Kirsten, a star volleyball player, had several college scholarship offers, and Mickey, unless he decided to play for a really small college, was finishing up his football career.

After our win, the coaches met in the office to go over a few things. An evening later, most of us were back in the offices, breaking down video and putting together a plan for the next game. I tuned the radio to *The Mosey Show* and got a blast of music that made me feel old.

Then Mose started talking, and man, I really hoped people were listening. Was it just that I was so fond of Mose, or was he really that good? He could have a talk show. He should have a talk show.

The Mosey Show went back to music, and Jim Hartline started talking about Tyreke.

"He's really got something. It's kind of all over the place, but he's special enough to make a lot of things work. He's so like Mose."

"Don't say that," I said.

Jim shrugged and smirked. "Why? You don't see it?"

"Just . . . I don't want to put too much on him."

But Jim was like a kid on a sugar rush reveling in a new candy discovery. Tyreke made his job, if not easier, at least a lot more fun.

"Makes me wonder what Mose would've been like at quarterback," Jim said. "We were set at QB when Mose was a junior, but do you think we would've moved him to QB as a senior?"

I hadn't really thought about it. Mose's injury came early in his junior season, but I'd always felt like he could play anywhere in the offensive or defensive backfield.

"He would've been great," Jim said. "Maybe we would've won another state title."

CHAPTER 18

I was headed to my office, walking through a school hallway decorated with framed pictures of Creekside's football teams from the last twenty years, when my phone buzzed. It was a message from a coaching colleague who moved on to the college ranks a few years ago.

He's now a relentless recruiter, always on the phone, calling and tapping out texts, going 24/7, analyzing and wooing recruits. His daily highs and lows can swing on the whim of a teenage knucklehead, but he loves the adrenaline rush.

I looked down at the text.

"Got more Tyreke video?"

Our new quarterback was getting some attention. Tyreke probably wasn't going to play quarterback in college, but he was going to play somewhere. He was still a baby, just sixteen years old, but college recruiting is all about projecting. What will a kid be like when he fills out, when his shoulders widen, when he won't be pushed over by a stiff breeze.

I didn't want to leave my time-crunched colleague hanging, so I stopped to text a quick response. As I finished my clumsy tapping, I looked up and saw the back of Mose's bobbing head across the office. It was our midday athletic period, and the players and coaches were out on the field, leaving Mose alone. He was wearing those monster headphones he loves, the ones that make his head twice as big, as he checked out video of our last game.

That's what I thought he was doing.

When I got halfway across the room, I noticed that the gliding, cutting, and strutting wasn't being done by Creekside's latest star. It was video of Mose, back when he was a teenage football invincible, sweeping past defenders, spinning away from tacklers, buckling the knees of those trying to guess zig or zag.

"Woooo . . . look at that!" I said with a laugh.

My voice caught Mose off guard. Startled, he straightened up in his chair, and as I leaned in for a better look, he turned his head away from me and the computer screen. I felt bad. I didn't mean to embarrass him, if that's what I did.

I didn't say anything more and walked over to my desk.

"Hey Coach," Mosey said without turning toward me. He clicked the video off the screen and pulled something else up as I sat down at my desk. He slid his headphones off, set them on the desk, and stared down at his lap. Mose, usually loaded with a comment for every situation, remained quiet. I felt awkward in my own office, and I thought about walking back out when I saw Mose rub at his eyes.

After a few more seconds, he spun around.

"Lookin' at old games to get ideas," he said. "More ways to get Tyreke out in open space."

"Oh yeah? Good idea. I'm open to suggestions."

"Not sure yet," he said with a weak smile. "But I'll come up with something."

"Sounds good. You know I always appreciate your expertise. You were a better player than me."

I say that a lot to Mose because I know he likes hearing it. As more time passes, fewer people remember the kind of player he was, and that's tough for Mose. When he was a kid, he got much of his identity from what he could do athletically. On the football field, the basketball court, the track—or even just dancing around in the locker room—he expressed himself through movement. He was much more than just an athlete, but he liked being "the athlete." In his mind, it was what made him special.

Mose went back to work for a couple of minutes, but then he spun back around, took a deep breath, and was quiet for a few seconds. I'm no expert at reading emotions—my wife would attest to that—but I felt like maybe Mose wanted to talk. We haven't had a lot of what you'd call "deep" conversations, but we're around each other a lot. I can sense that he feels lonely sometimes.

It would make sense. Most of his high school buddies have moved away and moved on with their lives. Many are now college graduates, some are married, and a few have kids. I think Mose has achieved some great things, but he still lives at home and relies on family members for help.

"I should go back and watch some of your games," I said. "Our offense was goin' pretty good back then."

"*Uuuuun . . . stoppable,*" Mose said with a nod of his head.

"We had so many options," I said. "Lance at QB, Darryl and Kevin in the backfield, and our receivers . . ."

"Smitty P," Mose broke in. "Too-tall Smitty."

"Get close to the end zone and we could just throw it up to him."

"Yep."

"And, of course, there was you," I said. "Amazing that we had so many good players and you still got on the field. How'd you manage that, again?"

"I was such a sweet talker. And quiet and respectful."

I laughed out loud, which I don't do often, but Mose gets to me. Give him an audience and he lights up, kind of the way he used to rise to every big occasion on the football field.

"I'll give you this, Mose. You were pretty special. That was the best team I've ever had, and you were a big part of it. The loudest part for sure. You were such a punky little dude. I was always amazed how brash you were, even around seniors who could cram you in a locker."

"My big bro, Coach. You grow up as the younger brother of Devon Posey and you're going to grow up tough."

"Was he that rough on you?"

"Oh yeah. Three years older than me and I was the only brother to pick on, the only target. He let me win nothing. Nothing. He gave me no breaks in hoops, and he tackled my ass hard in football. No little brother breaks."

"Turned out to be an advantage."

"Oh for sure. I could play with the big boys when I was a little boy. Now my mom . . ."

Mose started to smile.

"You know my mom—she's just the best, and I'm her baby boy. And she wanted to protect me from everything, and my dad was kind of like that too. It was good that my brother was there to kick me around, in a good way. Without him, I might've been soft."

"And quiet and respectful?"

That got a laugh from Mose.

"I'd say you've grown up okay. Your parents did all right."

Mose looked down and shook his head.

"So corny, Coach."

"I know. You've got to keep your edge. Don't worry, I won't tell anyone."

My phone buzzed again with a message from my coaching buddy.

"This coach is really hot on Tyreke. I guess he's starting to blow up."

"Of course," Mose said. "Big schools?"

"Not yet."

"They gotta move quick. The big dogs will be on the trail soon."

"You're pretty confident."

"It's easy to be. He moves like me."

I took a breath and nodded.

"Yeah, he reminds me of you. I've seen him talking to you quite a bit, so be a good mentor for him, okay? Show him how to be quiet and respectful."

"Oh Coach."

"Don't worry. . . . It's our secret, tough guy."

I smiled and turned toward the dry-erase board on the wall, which was filled with scribbles of plays, formations, and other stuff my wife calls "football hieroglyphics." Next to the board was a countdown clock, which showed three days, five hours, and forty-eight minutes until our next game. The seconds ticking away should've created a sense of urgency, but I felt content talking with Mose, sitting in the quiet office, next to an empty hallway that in ten minutes would be filled with students.

"Your show was great Saturday."

"Thanks," Mose said. "I'm working on my run for this week."

"How's it going?"

"Good. Still early, though. I don't turn in anything until Thursday."

"Does the radio station ever talk about making it longer or putting you on at other times?"

Mose shrugged.

"They say they like the show. I'm happy with that."

"Well, you're really good at it."

"Yeah, well, you know," Mose said with a nod—and a flash of the cockiness from his football days.

Mose looked over at the dry-erase board and stared for a few seconds.

"Got something to add?" I asked.

"Nah. Just thinking back to some of our plays. Coach Hartline and Pirate's Booty."

"Oh yeah, Pirate's Booty," I said. "Coach Hartline and his crazy names."

"Where'd he come up with that name?"

"No idea. Ask him when he comes in."

Mose paused for a second and then turned a little more toward me.

"I remember how scared I was when Coach Hartline first said I was going to throw the ball. Just like the jet sweep, he told me, but with a pass option."

"Wait a second," I said. "You admit to being scared?"

"Did I say scared? I meant excited."

"Right," I said with a smile.

"I was amazed that I was going to get to throw a pass. I went home and told my parents that I was going to start throwing passes. Devon thought you were trying me out at quarterback. I thought maybe you were getting me ready for it."

"For quarterback?"

"Yeah!"

"Wow," I said, smiling wider. "Well, you would've been tough to stop on the run. But it never would've worked, you know, because quarterbacks have to throw the ball to people. You wouldn't throw the ball to anyone."

"Coach, it was a pass *option*," Mose said, raising his hands, which always rested in loose fists, to punctuate his point. "If there was room to run, that was my option."

"And you always found room to run."

"Who was gonna stop me?"

"Good point."

"And nobody will ever top my completion percentage."

"You're right about that. One pass, one completion, one touchdown."

"One for one for sixty-two yards," Mose said.

My phone buzzed again, but this time it wasn't the rapid recruiter. It was Dave Holgate, my friend on the school board. My only friend on the school board.

Got news. Should be clear at 7 for a call

I knew it wouldn't be good news. But before I could give it more thought, Mose continued our conversation.

"Coach . . . you think I could've played QB?"

"Mose, you could've played pretty much anything."

"I mean like in college."

"Oh. Hmm . . . well, I'm not sure. But you could've played somewhere in college. Receiver, defensive back, that's what I always figured. Did you want to be a quarterback?"

"I liked having the ball in my hands."

"Yeah, obviously."

"When I got hurt my junior year, we were solid at QB," Mose said. "But we kind of struggled at quarterback my senior year."

"We struggled with a lot of things. It was tough getting used to not having you on the field."

"So you think I might've been a QB? I was thinking it's kind of like how you've moved Tyreke to QB, and the offense is a lot better."

I nodded. Then I smiled and pointed at Mose.

"I'll tell you this. Had you told me you wanted to play quarterback your senior year, I would've given you a shot. You would deserve the chance. . . . So yeah, you might've ended up at QB."

A few seconds passed.

"Have you've been thinking about that since Tyreke moved to QB?"

"Yeah. I thought of it before, you know, but now I'm like having these dreams where I'm a quarterback."

"Really?"

"Yeah. Back in high school, playing quarterback, doing my thing."

"Your thing?"

"Dominating."

"Oh, of course," I said, smiling again.

"Well, you know, it's my dream," Mose said, also breaking into a smile. "You know it's going to be on point."

"Sure. You dream about it a lot?"

"Always, always, always have dreams about football. But not much about playing quarterback until Tyreke came along. Must be something about him."

"You guys are kind of alike."

"I guess that's why I was wondering about me at QB."

He took a deep breath and looked down, and when he looked back up, his face had turned serious. He raised his right arm, with his hand still in a loose fist, and rubbed at his right eyebrow. He often did that when he was in deep thought.

"The dreams are so real, Coach. I run with the ball, and I can feel it tucked in my arm. I feel the muscles in my legs tighten and my cleats dig into the turf. I feel my foot flex when I make a cut. I feel the laces on the ball under my thumb and the ball rolling off my hand. I feel my fist pounding my chest."

Mose raised his right arm, hand still in a loose fist, and tapped it on his chest. He was wearing a Nike windbreaker, a go-to item in the Mose wardrobe, and I could see the boniness of his shoulders and arms. I wonder how he would've filled out in the years after high school. Six-one and 190 pounds, maybe? He certainly would've been big enough to play at a big-time school, and who knows the sizzling time he might've posted in the forty?

I cleared my tightening throat and looked away.

"You have vivid dreams," I said.

"God gives them to me. You've got to have faith. I still believe I'm going to walk again someday. Until then, God gives me these dreams. You know, with God, all things are possible."

"Absolutely," I said, looking back at him.

Mose sighed while nodding, like he was convincing himself of something.

"One day, Coach. One day."

"Like you said . . . faith."

"I know I'm getting stronger. Better curls with the hand weights. More feeling in my chest. One day, Coach. One day."

I smiled and nodded. It would be difficult to think of anything in the world I wanted more at that moment than for Mose to rise out of the chair. Forget football. I just wanted him to walk out of the office and toward the rest of his life.

"You know, I've had dreams about you playing, too," I said.

"You've told me."

"I mean recently," I said. "Not as good as yours, I'm sure."

"Tell me about them."

"You're playing defensive back for the Longhorns, but you look just like you did in high school, and I'm there watching, cheering."

"So what happens?"

"Nothing really specific. But you're out there."

"No big pass breakup? No big hit? No interception return for a TD?"

"No," I said with a light chuckle. "I guess I'm not that creative. But maybe more dreams are to come . . . for both of us."

"Texas Longhorns," Mose said with a nod. He put his right hand to his eyebrow and took a deep breath. "Me in the burnt orange. Yeah, I like that. Royal Stadium. Hundred thousand fans. Playing A&M or OU. That would be amazing."

He took another deep breath.

"I like your dream, Coach. Tell me when you have more."

CHAPTER 19

I called Dave Holgate that night for the news. It wasn't quite news, but it was more than a rumor, and I took it as fact. I also took it as confirmation of Bashum's intent regarding football.

"He wants to have a public-input session," Dave said. "He wants to start a discussion about whether football should be supported by the schools."

I thought Bashum had already started that discussion back when he was cutting middle school football. Time for another push, I guess.

"So he wants to cut football completely," I said.

"He wants to talk about it. I've never claimed to understand the guy. I've never known him that well, but he doesn't seem like the same guy as a couple years ago."

"Seems like a guy on a vendetta to me."

"Or maybe just a guy who sees an opportunity," Dave said. "There's so much momentum now across the country, with schools cutting back on football, some even dropping it."

"So he's going for the throat. Throwing deep after getting the turnover."

"Could be."

"I still say it's career suicide around here," I said. "I don't care what people are saying about football around the country or how many schools cut it. This is Texas. This is Dallas. People around here aren't ready for it. The backlash . . ."

"Maybe Bashum doesn't care."

"He certainly doesn't care about letting me in on whatever his plans are. Wouldn't you let the football coach know that you're going to have a meeting about cutting football?"

"He's waiting until after the season."

"Sure courteous of him. Letting us finish the season before he tries to finish the program."

* * *

If it were any other time of the year, thoughts of Bashum, the future of the football program, and the future of my profession could've consumed me. But we were smack in the middle of the season, and no matter what was looming, I felt a responsibility to the kids. They had worked hard for the opportunity, and for some of them, this was the time they had looked forward to since pee-wee football. This was their chance to be a part of Texas high school football, to be part of the legendary Friday nights.

And it's not like there was something I could do or say that would change Bashum's course. If he cared what I thought, I would've heard from him. I've always told my team not to worry about what other teams are doing, or what other people are saying, because it does you no good.

I took my own advice, and it worked, at least sometimes. There were some nights when the worry gnawed at me as I tried to fall asleep, but I stayed locked in on the season. The Creekside kids, who were hearing lots of rumors, did the same. The result was one of our best games of the season, a 31–21 win over Forney that felt like a fifty-fifty game at kickoff.

We took control early by running the ball with Paul Nelson. Forney didn't have the size to hold up against our offensive line, and if there was one gift we got from the football gods that year, it was that our offensive line stayed healthy. Ask any coach about the keys to a successful season, and keeping kids on the field will be at the top of the list. Unless you're one of the monster powerhouses, the drop from starter to backup can be a freefall.

Paul rushed fifteen times in the first half alone, and after we got three or four yards on each bruising inside run, the Forney defense had to pack in tighter. That helped Tyreke find open space on the outside, and he ran for a forty-yard touchdown in the first half and a twenty-five yarder in the second half. He also threw a thirty-yard touchdown pass on a play in which Cody took the snap as quarterback. Cody handed the ball to Tyreke, who ran right, stopped, and then threw into the end zone. Tyreke was getting better at selling the run, waiting for the safety to break from coverage, and then making a good pass. Good enough, anyway.

Our defense also played well, and our first winning streak of the season evened our record at three wins and three losses. I got some nice texts and tweets from former players congratulating us on the win. I thanked them but tried to downplay it because we had a game the following week that I felt was another must-win. Alex Cason, dedicated to checking in on his former teammates, said it looked like we really had things rolling now.

"Looks can be deceiving," I told him.

Alex, in the middle of his redshirt freshman season at Boston College, wanted to know more about what was going on with Creekside. A lot of former players asked about the cuts to middle school football, but Alex was more interested than any of them. Maybe it was because he was bored. He told me he missed the excitement and challenge of playing in games.

I filled Alex in on some things, even though I didn't really want to talk about it. I wanted to focus on the season, because the players deserved that. The team was steadily improving, and we extended our winning streak to three games against Terrell, a team that had made the playoffs the year before. I'm not sure we were the better team in that game, but we had the best player in the game, and he played the best game of his life. His extremely young life, since Tyreke had turned sixteen just a few weeks before.

Tyreke was pretty amazing in the 34–21 victory. He ran for a touchdown on our first drive and then for two more later. He also threw two touchdown passes, so he played a part in all five of our scores.

Tyreke had always shown flashes of what he could do, even as a freshman on the junior varsity team. He's just such a gifted athlete. But I've coached a lot of gifted athletes who weren't all that special on the football field. Sometimes, for whatever reason, it doesn't click, and you never get more than flickering teases of a superstar.

Tyreke was no longer a tease or a surprise. Everyone knew he was the primary reason for our three-game win streak, and I'm sure some people wondered why he wasn't at quarterback when the season started. Hindsight is twenty-twenty, right? I thought Cody deserved a chance to prove himself, and honestly, I had no idea Tyreke would take to the position so well. Moving Tyreke to QB was basically the disaster plan.

But that's not what I told the newspaper reporter who asked me about Tyreke. "We saw his potential and were confident that he would do a good job at quarterback," I said generically.

Tyreke was selected as the newspaper's Offensive Player of the Week, and the reporter wanted to talk with him. It was the weekend, so I called Tyreke's parents to let them know a reporter would be calling. Then I talked with Tyreke and reminded him to be careful with his words.

A few hours later, I called Lee Fountain about the story. I knew I was probably being overprotective, but I worried about Tyreke. Things had blown up quickly for him, and I thought about what might spill out of his inflated ego.

"Why so worried, Coach?"

"He's a good kid," I said. "But he's young."

"Why didn't you ask the writer who did it?"

"Because I don't know him like you."

"Okay, just a sec. Let me pull it up. There won't be much to it. Details of the last game, coach quote, player quote."

"Yeah. I know."

"Okay, here it is. Your quote is that we saw his potential and were confident that he would do a good job. And Tyreke's . . ."

Lee was quiet for a few seconds.

"I'm happy the coaches were confident that I could go in there and help the team."

"That's it?"

"Then he says he always knew if you would just give him a chance at quarterback, he would dominate because that's what he's all about."

"Don't mess with me, Lee."

I said it jokingly, but a part of me believed Tyreke might say something like that.

"Looks like he kept it pretty tame, Tuff. No reason to worry."

"Well, good. I wasn't trying to interfere. Just, you know, some of these young guys."

"I know. Tyreke's turning into something special."

"Yeah, he is. He's only played half a varsity season, so I don't want to get ahead of things, but he's certainly something."

"I'm happy for you guys. I know it's been a frustrating stretch."

"Thanks. Who knows what's to come, but with so many things going against us, it's nice to have something go our way."

CHAPTER 20

IT'S always a rollercoaster. Even the best seasons have low points and even the worst ones . . . well, you've got to peak at some point. I've never had a winless season, so I guess I can't speak for everyone.

But in high school football, we're talking about working with teenagers, a demographic that both astounds and confounds me on a daily basis. They're smart, funny, determined—all those great things—and then sometimes ridiculously illogical and unpredictable. Impassioned one moment, immature the next. I've read that it's because the prefrontal cortex in a teenager's brain isn't completely formed. It's like they've got all the components up there for a super computer, but a couple of the wires haven't been plugged in yet.

Because of all that, we high school coaches like to stay in the middle. Emotionally, I mean. You're never as good as some people think you are, you're never as bad, and everything eventually comes back to some kind of resting point. Peak one week, crater the next, and over the ten-game regular season, you are what you are.

That's why I wasn't stunned when my team, on a three-game win streak and pushing for a playoff spot, flopped against Mesquite Poteet. It had to come sometime, and that sometime was in an ugly 42–14 loss.

The good thing was that I didn't expect to beat Poteet. The loss evened us up at four wins and four losses, and with wins in our final two games, we would make the playoffs. Win one of two and we would still have a chance if the right teams won the other games and the headache-inducing tiebreaker scenarios went our way. We still controlled our playoff destiny.

The bad thing was that we didn't look like a playoff team in the loss. Our defense didn't stop the run the way it usually does, and our offense couldn't stay on the field. Tyreke struggled, and I guess that had to happen.

We put so much on his shoulders, expecting him to keep the ship afloat each week, and that wasn't fair. Eventually the hole in the boat was too big.

Tyreke looked lost as the defense plugged his running lanes and blanketed his receivers. He hung his head and slumped off the field, and it drives me crazy when a player does that. We all have bad games, make mistakes, get frustrated. I expect all of that. I also expect my players to run off the field with a look of purpose, not one of defeat. There will be no pity parties.

Tyreke finished the game on the bench and Cody got his first significant time at quarterback in several weeks. He threw a nice touchdown pass in the fourth quarter, and that was one of the few things worth remembering on the windy, damp night in late October.

After the TD pass, I could see Cody's smile behind the facemask as he turned to run off the field. He dropped the smile as he got near the sideline, I'm sure worried that the coaches wouldn't like that he was enjoying a moment in a lopsided loss, but nobody was going to give him a hard time. I patted him on the helmet as he jogged by.

On the Monday following the loss, I talked with Tyreke in my office. I told him how much I appreciated all the work he was doing and his willingness to learn a new position. I also told him that I didn't want him to feel the burden of carrying the team, even if he thought he could. And I told him that sulking around the field, whether in practice or a game, wouldn't be tolerated.

"Unacceptable for any player, but especially my quarterback."

"Yes sir," he said, looking down. "I know."

"I don't want you to feel like you have to carry the team, because you don't. But the team is going to look to you for leadership, even though you're young. QB has to be a leader."

"Yes sir, and body language is important."

"That's right," I said, a little surprised by his response. I hadn't talked with him about that.

"Did one of the coaches tell you that?"

"Coach Posey."

"Mose?" I said, breaking into a smile because I always liked the sound of "Coach Posey." If I could pay Mose to be a coach, I would.

"When were you talking with Coach Posey?"

"On Saturday. He calls me every weekend."

"I didn't know that. What do you guys talk about?"

"The game, mostly," he said with a shrug.

Maybe I was prying too much. Tyreke looked a little uncomfortable as he sat in the seat across from the desk. But Tyreke always looked a little uncomfortable when he was talking with me. Most players do when talking one-on-one with their coaches.

"Well, Coach Posey is a great person to talk to," I said. "He's a good coach. Knows his football."

"Yes sir. Could've been a great quarterback, too."

"Did he tell you that?"

"Yes sir," Tyreke said, chuckling a little. "He tells me that a lot."

"Oh geez. Mister Humble."

"I think he was saying I should listen to what he says because he could've been really good."

"Yeah," I said, nodding. "So what tips has he given you?"

"A lot about leadership. He told me because I'm young, I need to try harder at it, but that all the guys would be looking to me. He said I had to, like, you know, sell it like an actor. He said body language is important."

I was impressed. Good ol' Mose.

"Coach Posey is absolutely right," I said. "So tell me . . . how are you feeling about quarterback? I know things were tough Friday."

"I like it."

"Do you miss defense?"

"Nah, only a little. I like quarterback. I like having the ball in my hands."

I nodded and smiled. "That sounds like Mose."

"Yes sir, and he thinks I can play quarterback in college."

"Hmm. Well, you've got a lot of time to work on things. Listen to Coach Hartline, and he'll help you get there, if that's what you want. A few weeks ago, you were worried about not getting to play corner."

"Yes sir."

Tyreke turned his head to look out the window at the players headed out of the locker room.

"Well, whatever you want, Tyreke, you've got the tools. Just keep working hard on the field and in the classroom. Mrs. Collins tells me you got a ninety-two on your geometry exam last week."

"Yes sir," Tyreke said while allowing a legit smile to break through.

"What did your mom say about that?"

"She was happy. Said she's proud of me."

"Well, I am too," I said.

Geometry had been the one subject giving Tyreke some trouble. He wasn't near failing, but his parents weren't going to let him mess around. Parents can check their kids' grades online anytime they want, and Tyreke's mom and dad were all over that.

"Just keep on working hard," I said again.

"Yes sir, I will. And I'm working on shortening up my throwing motion."

"That's good, but remember, you've been playing quarterback for what, five weeks now? Be patient. . . . Was Mose saying something about your throwing motion?"

"Nah. Coach Hartline. He said he's gonna work with me on it after the season. And I'm going to a QB camp."

I was surprised how serious Tyreke was about playing quarterback. It was a good thing, because we didn't have many options on the horizon. The football cuts had led to some transfers, leaving our freshman and sophomore classes lighter than they had been since I came to Creekside. We needed something to build around.

"A quarterback camp?" I asked.

"It's in January. The coach running it talked to me after our game. He gave me his number and told me he'd stay in touch."

"A coach gave you his number?"

"Yes sir."

"From Poteet?"

"No, it wasn't last week. It was after the Terrell game. But he's not a high school coach. He coaches another team."

"What team?"

"Intensity."

Oh. Him.

I'm sure Tyreke saw the change in my expression. I leaned back in my chair, sighed, and shook my head. I've cleaned up my language over the years, but the "son of a bitch" in my head might've been audible. Tyreke had a stunned, slightly scared look.

"Have you talked to him since then?"

"No sir," Tyreke said defensively.

"Okay."

"But he texted me after the last game. Said to keep my head up."

I nodded, and I'm sure I looked pissed. I was, of course. But Tyreke hadn't done anything wrong.

"Should I not talk to him?"

"I'm not going to tell you who you should talk to. But remember this, and I should've talked to you more about this. Be careful giving out your number. People will want to get close to you, and you don't want some of those people close to you."

"Yes sir."

"Good. Well, I slowed you up for practice. Get dressed out."

Tyreke walked out of my office, and I stared blankly at the wall. I thought about that coordinator position at Putnam High School that I turned down. I could've been at a school where football was still a golden child and the stadium looked like a shrine to the sport I love. I could've been coaching my son; I could've been preparing a team with a legitimate chance at a state title; I could've had the security of knowing my football program wasn't lying under a guillotine. Man, I could've just laughed when I heard about the Intensity team, its eye-burning uniforms, and its hope to be the next IMG.

And then I laughed at myself. No pity parties, Coach.

CHAPTER 21

WHEN West Mesquite's star running back was slow to get up, I felt a little guilty.

I always hate to see a player get injured, and that includes the guys on the opposite sideline. These kids work so hard to get on the field, and for most of them, playing in high school will be the football high point of their lives. I don't want anything to get in the way of their moment.

So I felt for the West Mesquite running back when he walked gingerly off the field, helped by a trainer and coach. I saw the pain and frustration on his face as he reached for his left ankle, the one he had sprained a few weeks earlier. Here was this senior, trying to lead his team to the playoffs, and now his high school playing days were possibly over.

It was sad, but I felt relieved. Because on West Mesquite's first possession, when their star runner had carried the ball seven times on a ten-play touchdown drive, I knew we were in trouble. Our defense was pretty strong up the middle, but the linebackers aren't speedy. Our secondary didn't have a lot of flyers, either, so West Mesquite's back might've had two hundred yards against us.

But then he went down with the ankle injury late in the first quarter, and everything changed. We took control, led by Tyreke, who bounced back from his rough game a week earlier to lead us to a 28–14 victory. That gave us five wins and four losses, ensured we wouldn't have a losing record, and put us in great playoff position. Who would've thought it was possible back in August, when our potential quarterbacks were throwing wounded ducks and our receivers were dropping them?

One game was left in the regular season, and with a victory over a Northside team that had only three wins, we would be in the playoffs. Getting to the postseason is always an achievement, but just having a chance going into our final game was something special. I had never felt so fulfilled by such humble success. We still had to win one more game, but we were in the hunt on the final weekend and playing a team that we should beat. For a Creekside team that sometimes resembled a kindergartner's macaroni art project, with pieces of this and that thrown everywhere and big globs of glue trying to hold it all together, a playoff spot would be the summit of Everest.

Over at Putnam's stadium, the Panthers were clinching their third straight district title and talking about far bigger goals than just getting to the playoffs. Putnam is always talking that way when the playoffs arrive, but it was a first for Mickey, who spent the weekend going on and on about how much his team had improved and how Putnam was going to make a deep run.

Putnam still had one regular-season game left, but with its playoff position settled, many of the starters were going to sit out the game to avoid injury. Mickey expected to get some time at quarterback because Putnam's backup QB had some nagging injuries. Mickey played almost exclusively as receiver for Putnam, but he had QB experience, so he was Putnam's "emergency" quarterback. The coaches wanted to give him a few snaps in a no-pressure situation.

After our win, I again got calls, texts, and emails from former players who were following our turnaround. Alex texted me congratulations and then added that it was already "ass-freezing" cold at Boston College. He hoped the weather would be warm when he came back to Creekside for a Thanksgiving visit, and he also wanted to see one of our playoff games. We would have to make it to the third round for Alex to see one of our games.

"To get to the third round, I think we'll need you to play in the first two rounds," I told him.

"That would be great," Alex said. "Redshirting blows."

* * *

On the Sunday before our regular-season finale, I left church with my family and headed off for lunch with Solo. One of the greatest guys on

Earth, I'd say, and now the coaching profession was losing him. I couldn't believe it, or at least I didn't want to believe it.

"I'd like to say, 'You'll be back,'" I told him. "But I know how smart you are."

Solo smiled.

"I don't know if I'm that smart, but I did give it a lot of thought."

We both started in on our Whataburger goodness. Not exactly healthy stuff, but oh so good. I'm okay with knocking a couple years off my life if I get to keep eating A-1 Thick and Hearty Burgers.

"So full-on administration?"

"Yeah," Solo said with a look of slight embarrassment.

As football coaches, we're athletic coordinators of our campuses, but we feel more like coaches and teachers than administrators. When guys head to "real" administrative positions, we sometimes call it the Dark Side. But nobody can really blame them when an opportunity comes their way.

Solo and I had been having lunch together once a month for several years. Sometimes we reminisced about our time as young assistants, working on the same staff, but most of the time we talked about what was going on with our current teams, our districts, and our upcoming opponents.

Solo, who had been the head football coach and campus athletic director at Kemper High School for six years, was giving up coaching. He accepted a position as assistant athletic director in the Garland school district, where he had been an assistant coach earlier in his career.

"So now the time is right?" I said.

Solo finished chewing a bite of chicken sandwich, then raised his eyebrows and shrugged.

"I don't really know," he said, rubbing his fingers on a napkin. "I've been a coach for so long. It's going to feel strange. It already does, and I've got a game left."

"Wish you could go out with a nice playoff run."

"Me too. And I wish I could've done it for the kids and school staff. They've really been great. Three winning seasons and two losing seasons, and I was always treated the same. I've got a great principal and supe, you know."

"Yeah, thanks," I said. "Don't rub it in. Maybe I should jump off this ship and go to Kemper."

"They'd love to have you. But Mack, my offensive coordinator, wouldn't be too happy about it. He's going to take over."

"No surprise, and that's great. He can keep the staff together."

"Yeah, it's unofficially official. They've still got to go through the process. But it'll happen. I wish we could've had one last playoff run together, but it just didn't happen for us. Things didn't come together for us the way they did for you. I couldn't find a Tyreke."

I put down my burger and gave Solo a serious look.

"What? Don't I get some credit here?"

"Shut up. You know what I'm talking about."

I smiled.

"That guy, he's really something," I said. "And only a sophomore. If he can keep his head straight . . ."

"You think he won't?"

"Oh, I think he will. Tyreke's not a knucklehead. But he's young, you know, and everything going on with him is probably a little much right now. And oh yeah, you know that Intensity team I was telling you about?"

"Yeah?"

"Their coach showed up at our field. He was out there after the game, talking with Tyreke. Right on our field, recruiting Tyreke."

Solo started to laugh, and it turned into a snort because he had another big bite in his mouth. He shook his head as he finished chewing and then rested his chin on his hand and stared at me.

"What did you do?"

"I didn't know about it until afterward," I said, throwing up my hands. "Tyreke told me, just kind of randomly as part of another conversation."

"That's crazy. But not that surprising."

"Unfortunately."

"It's getting crazier every year."

"The recruiting?"

"Kind of everything," Solo said.

A family sat down at a table not far from us, and three young kids, two boys and one girl, couldn't sit still. They were like the bouncy balls I used to get out of the machines at grocery stores when I was a kid. They kept getting louder, and Solo and I looked over, but not with irritation. The kids weren't really being obnoxious, just loud and excited. I remember what it was like with my kids.

"Halloween was only a week ago," Solo said. "Still on that sugar high."

I nodded. The two little boys, maybe age seven and five or so, looked nothing like my boys. But they had the wild-eyed exuberance I remember, with smiles simultaneously sweet and mischievous. I see Mickey and Andrew in a lot of little boys now. So does Christine. I know it means we're getting old.

"It's all so to another level now, you know?" Solo said. "With the traveling seven-on-seven teams, sponsorships from Nike, Under Armour, Adidas—all that—scholarship offers for eighth graders, these bullshit camps, combines, and showcases that are money grabs from parents . . ."

"I know, I know."

"Then these kids are transferring all over the place," Solo continued, "and they're listening to guys like this Intensity coach. What's his name?"

"Driphus Coleman."

"He's got nothing to stop him, right? It's the wild, wild West, but even more aggressive. It's like the select basketball or baseball coaches going around promising kids stuff and telling them their team is better and they're going to get everyone a scholarship."

"Always with the scholarship promises," I said with a sigh.

"Of course, because that's what parents want to hear."

I looked over again at the kids by us. The younger boy had a blue and silver Dallas Cowboys star on his arm, so I thought the family might be going to the Cowboys game later that day. I went to my first Cowboys game when I was about that age, and it's one of the few things I remember from back that far.

The boom of the crowd. The announcer. The sun streaming through the hole in the roof at old Texas Stadium. My heart raced as I saw the players that I adored, although we were far away in the cheap seats. None of those seats are cheap anymore, and my dad never would've taken me to a game at today's prices. But when I went at age four or five, football had me for good. It was so spectacular. It was going to be my sport, and my dad encouraged it because he knew I would end up a big ol' lug like him.

"So what are you going to do about this guy?" Solo said, pulling me back into the conversation. "What did you say to Tyreke?"

"Not much. I don't want to be like the parent who forbids his kid to see someone. That always works out well, right? I just gave him the speech we all know . . . about how people are going to want to get close to him and that some aren't good for him."

"Sounds about right," Solo said.

"Whether it meant anything to him, I don't know. But Tyreke is a solid kid. Good parents."

"Then he should be fine. Good parents are like gold. Both for the kids and a football program."

"Yeah, you've got to win the parents first. . . . I guess that's something you won't have to deal with anymore."

"Not in the same way, anyway."

"And less stress."

Solo nodded.

"But less excitement, too," he said.

"Uh-oh. You're already missing it."

"Oh, I know I'm going to miss it. Certain parts of it."

"But the timing is right?"

"As right as it's going to be."

"Well, I know you'll be great, whatever you do. And if you ever want to come back and you need a job . . ."

"What about you, Tuff? You've talked about how the time will come."

"I think about it. Creekside is supposed to add a district A.D. But maybe that's all changing. Cut sports, and then nobody needs an athletic director."

"You want to stay at Creekside that much?"

"Oh, I don't know," I said with a sigh. "The district doesn't feel the same as when I started."

"So look somewhere else."

"Well, the district feels different, but the kids are the same. I feel responsible for them. It would be hard to walk away."

"I know what you mean. But I also, I don't know . . . coaching has always been kind of a young man's game, and it seems more like that now."

"Because you're getting older," I said with a laugh.

"Yeah, of course," he said with a smile. "It's easier to give in to the long hours in your twenties and thirties, when you don't see how fast everything goes by, and how fast the day comes when your own kids are heading out the door."

"Shoot, Solo, you're not as old as me."

"Sometimes I feel like I'm catching up."

"That's because you've got teenage girls," I said. "You can't blame football for that."

"Better not give me a hard time, Tuff. You're going to be there in a few years."

"Doesn't even feel like a few years. It's like Emma's sprinting toward the teens."

"I told you that little whoopsie baby was going to make things difficult on her old man."

I rolled my eyes.

"There are ways to prevent that, you know," Solo said deadpan, as if preparing to give a lecture. "You should've asked me before you got yourself another eighteen years."

"Oh shut up. What, are you working up a comedy act now that you're getting out of coaching?"

"Maybe I should."

"I'd stick with the coaching."

"Okay," Solo said as he broke into a smile and lifted his hands behind his head. He looked over again at the family next to us and then back at me.

"You know, I always thought I would stick with coaching. But things change over time. Different fits at different places in your life."

I nodded.

"And something else, Tuff . . ."

Solo looked over at the boys again and lowered his voice.

"You know, some of the stuff we're hearing about head injuries and concussions . . . it's getting to me."

"Really?"

"I know a lot of it gets blown out of proportion. But I do think football is getting more dangerous."

"More dangerous?"

"Yeah. I mean, we try to make it as safe as we can. But we can't stop the kids from getting bigger, faster, and stronger. These kids are so amazing, so different than we were back in the day. They're so conditioned, so powerful. The game has changed."

I nodded, but more in acknowledgment than agreement.

"But helmets are better," I said. "Equipment is better. Technique is better. We've got all these precautions to make it safer because we know so much more."

"But we also know more about concussions and head injuries," Solo said.

"Yeah, we do, and what's happened with some NFL players is sad. But I've had one player I've coached make the NFL. Only a few of my kids each year even play beyond high school. They're not accumulating years and years of hits."

"Not as many years, but still years. I've watched my nephew play. He's ten years old, not much bigger than him."

Solo pointed over at the older boy making faces at his baby sister, trying to get her to laugh.

"Yeah?"

"And my nephew's games are intense. The kids are already hitting hard.

Football has gotten more serious at a younger age. These little kids look like they can barely hold their heads up inside those helmets, and there are some legit hits out there. Those select teams for kids playing tackle football have them playing in the fall and spring. It's too much."

"Nobody should be playing that much," I said, "and those kids are way too young."

"What are those parents thinking? Some college coach is gonna discover their ten-year-old?"

I shrugged. My sons started playing tackle football at age ten, and if I did it over, I'd wait until they reached middle school. I was there to teach them proper technique, but there were no trainers at those pee-wee practices. We've got kids at age eight playing tackle football, and they don't know how to tackle.

Solo and I had discussed some of the reports about concussions before, and of course the NFL's mess with former players suing over head injuries. But we hadn't talked about football like this.

"You know, youth football is feeling the hit," Solo said. "Probably because parents are getting scared. And maybe they should be."

"All parents are scared for their kids, no matter what they're doing."

"Listen, Tuff . . ."

Solo leaned forward like he was telling me a secret.

"I don't know, I mean . . . I love football so much, and I appreciate football. It's been great for me. When I was a kid, I absolutely lived for it. Adored the Bears, you know. And in high school, football was everything. Those memories of playing, my great teammates, the bus rides, the friendships . . . I treasure those memories. All my time coaching, too. Remember how we used to joke that we couldn't believe we could get paid to be coaches?"

"Great times."

"Football is still great," Solo said. "But it's different, and people are starting to see it. The dang Ivy League doesn't even allow tackling in practices. No tackling in practices in college football! How do you prepare to play when you can't even practice it? And if they think it can't be part of practice, what does that say?"

"But we've all cut down our hitting in practice, too."

"Yeah, yeah," Solo said. "That's kind of my point. Kind of my fear. We're cutting down on the hitting because we're trying to protect the kids. But does that mean we're protecting them from the sport?"

I put my hands to my temples and rubbed my eyes.

"Listen, Tuff. I know it's overblown. I know the catastrophic injuries are rare. I know that deaths . . ."

He stopped for a few seconds.

"You heard about the kid in Missouri from last week?"

"Yes," I said.

"Just running down the field, looking to make a tackle . . ."

"I know."

"Just stumbled a little as a blocker came at him, and his head dipped."

"I know."

"And that was it."

"Freak accident," I said.

"And what about the kid who made the block?" Solo said. "He did nothing wrong. He was textbook, and now he lives with the guilt that someone died."

"I know. But think of the millions of kids playing football each year. All the kids who are never hurt. All the kids who get to have a football experience like you and me."

"Yeah, but maybe football has gone too far, too fast. These big, fast, strong players, no matter how we protect them, they're still going to collide and they're still going to be vulnerable."

I didn't know how to respond.

"When I was a kid," Solo continued, "my dad made me and my brothers play football. We had no choice because he said it would make us grow up right. And we wanted to play, anyway."

"Everyone played football then," I said.

"Pretty much. But now, if I had sons, I'd let them decide. I wouldn't discourage it, but . . . I'm just saying, I think I see things a little differently now."

I certainly saw things differently, but not like Solo. I wasn't naïve about football injuries, but my sons had never been seriously hurt. Mose's injury hit me hard, but it never changed my feelings about football. Mickey and Andrew loved the sport, and I loved the way the sport helped mold them.

I looked over at the boys at the table, who had finished up their hamburgers and were slumping in their chairs, overcome by the boredom of two seconds with nothing to do. The dad looked over at me.

"You guys going to the game?" I asked.

"No," answered the older boy.

"Just watching it on TV today," the dad said. "But I'm going to take them to a game one of these days. These guys can't get enough of football."

CHAPTER 22

IN the days leading up to our final regular-season game, I felt good about the team. We had come a long way, and despite some obvious limitations, we had a clear identity to build around. Our defense was good enough to keep us in most games, and on offense, we had a good line, a plodding but punishing runner in Paul, and then, of course, Tyreke. We still weren't very good at sustaining drives, but Tyreke was a threat to score every time he touched the ball. He elevated us to a playoff-level team, and we needed only one more win to make it happen.

But as we warmed up on Northside's field, an uneasy feeling crept in. I think it was because there was suddenly something to lose. In the first half of the season, we struggled so much that I didn't think about the playoffs. It was easy to give in to the feeling that the challenge was too big for a team that had lost several players to other schools. The September goal was to simply be competitive, and in the second week of November, we were one win from the playoffs.

We were also one loss from it all ending. After the game, I could be looking in the eyes of seniors realizing their playing days were over. I hated seeing that each season, and even the year when we won the state title, I saw that from the seniors. After the celebration, after the raising of the trophy, after the tears of joy, there were tears of genuine pain because it's hard to move on from such an exhilarating stretch of your life.

Fortunately, we started strong that night against Northside. By the middle of the second quarter, we were up 14–0 and Tyreke had run for his nineteenth touchdown of the year. On the play prior to his touchdown run, Tyreke had executed a screen pass perfectly, patiently waiting for two rushing defenders to get into the backfield before deftly dropping a pass over them. It's amazing how much a sixteen-year-old can improve in a month.

It's also amazing how much one guy can mean to a fifty-player team. And that one guy got hurt in the final minute of the first half.

It was a sprained ankle, and it didn't seem serious as Tyreke limped off the field. I thought he might just walk it off, and then the trainers could look at it at halftime, tape up his ankle for support, and we'd be good to go. But when Tyreke tested his ankle before the start of the second half, he didn't look good. He could jog in a straight line but couldn't accelerate quickly, and he stepped gingerly when making cuts. He grimaced as he planted his foot to pass.

Tyreke couldn't go back in. Without being able to run away from rushing defenders, he might get hurt worse. So we took the field for the second half with a 17–3 lead and Tyreke standing on the sidelines wearing a protective boot. Cody, pulled from his quarterback duties weeks earlier, was back taking snaps.

We hoped not to ask much of him. Our offense was going to be an extension of our defense, with scoring less of a priority than hanging on to the ball and running out the clock. We would take out time between each snap, shorten the game in every way we could, and hold on.

I was even more convinced of that strategy after our first possession of the second half, when we ran a receiver screen to Damion Reedy, a squirty little guy who can occasionally break a big play. Cody, with the adrenaline pumping through him, threw way too high for Damion, who is only five-seven in cleats. The ball tipped off his fingers and fell to the ground in front of a pair of Northside defenders. Had the ball deflected into the air a little higher, the pass would've been intercepted and maybe returned for a Northside touchdown.

Come on, Cody, I thought. Just no mistakes. I hated "playing not to lose" instead of playing to win, but it made sense. I trusted my defense, and without Tyreke, I barely recognized the offense.

We were still on top 17–3 when the third quarter ended. Northside, a team that had lost its last two games, looked ready for the season to end. We were a quarter away from a spot in the playoffs, and no matter what happened after that, we could say we were a playoff team.

The clock reset to twelve minutes for the final quarter, and as the teams headed back on to the field, I couldn't help but do some math. Northside had a third down coming up, and if we could get the stop and force a punt, our offense would run at least a couple minutes off the clock. If we could pick up a first down or two, we'd get the clock under eight minutes left and a two-touchdown lead would start to feel comfortable.

But comfortable was gone for good when our defense got burned on the first play of the fourth quarter. Northside's quarterback threw a quick pass to the receiver split wide left, and we were ready for the play we had seen several times that night. The difference this time was that the receiver had taken a couple of steps back after the snap, so the quarterback's throw to him went backward, giving the receiver the option to run with the ball or throw a pass.

Our coaches recognized it, but it was too late. The defenders had taken off in pursuit of the receiver who caught the first pass, and when he stopped, turned to his right, and threw across the field to the running back, we were toast. The running back caught the pass and headed down the right sideline for a touchdown.

The Northside band fired up the school fight song and their players celebrated on the sidelines. I looked up at the scoreboard. Eleven minutes and forty-eight seconds remaining. With a lead of only 17–10, it felt like an eternity.

The tension increased when Northside's kickoff, a "squib kick" that was intentionally bounced through the middle of our return team, took a crazy hop as our deep man tried to field it. The ball hit off his hand, and although he had time to scoop it up, he got swarmed by Northside tacklers at the fifteen-yard line.

Deep in our own territory, our offense was capable of much more bad than good. We played conservatively, went nowhere, and punted. Cody looked frustrated, but as he ran off the field, I tried to offer some encouragement.

"You're making good decisions," I told him. "We don't need to force anything. No freebies."

Northside got one first down before stalling near midfield and punting. The wobbly kick bounced down to the twenty-yard line, and as the ball bounced erratically, Damion might've suffered hearing loss from all the players and coaches yelling at him to get away from it. Had it touched Damion, Northside could've jumped on the ball and been twenty yards from a tying touchdown. Fortunately, he stayed clear.

Eight minutes left, and they couldn't tick away fast enough.

Running the ball made sense because it would keep the clock running, whereas incomplete passes would stop the clock and stretch out the game. But Northside was cramming its defenders near the line of scrimmage to stop the run.

On first down, Coach Hartline wanted to pass. Fake a handoff to Paul, and a receiver crossing behind the linebackers should be open. It was a fairly safe throw, it could get us some breathing room, and it might loosen up the defense.

Cody executed it well. He threw to David Palmer, who was crossing ten yards down the field and fell down almost immediately after catching the ball. It wasn't unlike a lot of catches David made that season. He never gained a lot of yards after catches, but he was tall—six-two—and usually found a way to fall forward.

Three plays later, we faced a third-and-one and Cody converted it for a first down on a quarterback sneak. It looked like he would be stopped short, but Cody fought through the tacklers to get the yardage. I could see his confidence growing, and he smiled when he came over to the sidelines after we called a timeout with a little less than five minutes left.

Cody stood next to me, squirting water into his mouth between heavy breaths, as Coach Hartline and I hashed out the next play. We decided on a jet sweep to Damion, who I reminded not to go out of bounds because that would stop the clock.

"Cut it up, D. If it doesn't open, just get what's there. No sidelines."

Damion followed through, getting five yards and staying inbounds. The clock was at four minutes left as we lined up for the next play. We were back in shotgun formation, as we almost always were, and the play was a designed run for Cody, with Paul as a lead blocker.

It worked better than expected. Our offensive linemen occupied the defensive front, and Paul bulled into an outside linebacker and a pursuing safety at the same time. That gave Cody enough room to get near the first-down marker before he was touched.

The first defender tried to stop him, but Cody was determined, just as he was when he fought for a first down a few minutes earlier. The Northside defenders gang-tackled him, but Cody kept driving his legs and moving forward. He passed the first-down marker and was still fighting for more when the ball was ripped from his hands.

Yep, ripped right from his hands. And the ball didn't just fall to the ground, it popped into the air to eye level.

A football can bounce many different ways. It's not round, you know. But this football bounced like a basketball, like a perfect bounce pass to a streaking player on a fast break. A Northside defender scooped it up and had a caravan of blockers behind him as he ran fifty yards for a touchdown.

The Northside crowd erupted, and even in the thickening, sickening, drama for my team, I was impressed by the fans on the other side. No matter what happened in this game, Northside was going to have a losing season, and it was going to end that night. But pride is a great motivator.

The point-after kick tied the game, and our players' faces were blank with shock. We had been ready to shift into cruise control after the second Tyreke touchdown of the first half. Now Tyreke was on the sideline, and we were tied against an inspired team, playing on their home field, with their band and crowd going crazy. It was all crashing down on us.

We weren't going to get in the playoffs on a tiebreaker. This was it. We needed to score, led by a quarterback who six weeks earlier had lost his starting job to a sophomore, and a minute earlier had lost the football just before the regular-season finish line.

CHAPTER 23

CODY put on a brave face, but I could see the anguish and fear in his eyes. He looked nauseous, and I was feeling that way. But I tried to remain calm—or at least look that way for Cody. I said nothing about what had just happened and talked matter-of-factly about what was going to happen.

"Okay, we've got nearly four minutes. Two timeouts. Plenty of time. We don't need to hurry. Let's make this the last drive of the game."

Cody nodded. I'm not sure what he was hearing or how much was sinking in. Things looked a little empty behind those blinking eyes.

"Let's go! You got this!" said Tyreke, leaning in and speaking with an angry tone. I know Tyreke was trying to help, but I brushed him back with my forearm. I wanted Cody to have a few moments of solitude before he took the field again.

As I stood next to Cody, prepping him and reassuring him, we got some luck. The kickoff bounced softly into the arms of our deep returner, and Damion found room to run along the sideline. He made it all the way to the forty before he was pushed out of bounds.

"All right, Cody," I said. "You got this."

Same words as Tyreke, but delivered differently, and I tried to think positively.

Although three-and-a-half minutes remained, Northside's defense had softened. Now that there was something to lose, the players were worried about giving up a big play. That helped us move the ball across midfield and creep toward field-goal range with a little under two minutes left. On third down, we faked a sweep to Damion going left and Cody ducked in on the right side for three yards and a first down. He pinned the ball to his chest with both hands as he was tackled.

Cody was breathing hard again, and I wanted a quick discussion with

Coach Hartline about our next few plays, so we called one of our two remaining timeouts. One minute and thirty seconds left.

We stayed conservative against Northside's tired defense, with two runs by Cody and a short pass to David, who stepped out of bounds to stop the clock. We had a first down, and with the ball near the twenty-yard line, we were in field-goal range. We lined up for our next play with forty-five seconds left, and the plan was to run one play straight ahead, get a few more yards, and then call our last timeout to get our field-goal unit on the field. But before we could snap the ball, Northside called a timeout.

Northside's timeout gave its defense time to rest, but it also gave me time to decide that I didn't want to rely on our kicker. I trusted him, but even a short field goal is no sure thing in high school. It would be a pressure situation, and we would need a good snap to the holder, who would then need to get the ball in position for our kicker. A lot of things could go wrong. Worst-case scenario: Northside blocks the kick and returns it for a game-winning touchdown. Unlikely, but possible.

So what if we threw a pass into the end zone first?

We would come out in a formation that we had run out of all night, with Damion split out to the left. When the ball was snapped, he would briefly block the cornerback in front of him. Cody would fake a handoff to Paul, and the safety would step forward to stop the run. That would give Damion, the second fastest player on our team, a chance to run past the cornerback, and if all went as planned, there would be no defender back to help in coverage.

I estimated our chances of completing the pass were less than fifty-fifty. But an incomplete pass would still allow us to run another play, get a little closer, and call a timeout to set up the kick. An interception was possible, but it was a pass Cody could make, and in my instructions to him, I left no gray area.

"If the defender stays close to Damion, just throw the ball out of the back of the end zone. An overthrow is okay."

I didn't think much about it. There was no time to think, really. If we tried a pass before a kick, we had two ways to avoid overtime, and I really didn't want to go to overtime. We were the team with something to lose, and the pressure would be on us.

"Sell the fake," I told Cody just before he ran on the field. "We need that safety outta there."

As Cody jogged back on to the field, I worried that I had put too much in his head. He might try too hard to sell the fake and fumble the ball, or he could tighten up on the throw and leave it short. Was I asking too much? I had pulled him as starter nearly two months earlier because he wasn't effectively throwing the ball, and now I wanted him to throw a game-winning, possibly season-saving, pass.

Second-guessing myself was nothing new. Coaches do it all the time. You try to make a decision, break clean from it, and move on to the next one. But you overanalyze, overthink, over-everything.

We lined up, and as expected, Northside was stacked against the run. Surely we would just hand the ball to our bruising running back and have him slam forward to get a few yards closer for the field goal.

Cody took the snap, made a good fake to Paul, and when I turned my head to see Damion, he was a yard behind the startled cornerback. Damion gained more separation as the cornerback turned and started to chase, and Cody let go of a pass that hung in the air long enough for Damion to get his fingers on it as he crossed the goal line.

Damion fell to his knees as he stretched to make the catch. He clutched the ball to his chest, landed on his shoulder, and then rolled several times like a kid going down a hill. He came to rest on his back and stuck the ball in the air.

A few seconds later, Damion was in the arms of Paul and one of our linemen, getting carried around the end zone. Half our team was on the field, celebrating like we had won a state title, drawing penalty flags. We were flagged for excessive celebration, and rightly so. Our players' discipline had crumbled, and I didn't blame them one bit. When I came to from the excitement, my headset was on the ground and so was my hat. Who knows what I was doing?

Actually, I do know—unfortunately—because I saw the film later. I'll spare you the details, other than to say that I'm too old for flying chest bumps.

We still had thirty-eight seconds left, but it felt like all the tension of the night was released at once. And it was more than just the tension from that night. It was the tension from that whole frustrating, ridiculous year. Some people might try to cut the life out of our football program, but they couldn't cut football out of our lives. That moment couldn't be taken from us, even if we didn't win another game that season—or another game ever.

The excitement of the moment made it difficult to regain focus. But fortunately, Northside didn't have a miracle response. We sacked the quarterback on two consecutive plays, and the clock ran out.

We went through the handshake line with Northside, and after that, members of both teams met at midfield and kneeled in prayer. That's not unusual in Texas, whether it's a preseason game or a tension-filled playoff matchup. The coaches don't lead it; the players do.

After the prayer, I gathered with our players on the field. What a collection of kids. Some had played almost the entire game, and some hadn't played at all, but they were all part of it. They all earned it.

"Okay guys. What a game. I'm so proud of all of you," I said, quietly and seriously. I was being that way intentionally.

"I'm so proud of you because, I can now say, officially, that . . ."

And then I yelled.

"The Knights are in the playoffs!"

The players roared, and it felt like it went on for a minute before trailing off with whistles and laughter. There was so much relief, so much togetherness, so much happiness in the players' faces that I was at a loss for words.

I looked over at Cody, whose sweat-soaked hair made him look like he'd been thrown in a lake. He'd actually been thrown into the fire, considering what I asked of him after Tyreke's injury. Cody had only a slight grin, but I could see him absorbing the moment. I knew what it meant to him.

"That pass, Cody," I said. "Perfect. Just perfect."

The team cheered, and Paul, kneeling next to Cody, shook him by the shoulders. That finally cracked Cody, who broke into a big smile.

"And that catch, Damion. . . . I mean, what can I say?"

Another cheer.

"I don't know about your yards after catch, but your average rolls per catch went way up tonight," I said, and the team laughed. "That was a spectacular catch, bud."

I took a breath.

"It was all spectacular, guys. Everything in between. You guys battled out there, and that makes me more proud than anything. You battled all season and you got to the playoffs."

I called up the captains, who always get the last word before we break. As I stepped back to give them room, Coach Hartline put his arm around me and slapped me on the back.

"Wow, Coach," I said, turning toward him. "Definitely one of the highs."

"You bet, Coach," he said.

Then Jim turned me away from the team slightly.

"Call Christine," he said.

"What?"

"Call your wife. She wants you to call."

"What's going on?"

"Don't panic. Everything's okay. But call her."

CHAPTER 24

"GORDON."

"What's going on?"

With the phone pressed to my ear, I walked away from the Creekside players and coaches who were leaving the field and heading toward the buses. They were walking slower than normal, trying to enjoy the moment for as long as possible. Fans and students were waiting outside the gate to the parking lot, and as the players approached, they clapped and cheered.

"Sorry, couldn't hear you," I said, pressing the phone harder against my ear.

"We're at Parkwood," Christine said. "But don't worry . . ."

"What happened?"

"Mickey got injured, but he's going to be fine. Probably a concussion. He's being checked by the doctor . . ."

"So wait, what happened?"

"He's going to be fine, Gordon. Come over."

Mickey had played football for ten years, along with basketball and baseball, and had never suffered a serious injury. It was remarkable how injury-free his life had been up to that point. When Mickey was little, he was a climber, always doing these Spider Man–like things up everything, and I worried he was going to fall off some structure at the park when we weren't there to keep him in check. But nope. He always made it home safely. A few sprained ankles. A broken finger. Cuts and scratches.

I took a deep breath, and for a few seconds, I just stood there on the field, watching the Creekside players walk to the buses as Christine talked. I needed to get over to the hospital, but first, I needed to pull myself together. I felt so scattered as people patted me on the shoulder and the players celebrated around me. The hairpin turn of emotion left me almost out of breath.

I felt both anxiety and relief. It could be so much worse than a concussion, but the risks of head injuries had been pounded into me, just like all coaches, and really anyone who had been paying attention in recent years. The word "concussion" was heavier than ever.

"What did the doctor say?"

"Mickey's okay," Christine said. "They're checking on him. Andrew and Emma are here with me. Just come over, and the doctors will have more information."

"But so he's talking and everything, and he's . . .

"Gordon, he's fine. Just come over. And drive safely."

When I arrived at the hospital, Christine filled me in. The doctors didn't seem too concerned. Mickey might've been unconscious for a second, but she didn't think so, and the doctors were probably going to release him that night.

He still didn't remember the play when he got hit. It happened in the second quarter when Mickey was tackled on a two-point conversion after a touchdown. As expected, he was playing quarterback because Putnam had already clinched the district title and the team's backup QB was banged up.

More than two hours had passed since Mickey was injured, and although Putnam coach Michael Greer was planning to come by the hospital, Christine told him it wasn't necessary. Mickey wasn't in any danger. She told Coach Greer to say thanks to all the players who were texting or calling to check on Mickey, who had left the game in an ambulance.

The ambulance ride probably seemed overly dramatic for a player able to walk off the field, but Putnam has an ambulance on site for every home game, and nobody really knew the severity of Mickey's injury. Few people had a clear view of the hit, which happened as Mickey stretched for the goal line between a pair of defenders.

He was stopped short of the end zone, and Christine said he popped up quickly after the play. When I looked at it later on video, though, I could see that Mickey took a couple seconds to get up and then struggled with his balance for a step or two. I think the Putnam coaches saw that, but it was Kingsley Savage who let them know something was wrong.

After "The Beast" jogged over to pat Mickey on the back, he thought Mickey looked a little out of it. Everyone else was running off the field, but Mickey had lost track of the game situation and didn't remember they had just scored a touchdown and gone for the two-point conversion. Mickey wasn't wobbly, Kingsley later said, but he seemed a little out of it.

Kingsley hooked his arm around Mickey's and walked with him. Before they got to the sideline, they were met by Putnam trainers and the concussion assessment began.

I didn't know the severity of Mickey's concussion, but I felt very thankful that night. I also felt a returning pang of guilt for letting him transfer to Putnam, where I couldn't track his every move on the field. And as I drove to the hospital, I thought about how Christine had probably told Coach Hartline's wife not to tell me until after the game.

What if Mickey had been seriously injured and I wasn't there?

Mickey was sitting up, but leaning back and looking tired when I first saw him. Christine left to drive Andrew and Emma home, along with Mickey's girlfriend. That left Mickey and me alone for a few minutes.

He looked apologetic. I don't know why.

"So how's your head?"

"Hurts a little."

"Same as right after the injury? Less?"

"A little less . . . I think."

"Well that's good."

Mickey's not a big talker, but he's not quiet either, especially when there's football to talk about. But I'm sure he was in no mood for conversation, and he wasn't supposed to talk much. The doctors said it was all about rest—"cognitive rest."

I didn't say much as we waited, but at least Mickey looked pretty good.

"Heard you threw a touchdown pass to Kingsley."

"I don't remember it."

"Was it right before your run on the conversion?"

"Don't remember. I remember being on the sideline . . . the doctor talking to me."

"And then you went in the ambulance?"

"Guess I failed the concussion test."

I smiled. "You didn't fail anything."

Mickey's phone buzzed, and his natural reaction was to grab for it next to him. But then he handed it to me.

"Not supposed to look at it," he said.

"I'm sure it can wait," I said.

"Could be Kirsten," he said.

"Like I said, it can wait."

He smirked. I'm always giving him a hard time about his girlfriend.

"It's Kingsley," I said. "Says Rip Dash is here. Rip Dash?"

"That's the receivers."

"What does that . . . oh never mind."

"Can they come in?"

"Do I look like someone who's in charge here?" I said with a shrug. I was trying to get him to smile, and it worked. At least a little. More of a smirk-plus-eye-roll. The concussion hadn't short-circuited that move.

"I think you're about to get out of here. I'll see what's going on."

I walked over to Mickey and handed him his phone. I stood next to him for a moment, looking at him, until I knew he felt uncomfortable.

"What?" he said.

I patted him on the chest, stepped back, and then stepped forward again and gave him a full-on hug. I could feel him tense up a little as I wrapped my arms around him. Then I kissed him on the top of his shaggy mop of hair.

It's probably not good to horrify someone who just suffered a concussion, but I didn't care.

* * *

Kingsley and two other Putnam players were waiting in the lobby as we walked out. They were all receivers—the Rip Dash squad, whatever that means—but it was hard to guess they all played the same position. Kingsley towered over the other two and looked like he could stack them together and bench 'em.

"How you doing?" Kingsley said in a much quieter tone than usual. Kingsley had been over at the house a few times, and his personality could be best described as bubbly. Yes, a bubbly beast. If he weren't six-three and built like a linebacker, his nickname would be as out of place as a Chihuahua named Brutus.

Mickey smiled, which was good to see, as he and Kingsley exchanged a hug and cool-guy handshake. (I'm sure they could explain it better).

"I'm okay," Mickey said. "You guys did fine without me."

"Nah, son, we need you back," Kingsley said before turning toward me and extending his hand.

"Coach Nehls."

"Good to see you, Kingsley. Congrats on the district title."

"Thank you, sir," Kingsley said. "And congrats to you guys. Mickey said you guys were in the playoffs with a win."

"Yeah, we're in," I said. "It was close."

Kingsley nodded and then turned back toward Mickey.

"So . . . you have to rest for a couple of days?" one of the players asked.

"Not sure."

We walked out of the lobby into a wind that felt like winter. The eighty-degree Wednesday from forty-eight hours earlier had turned into a frigid Friday night with stinging darts of rain, and although we were under a carport outside the entrance, I was ready to get out of there. And Mickey needed to rest.

"Heard about you committing to Notre Dame," I said to Kingsley. "Congratulations."

"Yes sir. It's a blessing."

"But your dad's a Texas fan, right? How's that going over?"

Kingsley laughed.

"My parents are already buying Notre Dame stuff," he said. "They just want to make sure I focus on the books."

"Of course. Know what you want to study?"

"Yes sir, business. Notre Dame's undergrad business programs are top five in the nation. I met with a few professors during my visit."

Talking with Kingsley, the beast seemed a lot more like a little boy. Eighteen years old and built like an ox, but still just a kid.

I thought about that as Mickey and his teammates parted with another set of man hugs. These guys might never have known each other if not for football, and now they referred to each other as brothers. They would head for different parts of the country in the coming years, but they would always share a bond. Because of football, those guys were at the hospital to support Mickey.

But the injury scared me. So did a lot of things about football, and it was not a sudden shift. Maybe the creeping thoughts were a sign of my age, I thought, because back when I played football as a kid, whether it was a rag-tag deal at the park or in full pads at the high school, I never once thought about getting hurt. I threw my body all over the place, played with joyous recklessness, and never thought of what could happen. But now, as a coach, a dad, an old guy, I'd watch games and think, *Please don't get hurt, please don't get hurt.* I knew that the dangers of football were overblown. I truly believed that, but still, I watched with an eye for injuries. Going soft, I guess.

Mickey and his friends looked so damn young. They were just boys, and they couldn't mask that with scraggly beards and muscle and machismo. They were still so fragile. Emotionally, for sure, but also physically, even if they felt invincible. And every week they were playing a game in which the competitors and collisions were bigger than ever.

We would protect them in every way we could, and we would take every precaution. But they were still going to play football at full speed— the only way they wanted to play and the only way the game should be played. Like Solo said, they were still going to collide, they were still going to be vulnerable, and they were still going to be kids.

CHAPTER 25

L EE Fountain had told me the package of stories would be in the Sunday paper, but I didn't need the reminder. The paper had been promoting the "future of football" series for a few days, and when the calls, emails, and texts started coming in Saturday night, I knew the story had been posted online.

It was pretty much what I expected.

Lee told me that Creekside was going to be the lead to the series because of our unique situation, and sure enough, we were center stage. Lucky us. All those years when I hoped we could get more attention in the paper, mainly because it made the parents and kids happy, and now I would've gladly been ignored.

ROYAL THREAT

High school football is still king,
but the crown might be slipping

A photo of Dr. Charles Bashum, with our superintendent looking pensive as he walked along a hallway at the high school, jumped out at me. He was in an online slide show of people and their quotes about high school football. Asher Wellington, the doctor quickly becoming famous for his anti-football remarks, was in there, too, as were many people who supported football. Not me, of course, because I didn't offer anything interesting or controversial or inflammatory. I didn't need to add fuel to the fire.

I began reading:

Creekside High School's recent achievements include individual
state champions in wrestling and track and field, a regional finalist

in baseball, and award-winning performances in marching band and debate.

But the school's most well-known achievement, at least beyond its own campus, is the state football championship. It was nine years ago, but it will be fresh in the minds of anyone who walks around the school.

The championship trophy is displayed in the school's front office, where visitors must sign in. A large poster of the team, along with a framed newspaper article, trophies from other playoff wins that season, and a game jersey are the centerpiece of the trophy case outside the school's main gym. The championship is also lauded on the back of the press box at the school's football stadium, and two miles away, "STATE CHAMPIONS" is painted on a city water tower.

This is a high school that loves football, obviously. But it is also a high school that, although it might seem unthinkable in the football hotbed of Texas, is considering giving up the sport.

"We are considering everything during this budget cycle," Creekside school district superintendent Charles Bashum said. "We are not targeting football, but we are not protecting it, either. It is not a sacred cow that can't be touched."

The "sacred cow" thing again. That was Bashum's favorite. Our football program had been called that so many times, I felt like I should be mooing. The story continued:

Creekside's football program has already been touched. The

Creekside school district dropped the seventh grade football program from its middle school last year, becoming the first Dallas-area district with a large high school to make the move. This year was the last for the eighth grade program.

Two other Dallas-area districts, and more than a dozen across the state, have decided to drop middle school football. Each has cited financial reasons, and some have pointed to increased injury concerns with the sport.

Bashum said he never wanted Creekside to be a trailblazer in regards to football, and he doesn't believe his district's decision has influenced others.

"Hundreds of districts across the country are evaluating football and deciding what's right for their students," Bashum said. "The cost of football is rising, and so are a lot of other costs for school districts. Football is no more or less important than anything else. There could be some districts that decide the money for football doesn't serve their students in the best way."

It was what I'd been hearing from Bashum for the last year. Football shouldn't be a sacred cow, everything should be considered at budget time, and it wasn't personal. But it certainly felt personal as I read how another public input session on the budget was planned for early December. If only the Creekside football team could still be playing then . . .

Not likely, but it would certainly make that public input session interesting. Hey, do you think we should cut football some more? Should we chop down the team that's deep in the playoffs, the team that's got the whole community excited?

Bashum would probably just postpone the public meeting until after we lost. And, being realistic, I knew we weren't going to be playing in

December. Even the rosiest-colored glasses wouldn't let us see that kind of future.

Could we have Alex back from Boston College for another postseason run? Could we have a couple of our defensive backs from last year and our best returning receiver, who I let transfer to Putnam?

Without those guys, it would be nearly impossible. We had a decent chance of winning in the first round if Tyreke could recover enough from his ankle injury. But the second round would be tough, and if we somehow got to the third round, it might be a mismatch like Alabama versus University of the Incarnate Word.

I would never tell my kids that, of course, and miracles do happen. Maybe Bashum will even open the budget session with a statement that he's come to his senses, football is too important to cut, and he doesn't want homecoming to be celebrated at a volleyball match. It could happen, right?

Back to reality. The newspaper's "future of football" story added to Bashum's momentum with details about how participation was down in the youth leagues and the new fears surrounding concussions. There were comments from parents who said they wouldn't let their kids play football, and the paper brought up how football leagues from the NFL down to youth leagues were dealing with lawsuits related to injuries.

And remember Chris Dozier, the kid who suffered the concussion playing for the eighth grade team at Bevell Middle School? That lawsuit was dropped months ago, but it still made it into the story. I'm just glad the kid's name wasn't mentioned, considering the threatening letters Bashum had received. The Dozier family didn't deserve any of that.

The newspaper said it sent anonymous surveys to more than three hundred school superintendents across the state. Of the two hundred returned, a fourth of the supers said cuts to the middle school football programs would be considered or at least not ruled out.

It was unbelievable. Or at least it would've been unbelievable a year earlier. In places outside Texas, maybe. But in Texas? In the Metroplex?

The newspaper's main story ended with this:

In other areas of the country, enough school districts have cut their high school football programs to create a trend. But in states such as Texas, where football is revered, where some high school stadiums are better than college facilities, and where nearly 60,000 fans watched a single championship game, it's hard to imagine an autumn without prep football.

Participation has dropped, however. And even if injury rates have not increased, the awareness of injuries has increased. Combined with the financial constraints of school districts, the result is a genuine threat to one of the state's cultural staples.

"Everything changes," said one superintendent. "The love for football hasn't changed, but maybe its place has changed, or it will change. The sun can still rise without football."

Pretty uplifting. I thought maybe I could work that into my next pregame pep talk.

Lee Fountain called me Sunday afternoon, wanting to make sure everything was good between us. I wasn't in a chummy mood, but I had no problem with his story. Other than the timing, I guess, with the way it rained on our playoff parade. I'm sure the paper thought it was perfect timing because the start of the playoffs meant everyone was thinking about football.

On the Saturday night when I and the other Creekside coaches read it, we were prepping for our first-round opponent, Sherman. Its district wasn't as good as ours, and I thought we had a good chance to win. A part of me was still feeling thankful, and a little lucky, to be in the playoffs, but I was pushing the "anything can happen in the playoffs" line with my team.

Sherman had some talented players, but it didn't have a lot of size and strength along the lines. It was a game I expected us to win, as long as Tyreke's ankle held up.

Tyreke's ankle was still a little tender, but it was nothing serious. We planned to hold him out of practice on Monday and Tuesday and then give it a go on Wednesday. Tyreke might not be at full speed by Friday, but he'd be fast enough to be dangerous.

Mickey spent the weekend after his concussion sleeping and lounging around the house, something not all that different than his typical routine. But Christine made sure he didn't watch television, so that took out a Saturday of college football. His head felt "tight" in the morning, he said, and he took some Tylenol. His head felt better by afternoon, and after not eating anything in the morning, he had a big lunch. He still seemed kind of sluggish, though.

"Any irritability?" I said when I got home.

"Not any more than usual," Christine said.

"And he still doesn't remember?"

"Don't think so. But he remembers there's a Cowboys game tomorrow. He wants to know if the TV Police will still be patrolling in the afternoon."

"Okay, well that's good," I said. "That sounds like Mickey."

The concussion protocol at Putnam, which was the same as at Creekside, called for Mickey to be symptom-free before taking a cognitive test that would be compared with his baseline test from before the season. If Mickey took the cognitive test Monday and the results were good, he could gradually return to exercise. If the recovery process went smoothly, Mickey could, by the school's rules, miss only one game.

Christine and I were already thinking about Mickey sitting out two games, which would give him a full three weeks to recover. But we didn't say anything to Mickey. I was just happy that he didn't put up a fight about needing to sit out of practice for several days. The concussion probably scared him a little. He'd never experienced anything like this. A broken finger that required a cast for six weeks was the most serious injury of his first seventeen years.

We decided that Mickey could skip church on Sunday morning,

allowing him more rest, and that he could watch the Cowboys game later in the day. Maybe that sounds irreverent, but I think even my father, the greatest, most God-glorifying man I've ever known, would've allowed that. He was a pastor in Texas. He knew that the flock needed to be home before the Cowboys kicked off.

✷ ✷ ✷

I didn't need to wake up until eight to have breakfast and get ready for church, but at seven, I heard the shower running upstairs. It made no sense, because Emma took her showers at night, and the only thing that got Mickey and Andrew awake that early was school or football practice. On Sunday mornings, it was usually tough to get them up and moving.

Emma and Andrew were still in their bedrooms, so I knew Mickey was in the bathroom.

"Mickey," I called to him through the bathroom door, trying not to speak loudly because the bedrooms were nearby. "Mickey," I said, raising my voice a little. I knew it was hard to hear over the shower.

"Mickey, open the door!" I said, getting closer to a yell.

The door was locked, but easy to unlock. We always keep the universal key to the bathrooms on top of the door frame. I popped the key in, opened the door, and walked into the steam-filled bathroom.

"Mickey!" I called to him again as I reached for the shower curtain.

Mickey beat me to it.

"What?" he said, with obvious irritation, as he craned his head around the curtain.

I took a step back.

"I'm just checking on you. How long have you been in the shower?"

"Why?"

"I'm just checking to make sure everything's okay."

"Why?" he said again. "I'm fine."

Mickey pushed back the hair that was dripping into his eyes. "So . . . what else?" he said, probably wondering why I was still standing there.

"Okay, well . . . good," I said. "But why are you up so early?"

"Early?"

"Going somewhere?"

"Yeah," he said, again with irritation. "School."

"Mickey," I said, stepping forward and staring into his eyes. "It's Sunday."

CHAPTER 26

THREE days later, I got a double dose of good news.

It was Wednesday, two days before our next game, and Tyreke was getting back up to speed. He looked pretty good, and more importantly, he felt pretty good. He was able to plant his right foot and throw without the ankle bothering him, and he didn't look hesitant when making cuts. It wasn't full speed or full intensity, but it was encouraging.

Mickey also returned to practice at Putnam on Wednesday, although only as a spectator. The results from his cognitive tests that day were positive, and the plan was for him to start stretching and light jogging on Thursday. He was still not cleared for any kind of contact drills. He needed to be symptom-free for seven days and then get cleared by a doctor before returning to any kind of contact.

I felt good about his recovery. But what about that confusion on Sunday morning?

It wasn't something to be alarmed about, the doctor said, because it happened within forty-eight hours of the concussion, and Mickey wasn't having continuing bouts of confusion. The important thing was to keep monitoring him and not rush his recovery. Mickey claimed that he had woken up other times of the year and groggily wondered for a moment what day it was. That's happened to me, too. But he had been in the shower for like fifteen minutes. It never clicked?

Whatever. We were going to take our time with Mickey. Give him plenty of time to heal.

I'm sure my high school football coaches, back in the early Eighties, would've laughed at the thought of sitting out of practice for an entire week after a player "got his bell rung." If you didn't get knocked out cold, it wasn't a concussion.

Hey Nehls . . . how many fingers am I holding up? Okay, get back in the game!

I feel like I've always taken concussions, potential concussions, and everything surrounding them very seriously. But the dangers of head injuries weren't front and center ten years ago. We got kids out of the game when something was suspected, and those kids didn't get back in the game. But in the days afterward, there wasn't the kind of follow-up we do now.

We had never heard of second-impact syndrome. Now we know it can happen when a second concussion occurs before the first one is healed. It scares me when I think back to how I played through a concussion. I'm sure I played through at least one.

It also scared me when I thought about Mickey, but he was doing well, we were taking things slow, and he wasn't going back to full contact until he was completely healed. I think he was tired of me and his mom asking how he was feeling. There was no ringing in his ears or headaches, he said. The "foggy feeling" was gone, and he didn't have trouble concentrating.

By Thursday, Mickey wanted to get back to practice. He said he was ready for it, but Mickey thinks he's ready for everything. He's eighteen, you know, that invincible age when boys think they know everything.

Texas weather can be really nice in the fall, but sometimes it feels like summer just runs into winter. And that second weekend of November, when the playoffs start, is a weather crapshoot. It can be close to seventy degrees at kickoff, or it can be subfreezing with a wind whipping you in the face.

For our playoff game, we got the good stuff: about sixty degrees with a light wind. It was a beautiful night as the red and silver Creekside Knights took on the maroon and white Sherman Tigers at Homer B. Johnson Stadium in Garland.

It was a battle of nerves for the players. We tried to treat it like any other game, but I know it felt different for the players. The week before had essentially been like a playoff game because we needed a win to keep our season alive, but this was the real deal. This was the last chance for the seniors to feel what it was like to be part of the Texas high school playoffs.

This could be the last chance for them to celebrate a win and stand in front of the fans as the band played the fight song. There were no more second chances or something-to-build-ons.

Most of my players had never been in a playoff game, and it showed. All the players seemed too pumped up and were overly aggressive, as if they were trying to win the game in the first five minutes. At the same time, they played tentatively, worried about making a mistake. It was a little ragged, and the combination of adrenaline and overthinking led to some poor decisions.

It also put us in an early hole. Fielding a bouncing punt, which is generally not a good idea, Damion took his eye off the ball to peek upfield. He bobbled the ball, and when he tried to pick it up, his nervous fingers didn't get a good grasp. The Sherman players closed in, and he panicked, and when he dove on the ball, it squirted away and was recovered by Sherman. The good field position set up Sherman for a touchdown and 7–0 lead midway through the first quarter.

It made my stomach hurt. I felt like we should beat Sherman, but we certainly weren't good enough to survive a lot of mistakes. That's part of the reason our next offensive possession was conservative. Coach Hartline and I worried that Tyreke might force a pass into coverage, because as potent as he had become at quarterback, he was still prone to mistakes. He had thrown two interceptions earlier in the season that were returned for touchdowns.

We played it safe, hoping to get a couple first downs that would get us near midfield before we opened things up. But a handoff and screen pass got us only four yards, and when Tyreke took off running on a quarterback draw on third down, the Sherman players saw it coming. I think their coaches could sense that we were playing scared, trying not to make another mistake.

We had to punt the ball away, and a few minutes later, the first quarter ended with Sherman up by a touchdown. We were about to get the ball back, and I knew we needed to hit the gas pedal, even if it might send us over a cliff.

My shoulders loosened a bit on the first play of our next drive, when Tyreke rolled out to his right and threw a twenty-yard completion. He looked good as he moved, and Sherman was so determined to stop our runs, both by the bullish Paul and the slippery Tyreke, that the passing opportunities were there. We drove for a touchdown to tie the game, and by halftime we were up 14–7.

On our first possession of the third quarter, Tyreke busted free for a sixty-yard touchdown run. Neither team did much with the ball the rest of the quarter, and then our defense came up with an interception that gave us the ball in Sherman territory just before the end of the quarter. We took advantage with a short touchdown pass that made the score 28–7 early in the fourth.

It was officially time to play it safe. Sherman cut the lead to 28–14 with four minutes left, but we got a couple of first downs to put the game away. There was no tension in the final minute, unlike a week earlier, so I could enjoy the looks on the players' faces as most of them experienced their first playoff win.

It was far from the biggest victory of my coaching career, and it was a game I expected to win. But you're always partial to the most recent wins, and after all that we had been through, it felt really good. It was also nice that I could share it with my family, because everyone was there—Christine, Emma, Andrew, and even Mickey, whose Putnam team didn't play until the next day. Mickey wasn't going to play, anyway. He had a doctor's appointment on Monday, and if he was cleared, then he could return to practicing at full speed.

Emma and Andrew stayed in the stands with Christine, but Mickey was on the sideline with the players. I loved having him there. He was wearing his old Creekside letter jacket and fit right in with his former teammates.

With thirty seconds left, Tyreke took the snap and kneeled. Sherman didn't have a way to stop the clock, and we didn't need to run another play, so the game was decided. Cody, hero of the week before who returned to backup quarterback against Sherman, was to my left, smiling and yelling. He looked so happy, and I wrapped my arm around his shoulder and pulled him in for a hug. A second later, Mickey emerged and patted me on the back and gave me a half-hug. I was surprised that Mickey was so central in the celebration, but before I could think long about it, I realized that Cody and Mickey were both holding me in position. They backed away and . . .

Whooooosh.

It was a warm night for November, but not warm enough for a shower of icy Gatorade to feel refreshing. I tried to duck, but it was too late, and the sports-drink waterfall hit me like a hard slap on the back. It ran down the back of my neck, soaked my shirt, and as an added bonus, the top of the cooler bonked me on the head as I tried to duck under it.

But I didn't mind. After the initial shock, I turned toward the players, smiled, and pointed at them in mock anger. I shook off some small pieces of ice and walked through the handshake line with a sticky wet shirt that, unfortunately, now outlined my body-by-barbecue. (I have decided that my New Year's Resolution for next year, once again, will be to lose fifteen pounds—at least).

The players gathered in front of the fans in the stands and raised the trophy as bi-district champions. A week later we would go for the area championship, and we would be a bigger underdog than Sherman was against us. But for the rest of the night, or at least an hour or so, I could soak in the team's accomplishment.

The players hugged, laughed, and talked with classmates and family members as little kids ran around the field, pretending to make amazing plays that they punctuated with over-the-top touchdown dances. Christine, who usually gives me a hug after games, patted me on my soggy shoulder.

"Fruit punch?" she said.

I shrugged and smiled.

"Gross," Emma said.

Christine gave me a hug anyway. So did Emma, without mentioning how much she hates football.

* * *

After finalizing the site and time of our next playoff game and talking with my coaches, I headed for home. It was a little before midnight when I got there, and although I was tired, my mind was buzzing. I took a shower, and that night's game ran through my head, along with plans for the next week. My mind still felt locked in, or at least locked awake, as I turned on the television for a few minutes. I didn't really watch anything. It was just on as I thought about everything.

Bashum. The future of the football program. Mickey. Emma wanting her ears pierced. Mose's future. It was all flashing through my mind like I was channel surfing. I knew I should go to sleep, or at least try to, and I decided to take a couple of Tylenol because my head was pounding. I couldn't find the bottle for a minute, and I was thinking of just trying to fight through it when I remembered that I had bought a new bottle after Mickey's concussion. I had been in the kitchen when I opened it, so it should be there.

As I walked to the kitchen, I remembered that after I gave Mickey some Tylenol, I stashed the bottle in a cabinet above the sink. I planned to move it to the medicine cabinet in the bathroom later and then forgot about it.

I grabbed the Tylenol, pulled off the lid, and for a moment, I thought it was a different bottle. What happened to all the pills? Was this an old bottle? Did we actually have some Tylenol in the house when I made that run to the drugstore Saturday morning?

Now I definitely wasn't going to sleep.

Chapter 27

MICKEY has done some crazy things over the years. I mentioned he was a climber when he was little, and he still has some of that daredevil attitude. Still, I feel like he's going to make good decisions most of the time. I could be too trusting, which I know a lot of parents are, but Mickey's a good kid.

I think he's usually honest with his mom and me. I'd like to say that's because of the way we raised him, but it's also because he's a terrible liar and he knows it. I can see through it, and with Christine, it's like the opposite of the Jedi mind trick. If Mickey even tries to tiptoe around the facts a little, his mom knows it. She gets to the truth.

It didn't take long to find out that Mickey's headaches hadn't gone away as quickly as we thought—or hoped.

"I had a cold the last few days," Mickey said as we talked in the kitchen Saturday morning. "You guys know that. Like a sinus thing."

"You think it was?" I said. "Did the headaches feel different than the ones earlier in the week?"

"Yeah, I think so," Mickey said. But as he leaned back against the kitchen counter, he felt his mom's stare. "I mean, kind of. Headaches are headaches."

"Not after you have a concussion," Christine said.

Mickey looked down and shook his head.

"But it's different."

We waited for more explanation, but there wasn't any.

"How is it different?" I said.

"The testing said everything was good."

"No, it just didn't find any problem," Christine said. "But that doesn't mean everything. And if you've been having headaches all week . . ."

"Not all week."

"But you've been taking Tylenol?"

As I said, not a good liar. And he knows it. Mickey shrugged and lightly nodded.

"So how are you feeling this morning?" I said.

"Good."

"No headache?"

"No."

"Good. Have you had any dizziness, trouble concentrating, anything?"

"No, Dad, I haven't been having any trouble with that. I haven't had any trouble with my classes or work. I told you that."

"Yeah, but you didn't tell me you were having headaches. Do you have a headache now?"

"After all this, I probably will."

"Don't joke around. Do you have a headache?"

"No."

"When was the last time you took Tylenol?"

"Yesterday."

"You're sure."

"Yes, I'm sure, Dad. I'm not an idiot."

"Relax."

I stared at him for a few seconds.

"So no headache today, and you feel okay?"

"I feel good."

"Okay, so then check in with mom and me tonight and tell us how you felt today. If you feel good, then we'll call this the first day with no symptoms."

"What?" Mickey said, with his voice raising because he knew where this was leading. But I shut him down.

"Listen, Mickey, and I'm serious. Very serious. I know how much you want to get back on the field, but you've got to recover. Part of the problem with concussions is getting a straight answer from the person."

"But I had a cold, and . . ."

"Mickey," Christine said, "your health is the most important thing."

"But I've already sat out all week, and I'm missing today's game. All my life I've waited for this chance."

"But you can't mess around with this, and your season's not over. And like Mom said, your health is most important."

Mickey leaned back, tapped his head against the kitchen cabinet, and sighed with irritation. Tears were beginning to form.

"So?" he said.

"So I hope you don't have any more headaches. I want you to tell us if you have a headache today, and I want the full truth. No 'maybe it's from a cold.' It doesn't matter. If you have a headache, tell us."

"Okay."

"Okay. And after seven symptom-free days . . ."

"But what if the doctor clears me Monday?"

"You're not seeing the doctor Monday," Christine said. "We'll cancel that."

"So I'm out for next week's game already?"

I nodded.

"After seven symptom-free days, a doctor . . ."

"But what if I'm fine now?"

The tears started, and I could see how much it hurt him. He gripped the front of his sweatshirt angrily.

"What if I'm just sitting out for no reason? What if I'm just losing the last football games of my life?"

"We don't know that you're fine," Christine said. "You're eighteen years old, Mickey, with your whole life ahead of you. It's so important to be sure."

"But we can't ever sure about anything, right?"

We all stood in silence for a few seconds. Then Mickey turned away and wiped at his eyes.

"This is so unfair."

"I agree," I said. "You deserve to be playing."

CHAPTER 28

BY the following Saturday, Mickey had been symptom-free for a week. That was great, but it meant nothing football-wise until he got medical clearance. So Mickey was going to sit out Putnam's second-round game, and on the following Monday, he would see the doctor.

"I'm ready," Mickey told me several times that week.

Of course he was.

As for my Creekside Knights, I felt we were as ready as we could be for our next game. But we were a sizable underdog against Wylie, and the Pirates looked a lot better than their record—eight wins and three losses—when I watched their game film. They had played a tough early schedule before winning seven of eight district games, and they rolled in their playoff opener. Wylie teams are always tough, and this year's team had several players with jump-out-at-you athleticism. It looked like we would need to clone a couple more guys like Tyreke to keep up.

"Gonna be tough," Mose said on the day before the game. He showed unusual brevity, perhaps because he didn't have a lot of positive things to add. I told him that if we won, he needed to play some kind of tribute for us on his radio show that night.

"Like what?" he said.

"Your choice."

"It won't be Springsteen, Coach."

I tried to exude confidence during our week of preparation, as did the other coaches. For defensive coordinator Reggie Glover, it didn't seem difficult. He liked the way our defense matched up against Wylie.

"I think we can stop their run," he said, "and when you pressure that QB, he'll make mistakes."

Pretty much any high school quarterback who gets pressured is going to make mistakes. Getting the pressure on him was the difficult part. But I liked Reggie's confidence.

This time we played at Clark Stadium in Plano, and the Saturday afternoon start was fortunate because storms were expected to roll in during the evening. The temperature was in the upper fifties when we kicked off, the winds were light, and the sky was clear. But by late in the second quarter, the temperature was dropping, the sky was milky gray, and we were leading by two touchdowns.

Creekside 21, Wylie 7. I was probably as shocked as anyone by what had been, by far, our best half of the season.

We punted on our first possession, but Wylie ran only two plays before giving us the ball back. Mason Gaines, our best defensive lineman, fought through a pair of blockers to get to the quarterback, who then rushed a throw that was picked off across the middle. That set up a touchdown run by Tyreke, who ran to his right and beat one defender before cutting up the field and slipping between two tacklers. When he got to the end zone, he simply dropped the football this time. No dancing, Heisman pose, or pretending to be Superman. Good Lord, I thought, was that some kind of sign we were fated to win?

Wylie drove to midfield on its next possession, but a holding penalty led to a punt. Tyreke then showed everyone that his ankle was fine. On a third-and-one, he faked a handoff to Paul and then ran right. He was too fast for the linebacker trying to chase him, and with our receiver doing a good job blocking the cornerback, he got five yards down the field before another defender had a chance for the tackle. He sidestepped him and the race was on to the end zone. The Wylie safety cut him off on the right sideline, but Tyreke cut to the left and the safety's legs buckled as he tried to make the play. Tyreke glided into the end zone, dropped the ball, and circled back toward our sideline. Another very subdued celebration. I hoped it was a sign of maturity, but it was only the first quarter, and Tyreke was probably just saving his celebrations for later.

Wylie scored on its next possession to cut our lead to 14–7 early in the second quarter, but we followed with another touchdown drive. Tyreke's long touchdown run helped open up some other things for our offense, and we scored on a third straight possession.

So there we were, with two minutes left in the second quarter, leading 21–7. We were on a roll, and after Wylie punted the ball back to us, I hoped we could build on that momentum. I didn't want to waste a possession, especially with Wylie getting the ball first in the second half, and the half-time break would give Wylie more time to make adjustments. Maybe we could squeeze in one more score before halftime?

I couldn't believe how winnable the game felt. If we could just get in the end zone one more time, and our defense could get a couple of stops in the second half, we might be on to the third round. We'd be playing on Thanksgiving week, which is a nice accomplishment for any team, and given the circumstances, would be darn near a miracle for my Creekside Knights.

But you can't get ahead of yourself, and even with a special talent like Tyreke, the risk-reward scale can tip at any moment. That moment came when Tyreke was getting chased and couldn't find an open receiver. All he had to do was throw the ball out of bounds, but instead he tried to throw a perfect pass to a well-covered receiver. I know he was trying to throw high to David, who had a smaller player covering him. But the pass came out wobbly and short, and the defender made an early break on the ball and snagged it.

He returned it fifty yards for a touchdown, needing to get by only one player who had a chance to make the tackle: the quarterback. Tyreke had no chance, as the defensive lineman who had been chasing him reveled in the opportunity to block a guy who he outweighed by a hundred pounds. He steamrolled Tyreke, who thankfully got right to his feet. He wasn't injured, at least physically. He might've been scarred in other ways as the Wylie fans erupted in cheers, but riding the highs and lows is part of playing quarterback.

We were still up 21–14 at halftime. We had played well before the interception, and if we played well in the second half, we would win. That's what I tried to get across to my players in the locker room, where they seemed dejected despite our lead. I didn't want them to stop believing in themselves and start thinking about how they were the underdogs. We didn't look like an underdog out there. We showed we could play with these guys.

But we couldn't do it for more than a half, apparently. Wylie scored touchdowns on its first two drives of the third quarter to take its first lead, 28–21. Wylie's defense found ways to stuff our inside runs and keep Tyreke from running free, and we punted three times in the third quarter and had only one first down.

With seven minutes left in the game, Wylie scored again on a sixty-yard pass play to make it 35–21. The touchdown came on a third and long, when it looked like we were going to get the ball back, and it was a backbreaker. From leading by two touchdowns to trailing by two touchdowns, that's a spirit crusher.

High school football is a weird and wonderful thing, though, and one play can change everything.

We had used Damion on sweeps earlier in the game, once for a short gain and once for a decent chunk that was part of our third touchdown drive. We went back to it on the second play of our next drive, this time twisting it into a trick play.

Before the drive started, I told David to limp off the field after the first play. Yeah, I wanted him to pretend to be injured. I suppose a hard-liner could question my coaching ethics, but I wasn't telling a player to fall to the ground and delay the game, as some defensive players might do to slow down a fast-paced offense. I didn't want to delay the game at all. I just didn't want Wylie to question the substitution of a starting receiver.

David knew not to be overly dramatic. Just grab at your calf, I told him, like it's a cramp. Don't fall to the ground. Walk gingerly to the sidelines and we'll send someone in there to take your spot. That player would be Cody, our backup quarterback who also played receiver.

After the first play, David hobbled to the sidelines, looking legitimately injured. I laughed when I looked at the video later on, and so did all of the players and coaches. He was our MVP—Most Valuable Pretender.

We got Cody on the field quickly so we didn't need to use a timeout, and Damion lined up in the backfield to the right of Tyreke. He took the handoff while running to his left, and when he got near the sideline, he pitched the ball back to Cody, who was running right.

While all this misdirection chaos was happening on the left side of the field, Tyreke was running down the right sideline. By the time Cody planted his feet and let go of the pass, it was too late for the Wylie defensive backs to get to Tyreke. The pass floated about thirty yards, and Tyreke barely had to break his stride to make the catch. It might've been Cody's best pass of the year, and after Tyreke ran into the end zone, we were again only one touchdown behind. We had only two first downs in the second half, and yet we were in the game.

We needed a defensive stop, and we got it, giving us the ball back with three minutes left. Our offense was in desperation mode, but that seems to be when Tyreke is at his best. He was scrambling all over the field, darting and dodging, finding his way to the first-down markers. It was nothing you could ever draw up as a plan. It was just Tyreke running around and his teammates finding people to block.

With ninety seconds left, we were at the Wylie twenty-five and still had one timeout. Plenty of time. I had already decided that if we scored a touchdown, we were going for two and the win. I didn't want to go to overtime against Wylie, and I'd take my chances with Tyreke. He was the best player on the field, and although only a sophomore, one of the best players I'd ever coached. I'd have him take the snap and give him the option to run, pass, or do whatever he thought might work.

But first we needed to get in the end zone. For Wylie, there was little mystery to what was coming. Tyreke would take the snap and run right or left, always with the option to pass. If we could get ten yards or so closer, maybe we'd throw a pass into the end zone to David, who could use his height advantage.

The touchdown was going to come on a Tyreke run, however. I was sure of it, even though the defense was focused on him. Tyreke is more than just physically gifted. He sees the field well, and he anticipates. He's gutsy and tough.

At that moment, as I put our season on his shoulders, it was hard to believe that I didn't see his potential a year earlier. As a freshman, Tyreke was a skinny kid who could run. But I wasn't even sure he would make the varsity this year.

Now, with a little more than a minute left in the game and possibly our season, we handed him the ball and told him to do what he does best. That's what Tyreke did on the next play, taking the snap and running left to the wide side of the field. He had his arm cocked in a throwing position, but was thinking run, and when he saw an opening, he cut up the field. Tyreke is a silky runner who can usually avoid big hits—a good thing, because he isn't a big guy—and he spun away from a potentially nasty collision near the ten-yard line.

But this time, Tyreke spun right into another tackler. The hit was square. Tyreke fell backward, the linebacker fell on top of him, and as our star was pinned to the ground, his arms flailed. Not in pain, but in panic, because he didn't have the ball.

A second later, a Wylie defender did. Fumble, fumble recovery, game over.

That was it. Possession over. Game over. Season over. For many kids, a life of football over.

Tyreke rolled to his stomach and made no move to get up. I was sure that he was suffering from heartbreak, not an injury, but I walked across the field toward him. He was on his feet by the time I got there, and he angrily ripped his chin strap away and pulled off his helmet. The guy with as much fight as anyone on our team was fighting back tears.

"You okay?"

He looked down and shook his head.

"Are you hurt?"

"I'm okay."

We walked back to the sidelines, and when we got there, I grabbed his jersey above the shoulder pad to keep him from walking away. He stood next to me, and we watched Wylie run out the clock. End of game, end of season, end of another autumn of work, struggle, joy, and pain.

"Sorry, Coach," he said.

I turned to Tyreke, and despite the heavy feel of the moment, I had to smile. I put a hand on each of his shoulders and looked into his eyes. Those eyes, which usually had a certain cockiness, a for-the-most-part likable cockiness, were hurting. The wannabe badass just wanted another chance to win the game.

"You have no reason to be sorry," I said.

We walked through the handshake line, and I thought about what I was going to say to the players. I would hate looking into those eyes, especially the seniors. It was like that every season. Only a few teams win the final game. For the others, the hopes and dreams end in painful realities. Win or lose in the final game, you get emotional when the weird, wonderful ride is over.

From the middle of the summer to the final game, from scorching hot days to icy nights, you are immersed in football. You pour your world into football, and then the season ends, always so abruptly, and you feel a little empty.

CHAPTER 29

EVERY year the Creekside football team has a Thanksgiving feast, a tradition we started when we made three consecutive deep playoff runs.

During each of those playoff runs, we had a playoff game on the Friday or Saturday of the holiday week, so we needed to practice on Thanksgiving. Practice would be in the morning and finish before noon, followed by a potluck lunch together. All the players' families were invited, and we'd have our Thanksgiving lunch together as a football family. Then everyone would disperse to spend the holiday with their other family members.

I don't say their "real" families because I've always felt like a football team is a real family. The players care about each other. They look out for each other. They get into some of the most ridiculous arguments you'll ever hear. It's a family.

The first year that we were out of the playoffs before Thanksgiving, we decided to still have a team Thanksgiving meal. And we've just kept doing it. Former players, often back in town from college, will stop by, and the parents of former players come by. The mom of a kid who played for me almost a decade ago, who now lives in the Chicago area and is married and has a baby daughter, still brings a big plate of cookies each year. They're chocolate chip with oatmeal and M&M's, and because I told you I don't cuss anymore—as much, I mean—I'll just say they're *really* amazing. Mrs. Kiesel brings the "Knight Cookies" in a couple of large plastic tubs, and she wraps a dozen separately for each of the coaches.

"I know how teenage boys are," she always says. "I want you guys to get some before they eat everything."

Yeah, teenage boys always seem to eat like it's their final meal, or their first meal in a week. Thankfully, the parents really come through with the food each year. So does a local barbecue spot, which provides big aluminum bins filled with sliced turkey. We get food from the barbecue place a couple of times a year in exchange for an ad in our football program and some signs outside the stadium. We might have to pay a little, but it's not much. The booster club takes care of it.

The line with kids piling up their plates included Mickey, who I hoped wouldn't go too heavy on lunch because he had football practice in the early afternoon. Mickey had been fully cleared by the doctor on Monday, seventeen days after he suffered the concussion. He felt great, he said, and Coach Greer was happy to have him back. I could never say that Mickey is a "game changer" for a team with as much talent as Putnam, but he's a contributor. And after cruising to comfortable victories in its first two playoff games, Putnam would start getting pushed. The next opponent was Round Rock, a strong team from Central Texas.

Also loading up plates were about a dozen of my former players, and all but one had big, bushy beards. I guess that's the trend. It makes them look a lot older, and that makes me feel older.

But I can still see the baby faces on those twenty-somethings. I remember how Ryan Worsham looked when he was a freshman, maybe five-foot-three, and his jersey draped over his narrow shoulders. Now he was at least six-feet tall, balding a little on top, and wearing a wedding ring. I guess I would describe Ryan as an average football player, but I don't think of any of my players as average. They're all different, you know. In good ways, bad ways, memorable ways.

Each was, and is, special. I know that sounds syrupy. I guess the thought of this football program not continuing gets me that way. Or maybe I'm just a softie. A lot of coaches are, I think, even the ones sweating to present a tough-guy look.

Behind Ryan was Mose, looking sharp in his typical head-to-toe dedication to Nike, with a backpack slung off the side of his wheelchair and iPhone in his lap. Beside Mose was the former Creekside golden boy. Alex Cason was back from Boston College, back to where he was a giant instead of a redshirt, and bantering with his longtime friend and debater. Mose gave instructions, and Alex loaded up two plates, and then they headed to one of the tables set up in our indoor workout facility.

Only four days had passed since our season-ending heartbreak. I told the kids to be proud of what they had achieved, to be proud of how they represented their school, to be proud of themselves. That moment hurt, I told them, but it was a moment, and a feeling, that they would want to hold on to. There were highs and lows, and we had experienced it all together, and that experience would be something we would always share. We were a family forever.

Those sad, swollen eyes that were so hard to look into that night were now warm and young again. As a coach, sometimes I remember the losses more than the wins. What could I have done differently? What mistakes did we make? That kind of thing.

But man, kids just shake stuff off. They cheered and laughed as they watched a highlight video put together by Mose. The oohs and aahs came out when Tyreke broke free for big runs, when safety Elijah Lawal made a diving interception, and when defensive lineman Mason Gaines flattened a quarterback and then pounded his chest and kissed his fist.

"Uh-oh, Gaines," Paul yelled. "Coaches gonna get on you for that!"

The genius of Mose showed in the final thirty seconds of the video, which faded to black for a moment and then showed this across the screen:

"And the Academy Award nominee for best actor . . ."

The players all started to laugh, pretty sure of what was coming, and they were right. The video faded back in to show David pretending to be injured in our final game. It zoomed in on him, and in slow motion, he limped off the field. It was really slowed down, and the players burst into laughter and then cheers.

"MVP! MVP! MVP!"

Yes, our most valuable pretender, but a solid receiver, too. If you're not very fast, you can still make plays if you have good hands and know how to fall in the right direction. David was one of those "average" players who I would always remember.

* * *

After our team lunch, Alex and Mose went back to my office. The two picked up right where they had left off nearly a year earlier, like an old bickering couple. They argued about football, movies, and food. I think there was something about a rap feud, which I knew nothing about, but it was fun watching them go back and forth.

Mose's phone buzzed.

"My auntie's here," he said. "Gotta go."

"So what time Friday?" Alex asked.

"One?"

"That'll work."

Mose dropped his phone into a pocket at the front of his wheelchair and started to leave. I stood up to follow him.

"The doors are locked on the outside, so . . ." I said.

"I got it," Alex said, waving me off. He followed behind Mose as they left the football office.

Alex returned a minute later, and when he sat in the chair across from me, it felt like he was back in high school again. He looked a little less scraggly and a little more grown up, but he was still a pup to me. A very large pup, but a pup.

"What are you guys doing Friday?"

"Just getting lunch," Alex said. "Mose says he's going to get me up to speed on everything."

"Mose is just the guy for that. He's into everything."

Alex nodded as he looked around the office.

"The office seems smaller."

"Yeah, well, maybe you're just bigger. So . . . how are things at BC?"

"It's okay. I hate redshirting, but it does get me a couple extra days home for Thanksgiving."

"Yeah, that's great. Thanks for coming by. The players loved seeing you again . . . and so did the coaches."

"It's good to be back. Feels weird. But it's good."

"You ever feel homesick?"

"Nah, I wouldn't say that. That's like some kid at summer camp. But I miss Texas some. We've already had a couple of snowstorms in Boston, and it's really different. Teammates are great, though."

"That's good. Mose still thinks you're crazy for turning down San Diego State."

"Yeah," Alex said, breaking into a smile. "Mose has told me that, you know, just a few thousand times."

"Wish we could've still been playing when you came back, but we just didn't have enough last week. We could've used you."

"But you've got a stud quarterback now."

I rolled my eyes. "Don't tell Tyreke that. He's already got plenty of confidence."

"He should be great next year."

"I hope so."

"So what about next year?" Alex said.

As I mentioned before, Alex has been more interested than any former player about what's going on with the Creekside football program.

"What's the deal with middle school football? Any chance they'll bring it back?"

"Doubtful. I'm just hoping to hold the line on the high school program."

"They could cut from the high school program?"

"They could do anything."

"When do you find out?"

"When the budget for the next school year gets formalized. Last year, it was January when middle school cuts were announced. They're going to discuss it Monday at the school board meeting."

"Can anyone go?"

"Yeah."

"Damn. I fly back Sunday. But I bet there will be a lot of angry people. You can't mess with football and not expect people to get pissed."

I nodded as I opened a desk drawer and pulled out a sheet of paper.

"I know some people are angry," I said. "A lot of parents. We've even had someone who's been writing letters, kind of threatening letters, to the superintendent."

I looked down at the letter and then up at Alex.

"This is the latest one," I said as I handed it to him.

He looked down at it.

"I think the guy's just venting, but the superintendent contacted police, and now I always get a copy when there's a new one. I'm glad the guy supports football, but I wouldn't want him to get into trouble."

"You get copies of all of them?"

"Now I do."

Alex nodded as he continued reading.

"Because you know," I said, "it could be serious."

Alex looked up, and his face was a shade paler than a minute earlier. That's when I knew. That's when he knew.

"*Shiiiit,*" he said, barely audible.

"So?"

"So you think it's me?"

"It's not?"

I've been working with teenagers for more than two decades. I'm not as good as my wife at reading these guys, but Alex wasn't a tough read. He's like Mickey. It's kind of a curse for earnest, well-meaning kids. They're usually terrible liars.

"Okay," he said, flipping the paper back. "I've written a few letters."

"How many is a few?"

"I didn't write them all."

"Who wrote the others?"

"I don't know."

"Other players?"

His face said it all, or at least enough.

"Look," I said. "I don't want to know more. Just stop writing them, and spread the word that I don't want any more letters sent."

Alex rolled his eyes and scooted his chair toward the desk. Then he lowered his voice.

"We never said we were going to hurt him or anything like that. We . . . I . . . just wanted to kind of show him that he's being unfair. I just thought maybe he'd back down."

"He's not going to back down. He's certainly not worried about making people mad. And, come on, Alex, there are better ways to show the merits of football than letters that call the superintendent an "ass-hat.""

Alex cracked a smile and then began to laugh. Then I did, too.

"I'm serious," I said, but I was still laughing.

"I know."

"Look, don't get yourself in trouble over this. Look at your opportunity at BC. Focus on that and let me take care of things here. We'll be okay."

"But he's saying all these things, doing all these things. He doesn't know what it's like or what it means to play football. It's like me saying Creekside shouldn't have a swimming team, or a band, or something like that. He's trying to kill the most popular thing at the school. Can you imagine no football?"

"No, but I only worry about what I can control."

Once again, that was more of a goal than reality. I was worried about a lot of things.

Alex sighed, tightened his jaw and shook his head.

"This guy might really get death threats if he cuts football," he said.

"But not from you," I said. "No more letters, okay?"

"Yeah."

"Good. Don't screw up your opportunity. I'll be really hacked off if you mess up what football's given you, especially on account of me."

Alex sat quietly for a few seconds and looked down at the floor. He didn't want to make eye contact, I'm sure. He was embarrassed. It reminded me of when he was a sophomore and threw interceptions. He would run to the sidelines with this crushed look because he was so hard on himself, such a perfectionist. A few times I had to kind of talk him off the ledge because he would get so down on himself.

He was just learning back then, but he wanted to impress me from the start. I undoubtedly threw too much at him early on, but I knew he was special. There's just something about kids like Alex and Mose and Tyreke.

"I'm sorry, Coach . . ."

"No, no, don't apologize," I said. "Just tell any other guys that . . ."

"Yeah, okay. Don't worry."

I slipped the letter back into a drawer.

We were both quiet for a few seconds. Then Alex smiled.

"So how did you know I wrote that letter?"

"I didn't," I said. "I thought maybe it was a player, that was all. But Mose took a look at it and thought it was you. He told me nobody else in the world would use the word hubris."

✳ ✳ ✳

I was on the sidelines three days later for Putnam's regional semifinal game. It was at Baylor's McLane Stadium in Waco, which served as a neutral site for Putnam and Round Rock.

Putnam's Coach Greer invited me to watch from the sidelines. It's easier to watch a game from the stands, but I liked being down there. I stayed out of the way and kept my eye on Mickey, who doctors had cleared for full contact five days earlier. He practiced without any complications, felt good, and was ready to go.

But I still felt a little on edge. All the sideline sounds, the ones that usually get my adrenaline pumping in a good way, seemed more intense: the cracking of shoulder pads and helmets, the grunting and heavy breathing, the players jawing back and forth. Even the screeching whistles seemed more aggressive.

Mickey didn't stand out in the game, catching two passes for twenty-three yards. But he walked off the field with a smile, and so did the Putnam players. Kingsley Savage had a pair of touchdown catches and Putnam held on for a 34–28 victory over Round Rock. The Putnam Panthers moved on to a state quarterfinal, and I moved on to worrying about my own football program.

CHAPTER 30

Iwas sitting in the Creekside High School auditorium watching the superintendent and members of the school board take their seats on the stage. A few months earlier I had been in the auditorium to see the Creekside students' production of *You Can't Take It with You*, a play that my high school had put on back in the Eighties.

More than thirty years had passed, and students were doing the same play. But in just the last two years, the Creekside football program had gone from king of the jungle to something like an endangered species. At least that's how it felt to me.

School board meetings usually take place at the Creekside City Hall, but the meeting on the first Monday of December was moved to the high school auditorium to handle the large turnout. Because when you're debating whether to whack football in Texas, people are going to show up.

The year had flown by. So much had happened since cutting middle school football was first proposed, but it felt like yesterday. Well, not yesterday, but certainly not like a year earlier. It was like the feeling I get when I pull out the Christmas lights each year. *Didn't I just put these away?*

It was time for another public forum on the budget for the next school year. The budget wouldn't be approved for several months, but this still felt like a moment of truth for football, or at least a moment of truth for Creekside football. Lee Fountain's article on the future of football kind of set it up that way.

The phasing out of the middle school teams had already knocked out seventh grade football, and the eighth grade team had just completed its final season. The district's chief financial officer provided some figures on the estimated cost savings from having all middle school football off the books for the next school year, allowing the return of "cost-containment," a buzzword welcomed back like a tax audit.

Middle school football was gone, and the district was saving money. Some kids wouldn't get to experience all the great things about football, and others would be playing in recreational leagues with coaches who didn't know what they were doing, but that didn't seem to matter. Bashum wasn't even trying to hide it.

"There could be some districts that decide the money for football doesn't serve their students in the best way," he said in the newspaper story. He kept saying the same things, but louder and more often.

"I want to make it clear that I'm not against football, or that I hate football," Bashum told the audience, and that's when I knew he was about to get into it. Just like the year before, but with a bigger knife.

"I know that there's a long tradition with football and that many people have an affection for it. And believe me, I've felt that."

The room was quiet as Bashum stopped for a moment and smiled weakly. He looked a little nervous, which was something new. He always seemed like an ice man to me. A superintendent robot.

"When I became superintendent, I pledged that I would do what's best for all students," Bashum said as he fell back into heavy seriousness. "And as part of that, it is necessary to evaluate all district programs. And as we talk about athletics . . ."

It was easy for me to demonize him at that point. I couldn't see our previous superintendent ever taking this route, and there were a bunch of times when I thought to myself, "Why did I get the superintendent crazy enough to take on football in Texas?" After all, only a few other Texas school districts had cut football programs, and none of them really had competitive teams.

"We need to evaluate football," Bashum continued. "There are growing concerns nationally about its safety, and with the rising costs of trying to address safety issues, we need to look at whether football belongs within the framework of the school district, and whether it's the best use of education dollars for the entire student body."

I'm not sure I'd be brave enough to sit up there like Bashum, so stoically, as the booing began. Why was he putting himself through this? It was hard to understand. It was hard not to admire him, though. Kind of like when some rushing defensive lineman would whip my butt and sack the quarterback. When I couldn't stop him, I'd be pissed. Pissed at myself, pissed at him. I would hate him. But sometimes I just had to appreciate what that guy could do and say, "Man, you've really got something."

Bashum had something, and it wasn't just some cold-blooded, hard-headed hatred of football. Maybe if I'd gotten to know him better when he was first hired, it would make sense. Or more sense. But he always seemed like a pretty closed-off guy to me.

The boos in the auditorium began from the front right of the audience, where about fifty football players were sitting, most of them wearing letterman jackets despite the heat in the room. The players were quickly shut down by the school board president.

"We're going to need everyone's cooperation to allow everyone who wants to address the board to have a chance," he said.

Assistant coach Michael Cooley stood up and walked toward the players, and I nodded to him that it was a good idea. He took a seat behind them, and I hoped that would keep things under control.

Then again, given what was going on, maybe we needed less control. I had been so worried about overreacting to everything, and so intent on keeping everyone from panicking, that I was probably too laid back about the whole thing. I was doing Bashum a favor by not fanning the flames.

But I had met with Bashum, and I had met with each of the school board members. I had gone over all the reasons why football was important, how it was more than just a sport for the players, what it added to the community—the kinds of things we've all known for years. The kinds of things they've known for years. I had presented the case for football so many times, and I was really, really tired of playing defense.

Three minutes per speaker, the school board president said. Given that more than fifty people had signed up to speak, they needed to have some limits. But good luck cutting off people on this subject. The thing could go on for a while.

It did go on for a while. The speakers took their turns and took their time. Most of them were football supporters, and as I expected, there were a lot of players' parents. The lineup of speakers was a lot like a year earlier, and although I'm happy so many people were willing to speak out for football, it felt like overkill. Just because of who they were talking to, you know what I mean? The superintendent had heard it all before, and so had the members of the school board. There was nothing that was going to change their minds now.

But of course I appreciated people like the woman who described herself as a "proud eighty-two-year-old American." Football is part of the soul of a high school, she said. It would be a travesty if her great grandson's high school did not have football.

"Will there be no more marching band? What about cheerleaders and halftime shows? What about all the people who come to the games?" she said as she spread her arms wide and turned away from the board members and toward the people sitting behind her.

Then she turned back toward Bashum and the school board.

"Shame on you!" she said, pointing at them.

Most of the crowd clapped and cheered in approval, but there were people there who agreed with Bashum. Considering they were so outnumbered in the auditorium, I was surprised so many were willing to speak publicly. They each talked about how football had been glorified for too long, and some sounded so similar that it was like they rehearsed together.

"We should be more concerned with developing successful students and successful adults than with developing football players," one woman said. "One hundred percent of them are going to be adults and zero percent of them are going to be in the NFL."

She said it with a "duh" shrug, as if she had just dropped a bombshell of knowledge.

"So what are we preparing these kids for?" she said, turning toward the crowd.

"It's preparing them for life," an audience member yelled to her.

"So he can like bench press three hundred pounds at a job interview?" she snapped back.

"Ladies and gentlemen," the school board president interrupted. "Please respect each person's time to speak."

Undoubtedly the most memorable speaker attacking football was a man who identified himself as a doctor. I didn't recognize his name, but it wasn't Asher Wellington, the notorious basher of football. Maybe Doc Asher sent this guy in his place.

"More than a century ago, a professor at the University of Chicago described football as boy-killing, man-mutilating, and education-prostituting," the doctor said, reading from a sheet of paper. "In 1905, the presidents at twelve prominent colleges met and came within one vote of killing the sport."

You can imagine where it went from there. Football is too dangerous. It breeds violence. It has no place in civilized society. It should be abolished.

"Adults can do what they want," he said. "But why encourage this for kids?"

Paul Nelson, my starting running back who two weeks earlier had played the last organized football game of his life, was one of three football players who signed up to speak.

"A speaker asked, what are we preparing kids for?" Paul said. "Football has taught me about hard work, teamwork, and a lot of other things. I'm planning to get a business degree at Texas, and I know the things I learned from football will help me. As for some of what I learned in calculus, or in chem class, or from reading classic literature, I'm not sure. But I know football has prepared me for the future."

Paul walked back to his seat and exchanged a fist bump with Mose, who was sitting with the players. Cody Shelton then got his chance, and I'm not sure he really wanted to speak. But he faced the superintendent and board, and with a nervous quiver in his voice, looked down and read from a sheet of paper.

"I was the starting quarterback and then I wasn't. It was really humbling getting benched, and honestly, I thought about quitting. I never told Coach that, but I really did think about it. But then I thought about my teammates, and how I didn't want to bail on them, and the coaches talked to me about commitment. I had committed to the team, not to just being the starting quarterback. I stuck it out, and I'm glad I did. I think . . ."

He looked down at the paper and pulled it toward him.

". . . having challenges made it mean more to me."

He looked up at the stage.

"It was a great season. Something I'll never forget. Thank you."

Cody walked back to his seat and defensive lineman Mason Gaines took his place at the lectern. Seeing Mason walk up there was stunning, because I couldn't remember a time when I'd seen him willingly speak to a crowd. He didn't speak a lot, period.

Coach Hartline nudged my shoulder.

"Are you kidding me?" he said.

I shook my head and smiled. There wasn't a lot to smile about on that night, but seeing one of my players grow up was a reason.

"Hello, my name is Mason Gaines," he said slowly in his deep voice, "and, uh. . . ."

Mason said it with a stone face. The paper rustled in his shaking hand, and I wanted to walk up there and save him. He looked so uncomfortable, I think everyone felt his pain.

"I'm one of the team captains, and I want to make sure y'all know how much football means to me. You know . . ."

He looked down at his paper.

"Football teaches you lessons for life, and . . ."

He dropped the paper to the table and sighed.

"I think I'm just going to have Mose come up here now. But the guys want me to say there are other players who signed up to speak, and they want to give their time to Mose so he has more time."

The school board president smiled.

"Well, we'll see."

Mason removed the microphone from the stand as Mose positioned his wheelchair next to him, and then Mason knelt next to Mosey to hold the microphone. A woman in the audience hopped up from her seat in the front row and offered it to Mason, and although he tried to wave her off, she insisted. So Mason sat in the seat, and then Mose maneuvered into position next to him.

Some in the audience probably didn't know Mose, but I think most knew his story. Not because he talked about it, though, because Mose pretty much avoided the subject. He always had other things to talk about, whether he was visiting kids at elementary schools or doing his radio show.

It was such a strange moment. I felt nervous, like it was one of my sons getting ready to take the field, or the court, or the stage. It's hard to explain how I felt, but my heart was pounding so hard I could feel it in my neck.

✳ ✳ ✳

It was quieter in the auditorium than it had been all night.

"Mister Superintendent, Mister President, and members of the school board, thanks for letting me speak. My name is Eric Posey, and I was a Creekside football player, and now I'm sort of a coach."

The football players whistled and cheered, and the audience responded by either laughing or looking sternly at the players. Coach Cooley stood up behind the players and quieted them down. But then someone yelled out, "Tell 'em, Coach Mose!" and the players laughed again.

Mason, still seated next to Mose, stood up and turned toward the players. He grimaced, did a throat-slashing gesture, and the players were quiet again. Mason didn't have to say anything to get his point across, and his seriousness told me that he knew what was coming, and also how much this meant to Mose.

"Yeah," Mose said with a smile. "The guys call me Mose. But I'm here as Eric Posey, because I want to talk seriously. And don't worry, I won't take a long time, although I appreciate my brothers lookin' out for me. I'm a deejay, so I know it's important to shut up after a while."

The audience laughed, and Mose smiled. At that moment, he had everyone. He could've gone on for three hours and nobody would cut him off. He looked down at the sheets of paper in front of him for a few seconds and then began.

"A lot of you know I got hurt in a football game. I was a junior, and it changed my life forever."

The room had been quiet when Mose began talking. But it got even quieter. It was so silent that I heard the buzz from the lights above.

"It probably seems strange that someone who was injured playing football would be here sayin' what I'm sayin.' Might be better for me not to say anything, right?"

Mose broke into a smile, paused for a moment, and then got serious again.

"But here's the thing. Injuries happen in football, there's no denying it. Injuries happen in all sports. Injuries happen in life. Terrible things happen in life, right? Disease, violence, wars, terrible things. I read the other day about six teenagers die every day in a car crash. It's really sad, man, but it makes me think of a famous quote."

He looked up.

"Blank happens."

The players chuckled, but the rest of the audience was quiet.

"Don't worry, I'm not going to say the word. But you know what I'm saying, and it's true."

My heart was still pounding, and I'm sure everyone else was mesmerized by Mose. I mentioned before that he could be a preacher. My God, or gosh, he would be a great preacher.

"Blank happened to me. And yeah, there are times when I think, why me? But if I could go back in time, the only thing I would change is not playing in that one game. Just not playing on that one play, that one freak play when I was injured. I would still play football. It's the game I loved, and I still love. I have dreams at night where I take the handoff, I'm running wide, getting the corner, and then gliding past defenders. I feel like I'm back playing on that championship team."

He took a breath.

"And then I wake up."

Mose paused for another second, and someone sniffled from a few rows behind him. I wondered if Mose had prepared this speech or if he was just rolling with it.

"And am I sad when I wake up? Yeah. But I know this injury isn't going to stop me. Man, I wanted to be a deejay before the injury, you know? And now I am a deejay. The injury hasn't changed who I am."

"You know what makes me most mad about getting hurt? That it took away football. It took away more than that, I know. But so could a car accident, or riding a bike, or riding a skateboard, or a motorcycle, or even something like going fishing. You're more likely to die in a canoe than on a football field. Did y'all know that?"

Mose adjusted his body in the chair and looked away from the stage for a moment. If it were anyone else, the board president might've asked if that was it. But you could tell Mose wasn't done.

"I still plan on walking again someday. I'll never . . ."

Mose's voice cracked slightly and he stopped. But he regained his composure.

"I'll never give up on that. And you know, I put all faith in God. If it's God's will, and that's part of the plan for me, then it will happen. Technology's amazing, man. You know Coach Nehls has a daughter who I've known since she was born. You might have seen her hitchin' a ride with me on my chair at one of the games. I told Emma my goal is to walk in ten years. I told her I'll dance at her wedding, even though she might never get married because Coach won't let her date till she's like thirty."

We all laughed. But the thirty-years-old thing is only a slight exaggeration. I'm the one who won't let her get her ears pierced, after all.

"So Mister Superintendent, Mister President, members of the school board, and everyone in here. What I'm sayin' is that blank happened to me, just like it does to all of us in some way. Blank happens. But a lot of great things happen, too. Remember the first time you drove a car? Incredible feeling, right? And it was pretty dangerous because you were still learning how to drive. Six teenagers die every day in car accidents. So should they just not drive? Should all people not drive? It's dangerous."

Mose looked over at Mason, who was still holding the microphone.

"Your arm getting tired?"

Mason smiled and shook his head. Mose slid a sheet of paper over so he could see the next one.

"One of the great things that happened to me was football. It taught me so many things. How to be disciplined. How to work hard. The reward of overcoming challenges. It taught me how to grow up. It made me part of something bigger than me, and those Friday nights are some of my greatest memories."

Mose was quiet for a few seconds. I don't know if he was collecting his thoughts or just pausing for dramatic effect. The guy's a master.

"I have a great family. My mom and dad are the best, my older brother is always there for me, my auntie is amazing. But I know other kids who aren't so lucky. Some were even my teammates. But on the football team, you have a team full of brothers. You have coaches who are looking out for you. You have a family. A football team is a family."

He paused again and took a deep breath. Then he smiled.

"You know, when I was injured, it's still fresh in my mind. I was so young, I didn't understand. I knew something bad happened, but until doctors explained things later, I didn't even know what a C-5 or C-6 verte-brae was. And yeah, I admit it. When I was lying on the field I was callin' for my momma, and I'm so glad she and my dad were there. But before they could get to the field, you know I was in shock and scared. But as scared as I was, I knew people were gonna take care of me. When Coach came out there and was by me, I knew my family was there."

Several minutes had passed. Ten, maybe? I don't know. But nobody said a word. Nobody made a sound at all.

"I know you've talked about saving money by cutting football, but people talk about investing in kids, and football is like an investment. And if this is all about football being too dangerous, I'm telling you, kids are going to play football anyway. Do you want kids playing for coaches who don't know what they're doing, or someone like Coach Nehls? Someone who knows what he's doing and you know is going to look out for you? Someone who can be your role model for like everything? Except about music, I mean, because you should hear what Coach listens to. I'm telling ya. So . . . much . . . Springsteen."

Another good laugh in the room. From me too, of course. When you're a coach, you're used to getting roasted.

"Thank you again for letting me speak today. I know you have tough decisions, and I wouldn't want to do what you do. I'm a words guy, not a numbers guy. But I can tell you, my life has changed because of football, and it's not how you think. My life is better because of football."

CHAPTER 31

A few more people spoke after Mose, but the list of fifty or so shrank considerably. Who wants to follow that?

I was still feeling—I don't know—partly numb from Mose's speech. It wasn't unlike the feeling I've had after watching an astounding football performance. Mose had a lot of those performances when he was that cocky kid with the skinny body who could glide between tacklers and float like a ballet dancer. He spoke with the same grace he had as an athlete. He was poetry in motion, whether in cleats or a chair.

That didn't mean it was going to change anything with Bashum and the school board. Those minds were made up. But I was so proud of Mose, and so excited for him as the players congratulated him. I swear they were in awe of him. Even Tyreke, who often seemed in awe of himself.

Whatever would eventually happen, even if Bashum and the board decided to take another step toward dismantling football, that was a good night. I'm a coach, so yeah, I want to win. But there's nothing more rewarding than seeing your players, the punky, peach-fuzzed teenagers, emerge as men.

"Wow. *Woooooooow,*" Coach Hartline said. "That was something."

No doubt. Mose's speech was so impactful that reporter Lee Fountain mentioned it in his story. He also mentioned that Mose was a former player, an assistant coach, and the host of a radio show on Saturday nights on *The Groove.* I thanked him the next day for mentioning the radio show, because I know he did that for Mose.

Coach Hartline and I were talking about Mose's speech as the auditorium emptied out. I put on my jacket and heard my name behind me.

"Coach Nehls?"

I turned.

"Hello Coach, I don't mean to interrupt," he said quietly. I didn't recognize him.

"You're not interrupting," I said, extending my hand.

"Okay, good," he said with what I guess I'd call a serious smile. "My name is Ronald Dozier, and we've never met, but my son is Chris Dozier, and he used to play football for Bevell Middle School. You might not know him, but . . ."

I knew Chris Dozier, of course. I was never part of the lawsuit, and it had been dismissed several months earlier, but I was not going to forget the name of the family that sued the school district.

"Nice to meet you," I said. "And yes, I know Chris."

Coach Hartline, standing behind Mr. Dozier, raised his eyebrows and then walked toward the auditorium doors. People were filing out quickly.

"Sorry that you're going through all this," Mr. Dozier said.

I didn't know what to say, so I didn't say anything.

"I wanted to ask you something," he said.

"Sure."

"Chris attends Richardson Faith Academy. But we still live in Creekside, and his mom and I were thinking he might start going to Creekside."

"Oh." I probably could've offered a little more enthusiasm.

"Anyway, uh, Chris really likes football. He can't play anymore, but we'd like to find something for him to be a part of. We were wondering if you might have an opening for someone to help with the team."

"Oh," I said again, this time with more warmth. "Like a student manager, or assistant . . . something like that?"

"Yes, exactly."

"We have something like that. I don't know what roles might be filled up, or will open up, but we always welcome anyone who wants to help."

"So Chris could be a part of that?"

"Absolutely. So how is Chris doing?"

"He's doing great, thank you." Mr. Dozier's face brightened and his shoulders loosened. "Really doing well, doing a lot better in school."

"Glad to hear it. Are you having Chris come to Creekside after winter break?"

"Probably for next semester. I . . . I mean we really feel like it would be good for him. And, honestly, we'd like to save some tuition money."

"I can understand that. I have three kids. Two sons and a daughter."

"We just have two. Chris has a little sister, and she goes to Bevell. But . . . we thought a private school might be better for Chris. And it's been fine, and it's not that he's unhappy there, but it's small, and I think he kind of misses some things."

"Well, Mr. Dozier, I can tell you that, if Chris wants to help with the team, we'll find a way for him to help."

"Thank you. That would be so nice. If you need a person to do video, that's something Chris is really into."

"Video, huh?"

"Oh yeah. He shoots all kinds of things and makes movies. He bought a drone with his own money so that he could do aerial shots. All kinds of stuff."

"Uh . . ." I chuckled, "we'll definitely find something for Chris to do. We always need video help, and Mose is kind of our tech expert . . ."

"The guy who was speaking tonight?"

"Yeah, that's Mose. He's really something, huh?"

"Yeah, he is."

"Mose is an amazing guy," I said, "and I'm sure he'd love to work with Chris."

"I'd love for Chris to meet him," Mr. Dozier said.

"We'll set something up."

Mr. Dozier smiled and took a deep breath. This was obviously a big weight off his shoulders. Maybe he had the wrong impression of me. Maybe he thought I would go off on him for the lawsuit or blame him for everything.

"Thanks again, Coach."

"You're welcome. I can't make any promises about anything, but Chris is welcome to be part of our football program."

"Thank you, and uh, Coach . . ."

He looked down for a second and then back up.

"I'm sorry for what's going on, and I hope what went on with Chris isn't part of it. We were just, I mean, he's our son, and we wanted to protect him, and I apologize if anything . . ."

"You don't have to apologize. You were being a parent."

He smiled and nodded.

"I'm glad Chris is doing better. We'll set something up with Mose."

The auditorium was nearly empty as I walked out the doors. My mind was still absorbing the conversation with Mr. Dozier, but then I remembered I should check my phone, which I had silenced during the meeting. I wasn't expecting anything, but that was usually when things started happening.

Yep. Eight text messages. All about Mose. No surprise there.

I walked out of the entryway of the auditorium and down the steps. I zipped up my jacket—it must've been the coldest night of the season at that point—and headed toward the parking lot. It was mostly quiet, aside from a few small conversations, including one that caught my ear.

It was coming from my left, around the corner of the auditorium and away from the parking lot. The voice was familiar, and although I couldn't place it, something about it pulled me in that direction. I walked over, and as I got closer, I recognized the voices of Tyreke and his buddy, Kerry Thurman. I couldn't see them, but Tyreke's voice is unmistakable, and where you find Tyreke, you'll often find Kerry, a sophomore receiver who split time on junior varsity and varsity during the season.

Then there was the adult voice.

"It doesn't matter what high school you're at, you can play."

It didn't take me long to recognize that voice, and it made me walk faster. I was almost into a jog as I turned the corner and nearly collided with Driphus Coleman. Yeah, the coach of the Intensity team. That all-star team, or home-school team, or academy team, or however you would describe it.

"Oh, hey," Coach Coleman said, obviously startled. He dropped back a step and made a ridiculous effort of overfriendliness. "Hey Coach, how are you?"

He smiled as he extended his hand, and I shook it without feeling.

"I was just out here supporting you guys, and . . ."

"You were out here supporting us?" I said, taking a step toward him.

"Yeah, you know, supporting football."

"Uh-huh," I said, and I took another step toward him. "But why are you talking to my players?"

"Just saying hi, Coach. They were here, I was here."

"Uh-huh."

I took a breath and stepped back toward the players.

"Tyreke and Kerry, how'd you guys get here? Who drove you?"

"Kerry drove," Tyreke said. "Bro just got his license."

"Then you guys get going, okay?" I said. "Be careful driving."

They walked off, and I turned back toward Coach Coleman. He had taken a step backward to give himself a more comfortable distance from me, but I closed the space with a step toward him. I could hear Tyreke and Kerry talking as they walked away. Their voices were squeaky with excitement. "Oh, shit, man!"

I should've walked away at that moment, especially knowing that the players could still be nearby. Anyone could still be nearby. The parking lot had cleared out, but anyone could've come around the corner.

And I wasn't thinking clearly. Certainly not logically. I was allowing myself to be consumed by a moment of emotion, the exact thing I warned my players about. Be disciplined, I always told them. Don't let your emotions lead to a personal foul on the field. Just walk away.

I should've followed my own advice as I headed down a path toward something much worse than a fifteen-yard penalty. The guy wasn't worth embarrassing myself or endangering my career. I actually remember thinking that, even as my head and heart raced.

Still, I took another step toward Coach Coleman. Our faces were only inches apart now, and his back was nearly against the bricks of the auditorium.

"Stay away from my players," I said.

"Coach, you're getting the wrong idea."

"You're over here talking to my players, and you jump when I come around the corner. Tell me how I'm getting the wrong idea."

"Look, Coach . . ."

Coach Coleman shook his head.

"Look, what?" I said. I tried to look him in the eyes but he looked down.

"It's up to them, right?"

"It's up to who?"

"The players," Coach Coleman said. He had regained his composure and was talking louder. Gaining confidence. He probably started to realize that I had too much at stake to really lose my cool.

He finally looked me in the eye.

"It's up to the players what they want to do when they're in high school," he said, "and who they want to play for."

The throb in my neck was back, and so was the warning bell about losing control. But as Coach Coleman stood in front of me, he was more than just a coach I didn't like. He was the greasy underbelly of youth sports. He was the screaming jackass coaches of third graders, who think they're Nick Saban or Bill Belichick because they've got a whistle, clipboard, and personalized workout gear for their team of eight-year-olds. He was the sleaze behind the traveling recruiting combines that prey on a kid's hopes and dig into his parents' wallets. He was the sponsors and money-hungry organizers of national seven-on-seven tournaments, all-star showcases, and bloated made-for-TV events that turn teenagers into profits.

Coach Coleman was all the bullshit surrounding the game I love. And he was the future of it.

"Stay away from my players," I repeated.

"Look, Coach, you don't even know if you're going to have a team.

How you gonna serve these kids if you don't have a team? I've got a team that can serve them. I'm just letting them know."

I stepped forward and pressed my finger into his chest. Coach Coleman isn't a little guy, but he's not a former offensive lineman. I don't try to intimidate people with my size, but in this case, I wanted to be close enough to look down at him.

"Back up, Coach," he said.

"Stop recruiting my kids," I said.

He gave a cocky smile.

"Why you keep calling them your kids? You might not even have a team."

I honestly don't remember scrunching up his jacket in my fists, but I remember feeling my forearms pushing his chest into the bricks. I remember my fists rising up below his chin, and I felt like I could pick him off the ground, push him through the wall, and drive him ten yards like a blocking sled. I felt like I could pull him off the wall like a rag doll and drive him back into it until that smile was gone.

"Get your hands off me, motherfucker!"

Coach Coleman's voice rose with his fear, and I enjoyed it. His voice was panicked, for good reason, and it hit an alarming pitch that should've snapped me back into reason before I did something that could change my career and life.

It still scares me when I think about it. I made Coach Coleman into far too great a villain and gave him far too much importance in the present and future of football. He was just one coach. Just a buzzard circling an opportunity, and God knows there are always a lot of them.

I'm not in football shape anymore, but I still work out with the players. I'm still strong, and on that day, feeling the way I did, I was strong enough to pick Coach Coleman off that brick wall and slam him back against it. I'm embarrassed how much I wanted to do it, and it frightens me how close I was to doing it.

What saved me?

It was my family. It was Coach Glover, who came around the corner, saw me looking like a high school bully, and pulled me off Coach Coleman. I'm not sure anyone else on my staff could've done it.

Coach Coleman was unhurt. At least he acted that way, and facing two former college linemen, he was ready to get out of there.

"Is this what you teach your kids?" Coach Coleman yelled at me. "Is this your example?"

He pointed toward Tyreke and Kerry, who were standing off to the side with expressions of excitement and fear.

"Get the hell out of here!" Coach Glover said to the coach.

I felt the sting of the cold air on my right hand and looked down. Two of my knuckles had scraped against the rough bricks as I pushed the coach against the wall. They were bleeding, which made me feel more ridiculous.

"The auditorium's still open," Reggie said. "You can clean up there."

"Thanks," I said, "but I'm just heading home. Just want to get outta here."

"You okay?"

"Yeah."

"You sure?"

"Yeah. . . . Thanks."

I took a long, deep, humiliated breath.

CHAPTER 32

I'M no better than anyone else at estimating crowds, but it's a big crowd, and a loud crowd, and the kind of crowd that no high school football player will ever forget. Thirty thousand? Forty thousand?

I'm not sure. I've seen bigger, a lot bigger, for high school games here in Texas. But this is still an amazing setting, and as I stand on the sidelines at AT&T Stadium, I know this is where a coach wants to be. It's December, the Texas high school playoffs are in the final stretch, and I'm on the field for the show.

But as I said when I started talking with you, before I began filling in all the details of the last year, I'm not a coach tonight. Right now, I'm just a dad with an invitation to be on the sidelines, where I can watch Mickey and his Putnam teammates take on Dallas Skyline in a state quarterfinal.

After my run-in with Coach Coleman five days ago, I wonder if Putnam's coach worries about having a hothead on the field. That's what I am now, you know. Nearly fifty years old, more than two decades in coaching, and now I'm the guy with the short fuse.

Well, I was the guy with the short fuse on Monday. And I cringe when I think back on how I lost control, on how I let myself down, and how it could've been worse.

It was bad enough. And because I knew the story would get out, probably in multiple versions with varying amounts of truth, I told my principal about what happened the following morning. I also wrote a letter of explanation to Superintendent Bashum, and I'll be meeting with him in two days. We were already scheduled to meet before I became Captain Meltdown, but now we'll have something else to talk about. I'm not sure if I'm more excited about the Bashum meeting or my age-fifty colonoscopy. It's a close one.

I was fortunate that Tyreke and Kerry didn't follow my instructions when I told them to go home that night. They were headed for the parking lot, but Tyreke saw Coach Glover in front of the building and told him what was going on. Quick thinking by Tyreke. Just like a quarterback, seeing the field, analyzing the situation. Man, he could be the greatest Creekside quarterback ever.

Or maybe Tyreke will be the first great Intensity quarterback—or transfer to another school. If Bashum convinces the school board to sweep another leg out from under our football program, could I blame Tyreke for leaving? How could I blame any kid who wants to play high school football?

The school district might give up on football, but that doesn't mean a kid will give up on his dream. If he wants to play, he'll play somewhere. If schools stop offering football, the kids will still find teams. It won't be as exciting, memorable, or safe, but it will be football.

And football, at least for now, is still king. Thirty thousand, forty thousand, whatever number is in here tonight, it's a spectacle. Putnam's blue and silver on one side, Skyline's red and black on the other. Some of the red on Skyline's side comes from Allen fans, who watched their team win the quarterfinal that preceded this one. This is a doubleheader day at AT&T Stadium, which was host to four games in a day two weeks ago. On those quadruple-header days, there are people who will get here for the morning game and stay until the last one finishes around midnight.

I couldn't do it, but I'm not surprised some people do. This is Texas (y'all).

There are only two games today, but Putnam and Skyline are putting on a great show. Through three quarters, neither team led by more than a touchdown and there were four lead changes. Early in the fourth quarter, Putnam returned to the happy side of the lead-change seesaw with a touchdown that gave it a 28–24 lead. The TD was scored by "The Beast"—Kingsley Savage—on a long pass play.

I don't have much to report on Mickey. Two catches for about fifteen yards. He also ran once on an end-around that picked up three yards and made my chest tighten. When he stepped out of bounds and avoided a potentially big hit, I relaxed. I know we were cautious with Mickey's recovery, and he had already played a week earlier, but a parent is a parent. Even when the parent is a coach.

Mickey hasn't had a big game, but he didn't expect to have a lot of big games at Putnam. Winning is the important thing, and Putnam is now in position to put the game away. Moments ago, Kingsley caught another pass to set up a touchdown run, and with less than three minutes left, Putnam is up 35–24.

If Mickey had stayed at Creekside, he would've touched the ball on almost every offensive play. At Putnam, he hasn't touched the ball since the first half. But I can tell that he doesn't care. The way he smiles on the side-lines, the way he celebrates with teammates . . . the way he's now looking up at the Jumbotron and watching a replay of the touchdown. He's part of a football family that's on a journey the players will never forget. This is what he always wanted, and it's what I always wanted for him. It's why I had to let him go to Putnam, just as I'll have to let him go to college next fall.

The Putnam fans are celebrating, but the game isn't over yet. Skyline is driving down the field desperately and effectively. Fifteen-yard pass. Quarterback scramble for ten more. A dump-off pass that the receiver breaks for twenty yards against a prevent defense. And then a touchdown pass across the middle, followed by a two-point conversion that cuts Putnam's lead to 35–32. Skyline's band pumps out the school fight song, and for the Putnam crowd, the nerves creep back in.

But there's only one minute left and Skyline is out of timeouts. Skyline's only hope is to recover an onside kick, and that means Putnam is putting its "hands team" on the field. That includes Mickey, who runs on to the field with Kingsley and Putnam's other sure-handed players. Skyline's players gather in the middle of the field around the kicker, then suddenly all shift to their right, to the side of the field opposite me. Putnam's players scramble in response, and now the kicker is ready.

If Skyline recovers, it has a chance to get in position for a game-tying field goal. If Putnam recovers, this thing's over.

The football takes two small bounces before one end catches the turf and sends the ball about ten feet in the air. It's a well-executed onside kick, creating a jump ball for the Skyline and Putnam players. Mickey's hands are as good as anyone's, but it's the reach of Kingsley that secures the win for Putnam. "Beast" pulls the ball out of the air and clutches it to his chest just before a collision of players obscures my view.

Skyline players will fight for the ball, but they're not going to get it from Kingsley. I've seen that kid's arms and shaken his hand. Game over.

One official is pointing Putnam's direction while two others pull players off the pile. Kingsley rises from the scrum with the ball in his hand, and the Putnam crowd erupts in cheers. The band begins playing, and I pump my fist.

I know it's not my team, that it's not my family. But I feel the electricity rising through me. That's Mickey's team, and I know how much it means to him. This is what he's worked for.

Wait. What?

Those are Mickey's cleats. I know that blue piece of tape. Mickey always puts it on the soles of his cleats. Those are his feet, not moving, attached to his body, not moving.

"Hey!" I scream.

I'm not sure what else I'm yelling as I run through the crowd of players on the sideline. I crash into one of them as I try to make my way to the field. I'm not sure how many thoughts a mind can have at once, but my mind is chaos as I run toward Mickey.

Is he unconscious? Oh God, what's going on? Why is he . . . what happened . . . where are the trainers?

Second-impact syndrome flashes through my brain. No. We were careful, over-the-top careful. We let him heal. We were overprotective.

I can feel the heaviness of my body as I run toward the middle of the field, gracelessly stomping toward what I might not want to see. The crowd is still cheering, not seeing what's happening, probably thinking I'm part of the celebration.

My mind is still racing. All those NFL players who've suffered concussions. Their lawsuits. Chris Dozier and his parents talking about long-term damage. All the thoughts are in there, and little of it makes sense. I can't even think straight, and I can't believe I'm on the field. This isn't even my team, and . . .

Okay, he's moving.

He's not unconscious. The trainers are there. Okay.

Okay.

I'm doubled over, exhausted, gulping for air, seeing stars. God, I'm out of shape. I'm so out of breath I can barely think. And now, as the crowd quiets, I'm standing in the middle of the field and everybody's looking at me, the maniacal dad who has run on the field.

I know I need to back off. But that's Mickey, the second grader who scored imaginary touchdowns with the tiny plastic football. The fourth grader who made up plays to run at the park across the street. The sixth grader who told me he was going to play for the Longhorns one day. The high school senior who had dreamed for so long about when his football time would come.

Time has flown by. I can still remember, vividly, when Mickey was a baby sleeping in our room at night. He'd keep me up with his crying, and then he'd keep me up when he was too quiet. Sometimes I had to walk over to the crib and see his chest rise and fall before I could fall asleep. I was so afraid that something would happen to him, that something would go wrong. I never felt that way when he was playing football, and I can't explain why. Maybe because I wanted so badly for him to love football the way I do.

I feel a hand on my shoulder. It's Coach Greer.

"Sorry," I say, instinctively.

"No reason to be."

Mickey is talking with the trainers. He's pointing to his arm, and it could be serious. A shoulder injury, possibly. Maybe a broken arm. It could be the end of his days as a high school football player.

That would be really sad. But I'm so thankful.

CHAPTER 33

"**S**O how's your son?" Superintendent Bashum asks.

"He'll be fine. Hairline fracture of the humerus, right below the shoulder. Doesn't need a cast, just needs to wear a sling for a month or so."

"But football?" he says as he winces, showing he cares, or pretending to.

"He's out."

Yes, Mickey's out. Not a serious injury, but he won't be able to play in the state semifinal that will match two of the state's biggest schools: Putnam and Allen. It should be quite a game, and Mickey's devastated. After not missing a snap because of injury for the first eight years of playing football, Mickey gets hurt twice in a month. Simple bad luck.

"Sorry to hear that," Bashum says.

"Yeah, well . . ." I shrug, feeling like a kid sent to the principal's office. I actually was a kid sent to the principal's office once—just once—when I was eight years old. I gave my friend answers on a multiplication worksheet, and I knew it was wrong, but it got him to recess sooner. We always played Nerf football during recess, and I wanted him on my team. So many memories in my life are connected to football. What would I do without this sport?

Four decades later, I'm not expecting a lecture. But I'm bracing for something kind of like that. Any meeting with Bashum is awkward, and it's worse in the wake of trying to push another coach through a wall, especially when that wall is attached to your school. And it was right after a school board meeting. Nice going, me.

"As for what happened last week, I don't want to talk about it unless you want to. I appreciate that you let us know right after it happened, and Dave Holgate gave me some background."

I'm relieved, but not sure what to say. "Thank you" doesn't seem right.

Dave is the one I should thank. He's always had my back. If the other school board members were like him, Bashum wouldn't have a chance of cutting football.

"So this coach showed up at a game?" Bashum says.

"Yes. . . . But I'm disappointed by the way I reacted. Nothing positive comes from it."

"Well, we all have our moments."

"Thanks."

So now I'm thanking the guy who's cutting football.

Bashum looks down and taps the tips of his fingers together. He pauses for a moment, and I catch a glimpse of the photos on the bookshelf behind his desk. A family shot with his wife and two daughters somewhere in the mountains. A photo of a toddler that I assume is a grandchild. He must have a dozen framed photos behind him, including the black-and-white football shot, still right at my eye level, just as it was the last time I was in the office a few months ago. The photo looks like it's from the fifties or sixties. How old is Bashum, anyway?

"I want to make something clear," Bashum says. "I don't hate football."

I nod. I don't know if he's waiting for a response from me, but all I manage is "Okay."

"I just wanted to say that because I'm sure you think I do. I know most people will assume that, and I know the majority of people in this district don't want to cut football. I know where I am, I know the saying that football is like religion, and despite all that . . ."

He smiles.

"Well, basically . . . I'm not crazy."

"Okay." Am I supposed to respond in some other way?

"I also know football is important enough here that I might not last as superintendent. I've received enough emails, letters, phone calls, threats— you name it—to know the path is rocky. I'm not going to win a popularity contest."

Is he looking for sympathy? I'm nodding like a bobblehead. But

Bashum's leading up to something. Something like the "You're really nice and I like you a lot" that comes before getting dumped.

"But . . . football is on the decline," Bashum says. "I really believe it is."

He says it like he's apologizing.

"And I believe that decline will accelerate. We've got school districts across the country cutting middle school football, some cutting freshman teams, some cutting football completely."

"And that's a good thing?" I say.

He pauses for a moment.

"It's a thing. Five years ago, I couldn't have imagined someone talking about cutting football at the national superintendents meeting. Now there are multiple discussions planned for it."

"Discussing it is different than doing it."

Bashum gives a grudging nod.

"Of course. But I'm telling you, Coach, some are doing it. And they will be doing it. More and more will be doing it."

"Why? What has changed in the last five years? It was just five years ago when we built our indoor facility. Millions of dollars for that. What has changed?"

Bashum rolls back his chair, presses his hands into the armrests, and begins to stand. I see a flash of strain on his face as he rises up, but he tries to hide it by looking away. He turns toward the shelves on the wall behind him, stares at something for a moment—maybe the pictures—and then turns toward me.

"Sorry, I just needed to stand for a moment. No matter how I sit, sometimes my back just kind of locks on me."

"Sorry to hear that. I didn't know you had problems with your back. You run, don't you?"

"Yeah, I do," Bashum says, leaning forward against the chair's backrest. "I probably shouldn't anymore. I've run for years, have done four marathons, but what used to be good for me doesn't seem to be anymore. I'm slowly realizing that."

He takes a deep breath, lets it out slowly, and sits back down.

"The indoor facility is great," he says. "And you know, if I had been here as superintendent five years ago, we probably still would've built it. That's where things were five years ago."

"That's what I mean," I say, scooting forward in my chair. "What has changed?"

I brace for Bashum's take on the football-is-evil-connect-the-dots game that has become a national sensation.

"Everything has changed," Bashum says. "It really has. The research on brain injuries. How all the hits accumulate. The NFL ignoring it. The lawsuits. How some insurance companies refuse to cover football. And you've seen how football participation is dropping."

"Not by much."

"But it's dropping."

"It's only been a couple of years. There are still more than a million kids playing high school football. More boys play football at Creekside than every other sport combined."

Bashum nods as if he's soaking it in. But this isn't new information. None of what I'm saying is new to him. I'm going to keep talking, though.

"I know some school districts outside Texas are cutting football. But football there isn't what football is here. Why Creekside? Why now? Football is at the core of this school."

"Should it be?" Bashum says, raising his eyebrows.

Every coach has heard this argument. Football is given too much importance. It's just a game. Why does everyone care so much?

But it doesn't matter why people care so much. It matters that they do. It bonds the community together like nothing else. When we went to the state title game, we had more than fifteen thousand people on our side of the stands. You can't get fifteen thousand people together in Creekside for a parade or any other celebration. You could announce you were handing out free pizzas and you wouldn't get as many people as come to our games.

"Football means so much around here," I say, "so much to these kids."

"I know," Bashum says.

"So why take it away? Why take away something that means so much?

Listen to former players talk about what football meant to them, taught them, did for them later."

Bashum shakes his head and extends his palms toward me.

"I know there are valuable lessons in football. But can't those lessons be learned in other sports, in other ways?"

"I don't know. But you're talking about risk. You want to take that risk with kids? The NFL is more popular than ever. So is college football, and we had nearly sixty thousand fans at the high school state title game last year, and those people could've watched it on TV. People love high school football."

"I know that," Bashum says.

I think he's getting annoyed now, but sometimes the truth is annoying. And the truth is, football is too big to be killed by one superintendent or school board. Kids are still going to play it, even if there is no high school program. If you cut Creekside football, you're not cutting football, you're just taking a knife to the trained coaches, the support staff, the safest facilities, the best equipment.

"Dr. Bashum, you're going to send these kids running to guys like the Intensity coach. Those guys are waiting with open arms. Cut football in Creekside and you're creating more danger for these kids."

"So it's the responsibility of the school district to take this on?" Bashum says. "Despite the cost, despite the danger, a school should support this?"

"I'm not saying what should happen. I'm saying what will happen. And if you're talking about danger, think of how football has evolved. Better equipment, rules changes."

"But it doesn't change the game. We're talking about growing bodies, vulnerable bodies, slamming into each other over and over. It's more violent than when I played. It's hard for me to watch, honestly. I think of the kids out there."

"I think of the kids, too. But I think of the moments they're experiencing. The moments they'll never forget."

We both take a breath and sit back in our chairs. We could talk for hours, and I'm sure it wouldn't change anything. Bashum wouldn't push everything this far and then be swayed by me saying the things I've said for months.

"Your former player who spoke the other day. Quite a young man."

Bashum is talking about Mose, of course.

"Eric Posey. Yeah, he's something."

"I'm glad you've kept him involved. I can tell it means a lot to him."

"He means a lot to me."

We're both quiet for a few seconds.

"Does what happened . . ." Bashum says before pausing for a moment. Maybe he's not sure if he should keep going, but then he does.

"Does what happened to him ever make you think about . . ."

"Yes."

"Not saying there was anything you could've done, but . . ."

"Yes, I think about it."

Of course I've thought about it. It still tears me up sometimes. For all the wonderful things I see in football, I also see in Mose how it can alter a life. I love to see Mose when he comes to the school. I love to talk with him, spend time with him, just to have him around. But how can I not think about how different his life would be without football? Without one play?

"Sorry," Bashum says.

I nod and we're both quiet again. Bashum leans forward, stretches his back, and then rests his chin on his fist.

"I appreciate you coming in here today," he says, rubbing his chin, "and I respect what you do for the kids. That makes it painful when I say I can't guarantee you're going to get to coach football here. I'm not going to hide from my belief about football."

At least he's not leaving me in the dark.

"It's not easy," Bashum says. "I wish football could make changes. I wish it could've made those changes years ago. I know you disagree, but I believe the dominoes are starting to fall. And I'd prefer to be at the front of the falling dominoes, before we invest more in football and open a second high school campus."

I'm trying hard not to look disgusted. I didn't expect to win this conversation, but God, I don't want to hear about the dominoes again.

"You really think schools like Allen and Putnam and Highland Park and Southlake Carroll are going to cut football? You think Allen, with its sixty-million-dollar stadium, is going to give up on football?"

"They won't give up on it. But a decade from now, will they have enough players for it? It could be a decade from now. It could be twenty years. Youth football grew for years and years, and now it's dropping. When parents start steering kids in other directions, the dominoes are falling. Lawsuits, injuries—those will only speed things up."

That's how Bashum sees it, and maybe others see it that way. But what I see is a cornerstone of American life that can't be swept away in a few years or decades. Football is too big to die. It's too big to let itself die. It can change, it has changed, and it will continue changing.

"It's a cultural icon," I say.

"So were typewriters and telephone books," he says.

"Come on, that's no comparison."

"Okay, Coach, but remember back to when you were a kid. I know you're younger than me, but I bet when you were growing up, a lot of people didn't wear seatbelts."

"Yeah."

"Some cars didn't even have seatbelts in the back seat," Bashum says. "I remember on our family road trips, my brother, sister, and I would lie in the back of our station wagon with no seatbelts. We'd have pillows and blankets and we loved it. It's a great memory."

"Yeah, I did the same."

"Everybody did. But you wouldn't let your kids do it now. It's not even legal."

"You really think of football like that?"

"I just mean times change," Bashum says. "But I also know it's hard to change. We can't just cut all the football teams right now."

"But if you cut any of the program, you've killed football. It's over."

Bashum takes a breath and folds his hands again.

"I can only say what I believe is best for the school district and then let the board members make their decisions."

Bashum sits up in his chair and seems to wait for my response. But I've got nothing left to say. I don't agree with him, but we knew this conversation wouldn't end in agreement.

"One more thing," Bashum says. "When we open a second high school, we'll add a district athletic director, and you would be a strong candidate with your history with Creekside. I know you like coaching, but you don't have to be a football coach to impact the lives of kids."

In one breath, I'm told that my football program has been sentenced to death, and in the next, I'm complimented and offered a job. God, it feels like I've just spun around in my chair ten times. It's probably best to end the conversation.

But there's that black-and-white photo again. I need to know about it.

"So . . . is that you?" I say, pointing to the photo.

"Oh," Bashum says, turning and grabbing it. He looks at it for a second, takes a deep breath, and then sighs.

"This is actually my nephew, Gabriel. I'm flattered you thought it was me. Gabriel was a much better player than me. I was just a backup defensive back and special-teams guy. Gabriel was really good. A linebacker."

"When did he play?"

"Not that long ago. He graduated six years ago. The black-and-white photo . . . they were doing a throwback theme or something. Taking photos in those old poses."

"Where did he play?"

"Riverside, California. That's where my sister lives. And then after high school, Gabriel played at a junior college."

"Anywhere after that?"

"No."

Bashum looks down at the photo for a couple of seconds, puts it back on the shelf, and then turns back toward me.

"He died three years ago."

Oh God. The air is sucked out of the room and the silence is heavy. I need to do something or say something, but I'm locked up by the awkward-ness. I can't even think . . .

"God, I'm sorry," I say quietly. "I shouldn't have brought up that photo."

Bashum turns back toward me and smiles grimly.

"It's okay. Gabriel was a good kid. I think you would've liked to coach him."

"I'm sure," I say, still feeling like crap for leading the conversation here.

"Yeah, Gabriel was a great kid, and wow, how he really loved football. He wanted so badly to play in college, to play for USC, to be a Trojan. You talk about people who have a passion for something . . . that was Gabriel and football."

I smiled. "Sounds like a guy a coach would love."

Bashum nodded.

"Football was always what drove him, and that made it hard for him to let go of it. After high school, he kept trying to recapture the glory days."

"We can all be a little guilty of that, right?"

"Sure," Bashum says. "But sometimes I think we build things up too much for these kids, make them stars of the world before they've really done anything. Gabriel just couldn't move on. That dream was too big and too important."

Bashum puts the photo off to the side and taps his fingers together. Thirty minutes ago, I didn't even know Bashum had a nephew who played football. Now I'm preparing myself for a story about how he died, because I know that story is coming.

"I'm really sorry," I say without thinking, not knowing what would be the appropriate thing to say. I just knew I needed to say something.

"Gabriel wanted it so badly," Bashum says, and I realize now that he's going to tell me the whole story. Maybe he planned to tell me all along, and I just opened the door to it.

"Gabriel wanted that dream so badly that when he finally realized he couldn't have it, he gave up on everything else. That's what his mom says. She says he took steroids, although he never got caught. I don't know. But when he injured his knee in junior college and his football days were over, he just dropped out."

"Dropped out of college?"

"Dropped out of everything. Got depressed. I didn't see Gabriel much because I was a thousand miles away, but that's what my sister says."

I give an empathetic nod, which is all I can do. Then I wait for what's coming next.

"So anyway, his life got off track over the next couple years. He drifted around, got in some trouble, got more and more lost. I don't know a lot about what happened, but . . ."

Bashum takes another deep breath and lets it out slowly.

"He eventually decided he couldn't do it anymore."

Chapter 34

"HEY there, young lady."

Christine rolls her eyes and smiles.

"You must be looking for someone else, Mister," she says while leaning a hip into the kitchen counter and looking down at her iPad. If she's checking Facebook, I'm sure to hear a lot of stories tonight.

We're going out. Nothing that special, just dinner and a movie. But it feels special after the football season is over and Christmas passes, when we have a pocket of calm that allows us some time together. A date night for the couple that's been married twenty-four years.

"So I was thinking, young lady . . . maybe you'd like to go on a date sometime."

"Oh, well . . . maybe," she says. "But tell me, how do you feel about kids? I have three."

"Really? What a coincidence. I have three kids, too."

"Oh yeah? Do you have two boys who can clean out a refrigerator in one day, and a daughter who believes the world is going to end if she doesn't get her ears pierced?"

"Hmm . . . That sounds like a lot to handle. But another thing about me . . . I'm a football coach."

"Football coach? Oh, in that case, I don't know. I've heard about you guys."

"So there's no way I can convince you?"

I give Christine a hug as Mickey comes into the kitchen.

"Gaaawd," he groans. "Break it up, already."

Mickey opens the refrigerator door and stares in like a hunting predator. It's Sunday afternoon, and we went out to lunch a few hours ago, and he's hungry again. If Mickey were to list his top two hobbies, they would be sleeping and eating. There are a lot of similarities between an eighteen-week-old and an eighteen-year-old.

"Can I eat this?" he asks, pointing to some chicken salad.

"All yours," Christine says.

Mickey flops into a kitchen chair with little regard for his healing arm. Nearly three weeks have passed since he injured it, and the pain is replaced with impatience. He moves his arm around a lot in the sling. Too much, maybe, but we'll get another x-ray next week and hopefully it will show that the healing is going well.

Mickey only missed one game because of his injury. In the state semi-finals against Allen, Putnam fell hard. Kingsley Savage had one last "Beast" moment, a touchdown catch in which he leapt between two defenders, but that was one of the few highlights for Putnam. Allen broke the game open in the third quarter and then won the state title last week.

Mickey was down about the way everything ended, but he had a good ride. Now he's finalizing plans for college, which will not include football. I think he's at peace with it. He's ready to make his mark in other ways and, hopefully, not that far away.

"Here's money for the pizza tonight," I say, handing him two twenties. Then I pull them back. "Unless you want to cover it."

"Yeah right," he says.

"So who's coming over?"

"Dalton, Chris, and Kingsley."

"Kingsley's coming?"

"Yeah."

"You better get another pizza," I say. "With your brother, that's five. You guys will wipe out two pizzas."

"I'll need more money."

I look at Christine and shake my head. Then I find another twenty in my wallet.

"You realize we're leaving the house to five teenage boys," I say, "including one who goes by the name Beast."

"Kingsley is the one I'm least worried about," Christine says. "You should read what he wrote about alienation and the loss of innocence in *The Catcher in the Rye.*"

"So he didn't use the word prolly?" I say, and Christine fakes a punch to my gut.

I have no worries about leaving them alone at the house. Emma has already left to stay over at a friend's house. It's a Sunday, but it feels like a Saturday because we're in the middle of winter break.

"What are you guys going to do?" Christine asks.

"Just going to watch football and play video games," Mickey says. "And then go on the roof, throw things at people, be delinquents or something."

"Uh-huh," Christine says. "Will you vandalize some cars, too?"

"If there's enough time," Mickey says before taking a swig from a water bottle.

* * *

The movie starts in about thirty minutes, so we're here in plenty of time. But Christine has a thing about being late. She's such a planner that we end up arriving early to everything. Better that than late, I guess, but I'd rather spend a few more minutes in the restaurant than watching ads on the movie screen.

We're sitting in the car listening to the end of Mose's show. I don't listen to the show that often because it's mostly music, and not my kind of music. But Mose sends me downloads of each one, and usually I fast-forward through it, searching for the times when he talks.

"He sounds older on the radio," Christine says.

"That's the professional in him," I say.

Our dinner conversation was more football-related than usual. We had other topics to hit, such as Mickey's college search, Andrew's new braces, Emma's friend who might be a bad influence, and a kitchen remodel that we've discussed for two years.

But football gave us a lot to discuss. We talked about me eventually becoming the athletic director at Creekside, and how Bashum made it sound like the path to the job was clear. The hours would certainly be better than as a football coach, and those hours become more precious as you get older. You feel like you have all the time in the world when you're in your twenties and thirties. Then suddenly you're nearing fifty and trying to soak up the time with your kids before they're having kids.

It's just that I really love coaching. I love being "the head coach," and it's not some narcissistic thing. It's the power that you have to do good. Or bad, and unfortunately, there are a few guys who lean that way. But getting to see the players every day, seeing them grow, seeing them struggle and then achieve, seeing them emerge as men—that's amazing. You get a rush from that opportunity, that power in your life.

"You don't have to be a football coach to impact the lives of kids," Bashum told me, and he's right.

But being a football coach is the best way I can impact kids, and despite everything that's going on with Bashum and the school board, I'm looking forward to the next season. I'm looking forward to our return to school, when I can see Tyreke again strutting down a hallway. I'm looking forward to seeing the new crop of Paul Nelsons and Cody Sheltons and Elijah Lawals who will be on varsity next season. We'll start with bright-eyed enthusiasm, give it everything we have, and see where the ride takes us.

But what about all those dominoes?

Of course I think about it. Bashum isn't the only one who says the football dominoes are falling, and I can't ignore how the perception of the sport has changed. Football has an image problem. It also has some real problems, including how to best protect players who keep getting bigger, stronger, and faster and at younger and younger ages. Protect the kids and you protect the future of the sport.

But high school football is more than collisions. It's more than the spectacular and crazy plays you see in video clips. It's more than the moments when your body tingles with excitement, whether you're in the stands or on the field.

During the high school football season, there's far more grind than glamour. But all the practices, all the workouts in the weight room, all the planning, and all the prep work is special, too. During the offseason, the kids always say they can't wait until fall, when the Friday night lights are back. But the offseason, months like January and February, that's when I have some of my favorite coaching moments.

That's when a team comes together, that's when you become a family, and that's when I'm most certain about the role of football in these kids' lives. I see them bond; I see them improve; I see them mature. I see them every day, and it's a blessing. I try to be a blessing to them, too, although I'm sure they don't feel that way as they're running sprints in August.

I might never coach another state champion, and I might not coach another kid with the talent of Mose or Alex. I'm not even positive I'll get to coach Tyreke again. Nothing's for certain with the way things are going at Creekside, and nothing's for certain with football. You know, the dominoes.

Maybe they're falling, I don't know. But until they fall on me, I'm going to do what I've been doing. I still feel the passion. Sometimes a little too much passion, I suppose, as I look down at my knuckles that were bloody a few weeks ago. A small scab remains from my night as a vigilante.

Me, a vigilante. That's hilarious. But I'll fight for what I think is right, and I'll fight for football.

Football isn't what I'm really fighting for, though. It's the kids. And as long as they still want to play football, I want to be a part of it. I know football isn't life. In fact, I always tell the kids not to identify themselves as football players. Just tell people you play football, I say, because your value goes way beyond what happens on the field, and no matter what happens, life goes on.

We'll try to win every game, of course. That's always the goal. But there's a difference between a goal and a purpose. And even when we can't reach our goal of winning, we can always serve our purpose as a football program. We're here to help kids develop into young men.

✳ ✳ ✳

On the radio, *The Mosey Show* continues, and Christine and I talk through a song that normally wouldn't keep us in the car. We've been parked for five minutes.

"This is a long song," Christine says.

"So . . . ready to go in?"

"No, let's wait a second," she says. "Mosey will be back on in a minute."

Christine never listens to Mose's show, so it's starting to feel like something's up, like a bunch of people are about to jump out and yell "Surprise!" or something. And I have reason to worry, because when I turned forty on the night of a game, my players attacked me with shaving cream—provided by Christine. I hate to think what will happen when I turn fifty.

Mose is finally back, bringing that smooth, deep voice with a hint of Texas drawl. Christine is right that Mose sounds older than his mid-twenties. He makes it seem so easy, and for him, it kind of is. But I know he spends a lot of time preparing for his show because it's important to him.

"All right, everyone, we're coming up on the end of the show," Mose says, and a disappointed "ooooooh" follows. It's a recording that they use each week when the show is coming to an end.

"Thank you, my loyal, fake, studio audience," Mose says with a laugh. "And I appreciate y'all listening to this special Sunday edition of *The Mosey Show*. Thanks to everyone here at The Groove for giving the show an extra night this week. Deejay Reggie B will be back next Sunday, and I'll be back on my normal Saturday night at nine."

He's silent for a moment.

"All right, so we're down to the final song of the show. Usually it's a dedication from one of you listeners, but I have one of my own tonight. That's right, I'm taking this show's last song of the year and stealin' it. Selfish, right?"

Mose chuckles.

"Our next show will be after New Year's, so I got to thinking about resolutions. I read that only like eight percent of people stick to their resolutions, so I've got one for you. It's simple. Just be happy with yourself and appreciate all the good things in your life."

He pauses again.

"So I'll go first. I've got the greatest family in the world, with mom, dad, my brother, my auntie. I've got all my great friends and you listeners out there, and I've also got a family at Creekside High School, where I'm an assistant coach. So, anyway . . ."

Another pause.

"The head coach over there is a guy named Tuffy Nehls."

I think my heart just skipped a beat, and I can feel the sweat starting on the back of my neck. I'm not sure I like where this is going. I don't need this kind of attention.

"I know you're like, what? Tuffy? I guess when he was a player, somebody thought he was tough, so he became Tuffy. Something like that. Anyway, I've known Coach Nehls for ten years, and I've been telling him, since I started this show, to tell me a song to play for him."

I'm still not sure I like this, but I start to laugh because Mose really has been bugging me for months to pick out a song. I thought he was joking at first, but then he kept asking.

"You would think it's easy to pick out one song—just *one* song—but Coach Nehls . . ."

Another pause.

"Well, Coach's real first name is Gordon, and he is about as hip and fresh as his name. I told him that I play some old school stuff, so come up with something. Coach finally got back to me, and I'll give him a break . . . he did okay. Kool & the Gang, Prince, and Earth, Wind & Fire. Pretty good for an old guy, I mean an older guy, named Gordon."

Mose chuckles again. I love how he amuses himself.

"But, you know, if I'm going to dedicate a song to Coach, it's got to be right for him. And so listeners, as I remember that good deejays know when to shut up, I ask for your patience, understanding, and—man—probably forgiveness during the last five minutes of this *Mosey Show.*"

One final pause.

"So here it is."

The drums pound and I start to laugh as I recognize the song immediately. So does Christine because she's heard it so many times. The horns and guitars rush in, and so does an emotion that waters my eyes.

I turn my head to look out the driver's side window as Springsteen's "Born to Run" gets rolling. Christine turns up the radio, and I can see her, in the reflection of the window, looking over at me.

She's waiting for me to turn back toward her, but I'm not going to do it. I'm going to keep looking out the driver's side window, focusing hard on nothing, staying tough as nails.

ACKNOWLEDGMENTS

WHEN I started writing *Fourth Down in Texas*, I had a lot of ideas. What I didn't have was a name for the coach telling the story, who for several weeks was simply "Coach" before becoming Tuffy Nehls.

Where that name came from, I'm not sure. But it's easy to pinpoint the origins of the character of Coach Nehls, who was inspired by the hundreds of coaches I've known over the last two decades. Those coaches were gracious with their time, whether we were talking about their teams, the joys and challenges of coaching, or football in general. I always enjoyed listening to coaches talk proudly about their players' accomplishments, many of which had little to do with football.

A special thank you also goes out to Greg Riddle, a tremendous editor and the secret weapon of *The Dallas Morning News* sports department, for his insights and help shaping the story. Mark Falkin provided valuable feedback and editing, and when the writing was nearly complete, Bill Webb's expertise and enthusiasm got the novel to the finish line (or into the end zone).

Finally, a thank you to my wife, Janell. She's not a big sports fan, unless our sons are on the field or court, but she read this novel first, in bits and pieces, over the many months that I wrote it, and then shared her thoughts. She might not know a bootleg from a blitz, but she's the person I trust most of all.

About the Author

MATT Wixon spent eighteen years at *The Dallas Morning News* as a writer and columnist, and for much of that time, he covered high school football. He was named the Texas High School Coaches Association's Sports Writer of the Year in 2013, and the Associated Press Sports Editors ranked his work among the top ten nationally in projects reporting in 2010, 2015, and 2016. In his final year at The News in 2017, he was named Media Person of the Year by the Dallas chapter of the National Football Foundation.

Wixon now works in sports communications for the Frisco Independent School District north of Dallas, near where he lives with his wife and their three sons.

www.mattwixon.com
Twitter: @mattwixon